William Sparrow Simpson

Chapters in the History of Old S. Paul's

William Sparrow Simpson

Chapters in the History of Old S. Paul's

ISBN/EAN: 9783337326074

Printed in Europe, USA, Canada, Australia, Japan

Cover: Foto ©Andreas Hilbeck / pixelio.de

More available books at **www.hansebooks.com**

CHAPTERS

In the History

OF

OLD S. PAUL'S.

BY

W. SPARROW SIMPSON, D.D., F.S.A.,

MINOR CANON, LIBRARIAN, SUCCENTOR, AND JUNIOR CARDINAL IN S. PAUL'S
CATHEDRAL; ONE OF THE HONORARY LIBRARIANS OF HIS GRACE
THE ARCHBISHOP OF CANTERBURY.

LONDON :
ELLIOT STOCK, 62, PATERNOSTER ROW.
MDCCCLXXXI.

PREFACE.

FOR some time past my hours of leisure, which have been only too few and far between, have been devoted to researches in the History of the Cathedral of S. Paul. I have enjoyed for twenty years the great honour of being a Member of the Cathedral Body and Keeper of its Records, and each succeeding year has but increased my love for the stately Sanctuary and its solemn Services, and augmented my interest in its venerable Archives. In the present volume I have endeavoured to embody in a popular form some of the results of my studies, in the hope that many who are repelled by Original Documents expressed in mediæval Latin, may read these desultory Chapters in the History of Old S. Paul's, and share with me in the absorbing interest which gathers round the subject.

Where I could tell the Story of S. Paul's in the words of some old Chronicler, I have always preferred his quaint phrases to any sentences of my own : at the same time I have freely used the documents and other materials gathered together in my previous books upon the History of S. Paul's, and I have done so with the less hesitation because the first of these was privately printed, and the second was issued only to the Members of a learned Society.*

I must ask indulgence for the familiar cicerone style of Chapters IV. and V.: it seemed likely to make the stroll about the renowned Cathedral

" With glistening spires and pinnacles adorn'd "†

less tedious if the Reader and the Author walked arm in arm together.

---

* *Registrum Statutorum et Consuetudinum Ecclesiæ Cathedralis Sancti Pauli Londinensis*, 4to., London, 1873, privately printed for the Dean and Chapter ; and *Documents illustrating the History of S. Paul's Cathedral*, 4to., London, 1880, issued by the Camden Society.

† *Paradise Lost*, Book iii. v. 550.

CONTENTS.

CHAPTER VII.

CHAPTER VIII.

CHAPTER IX.

CHAPTER X.

CHAPTER XI.

CHAPTER XII.

CHAPTER XIII.

CHAPTER XIV.

ILLUSTRATIONS.

"But let my due feet never fail
To walk the ftudious cloyfters pale,
And love the high-embowed roof,
With antick pillars maffy proof,
And ftoried windows richly dight,
Cafting a dim religious light :
There let the pealing organ blow,
To the full-voic'd quire below,
In fervice high and anthems clear,
As may with fweetnefs, through mine ear,
Diffolve me into ecftafies,
And bring all heaven before mine eyes."

Milton, Il Penferofo, 155—166.

*THE EARLY HISTORY OF RELIGION
IN LONDON.*

CHAPTER I.

THE EARLY HISTORY OF RELIGION IN LONDON.

PON the fummit of a hill, floping gently on its fouthern fide to the broad waters of the Thames, and on its weftern to the rapid ftream of the Fleet, ftands, and has ftood for many centuries, a church dedicated to the great Apoftle of the Gentiles. When was it firft founded? Whofe voice firft proclaimed the Holy Name of JESUS to the pagan inhabitants of ancient London? Who was the firft Apoftle of this, the very heart of England?

The compilers of the Statute Book of S. Paul's Cathedral were not troubled with any doubts about the matter. They reply, with great definitenefs of language, on this wife: " In the year from the Incarnation of the Lord one hundred and eighty-five, at the requeft of Lucius the King of Greater Britain, which now is called England, there were fent from Eleutherius the Pope to the aforefaid King two illuftrious doctors, Fagnus and Dumanus, who fhould in-

cline the heart of the King and of his fubject-people
to the unity of the Chriftian Faith, and fhould
confecrate to the honour of the one true and fupreme
God the temples which had been dedicated to various
and falfe deities."* The Chronicler proceeds to record
that thefe holy men, taught by the Spirit of God,
founded three metropolitical fees, and that the firft of
thefe was London.

But, alas, the exact ftudy of hiftory remits thefe
pofitive ftatements to the land of fable. " King
Lucius and the miffionaries of his Court have quietly
withdrawn into the dim region of Chriftian myth-
ology."† Almoft the only relic ftill furviving which
throws any light upon the religion of early London is
the little Altar of Diana found on the fite of Goldfmiths' Hall, and ftill preferved as the choiceft ornament of the Court Room of that wealthy Guild.
Clouds and mift hang over the early hiftory of the
Chriftianifing of the capital. Auguft forms float
acrofs the haze, but we cannot name them nor difcern
their features.

It muft be remembered that we are not now con-
fidering the larger queftion of the Chriftianifing of
England, but are limiting ourfelves to that of the
evangelifation of London. If, as Dean Milman fays,
" the converfion of King Lucius is a legend," we muft
not forget that he adds alfo thefe memorable words,

---

* *Statuta S. Pauli*, p. 10.

† Dean Milman's *Annals of S. Paul's*, p. 3.   See alfo the
firft chapter of Canon Bright's *Chapters on Englifh Church
Hiftory.*

" There can be no doubt that conquered and half-civiliſed Britain, like the reſt of the Roman Empire, gradually received, during the ſecond and third centuries, the faith of Chriſt. S. Helena, the mother of Conſtantine, probably imbibed the firſt fervour of thoſe Chriſtian feelings which wrought ſo powerfully in the Chriſtianity of her age in her native Britain."* And certainly, at the great Council of Arles, held in the year 314, Reſtitutus, Biſhop of London, appears amongſt the liſt of prelates who were preſent : he was ſucceeded, many years afterwards, by a certain Faſtidius, Biſhop of Britain in 431.

Jocelin of Furneſs, a monk of the twelfth century, has indeed compiled a liſt of fourteen metropolitans of London. But upon this catalogue, Canon Stubbs† obſerves that " it is a moſt uncritical performance ;" adding, however, that " the compiler evidently acted in good faith, and put down no more than he found in his authorities."

Of the lateſt of theſe prelates, Geoffrey the Chronicler relates that when the Saxons drove the Britiſh fugitives into Wales and Cornwall, Theon, Biſhop of London, and Thadioc, of York, fled into Wales with the Archbiſhop of Caerleon and their ſurviving clergy.‡ The traditional date of this flight is 586.

With the cloſe of the ſixth century we reach the æra, memorable for ever in the hiſtory of our country, the æra of the great revival of religion wrought by the

* *Latin Chriſtianity*, ii. 226.
† Canon Stubbs' *Regiſtrum Sacrum Anglicanum*, p. 152, where the catalogue may be ſeen.
‡ Canon Bright, p. 33, citing Geoffrey, viii. 2.

band of Chriftian miffionaries headed by the Apoftle of England.

Soon after Eafter, 597, Auguftine and his companions croffed the Channel. They landed at Ebbsfleet, near the grand Roman caftle at Richborough, which crowns a flight eminence between Sandwich and Pegwell Bay. The little army of forty men advanced, bearing a filver crofs and a painted panel upon which was depiĉted the Crucified Jefus.* Ethelbert, the fincere and noble-hearted King, receives them generoufly and hofpitably ; he finds that he has entertained angels unawares ; he obtains a rich reward, for he is converted ; and on Whitfun Eve, according to the Canterbury tradition, he is baptifed. In due time he becomes the founder of the Cathedral Church of S. Paul. The Manor of Tillingham, one of thofe with which the royal bounty enriched the church, ftill remains in the poffeffion of the Dean and Chapter. S. Gregory had defired that London fhould bcome an archiepifcopal fee, Auguftine thought otherwife, and referved the primatial dignity for Canterbury. In the year 604, fays Ralph de Diceto, the hiftorian and Dean of S. Paul's,† " Ethelbert the King built the Church of S. Paul, London," and he goes on to record that Auguftine himfelf confecrated Mellitus as Bifhop of the fee.

And where in ancient London did Mellitus call together the affembly of the faithful ? Did he find a

* See Bright, pp. 45, 50, and Dean Stanley's admirable effay in his *Hiftorical Memorials of Canterbury.*

† Whofe *Hiftorical Works* have recently been edited by Profeffor Stubbs.

heathen fanctuary where S. Paul's now ſtands, furrounded with umbrageous trees ; and did he, in the
fhadowing wood, find a meet fhrine for God's true worfhip?

> " The groves were God's firſt temples.   Ere man learned
>   To hew the fhaft, and lay the architrave,
>   And fpread the roof above them—ere he framed
>   The lofty vault, to gather and roll back
>   The found of anthems ; in the darkling wood,
>   Amidſt the cool and filence, he knelt down,
>   And offered to the Mightieſt folemn thanks
>   And fupplication.   For his fimple heart
>   Might not refiſt the facred influences
>   Which, from the ſtilly twilight of the place,
>   And from the gray old trunks that high in heaven
>   Mingled their moffy boughs, and from the found
>   Of the invifible breath that fwayed at once
>   All their green tops, ſtole over him, and bowed
>   His fpirit with the thought of boundlefs power
>   And inacceffible majeſty."*

" The firſt cathedral of this fee," fays Maitland,
" was built in the pretorian camp of the Romans,
and destroyed under Diocletian." There are many
examples in England of churches ſtanding in the
midſt of ancient earthworks. "This cathedral," he
continues, " was rebuilt under Conſtantine, and again
deſtroyed by the Saxons in their times of Paganifm ;
after which it was reſtored by Ethelbert."

No records remain which can give us any certain
information as to the earlieſt fanctuary which crowned
the Pauline Hill. Perhaps it was but a very fimple
ſtructure of rough trees, hardly fhaped by the axe,

* W. C. Bryant, *A Foreſt Hymn.*

like that ſtrange method of conſtruction of which an example ſtill remains at Greenſtead, near Epping. The woods and foreſts near to London would have ſupplied abundant material for ſuch a purpoſe. Perhaps it was a humble chapel built of ſtone, ſcarcely more elaborate than the rude cells at Ripon and at Hexham. No tradition, however, remains, which can ſupply us with a ſketch of the earlieſt fabric.

We do not even know the form and extent of Ethelbert's Cathedral. Bede, and Ralph de Diceto* following him, confine themſelves to the feweſt poſſible words : "Ethelbert the King built the Church of S. Paul in London." Dean Milman† applies to it a ſingle epithet: it was "magnificent." Profeſſor Owen built up the *Dinornis* from a ſingle bone, but the moſt ſkilful architect could ſcarcely reconſtruct Ethelbert's Cathedral from a ſingle epithet. Nor would it help him much were we to add another brief ſtatement, that Biſhop Erkenwald, of whom more will be ſaid preſently, "beſtowed great coſt on the fabric thereof."‡

Fire, always the bitter foe of S. Paul's, would not ſpare the work of the royal founder ; for in 961, the *Saxon Chronicle* relates, "The monaſtery of S. Paul's was burnt, and in the ſame year reſtored."§ And again, in 1087 or 1088, for the authorities are not agreed, the City of London and its cathedral were

* *Hiſtorical Works*, i. 107.
† Milman, *Annals of S. Paul's*, p. 9.
‡ Dugdale, *S. Paul's*, p. 3.
§ Newcourt, *Repertorium*, i. 2.

both confumed by the flames. The *Chroniculi S. Pauli** fay that the great conflagration happened on the feventh day of July in the year 1087.

But although little or nothing is known as to the form and extent of the primitive fanctuary of the firft Chriftian inhabitants of London, and although the later church of the generous Ethelbert has found no accurate and minute hiftorian, Mellitus, the firft bifhop of London after the arrival of S. Auguftine, ftands out as a very real perfon, and as one who made his mark upon the hiftory of the church. He appears confpicuoufly upon the broad canvas of the venerable Bede.

Mellitus was confecrated by Auguftine himfelf in the year 604, and filled fucceffively the fees of London and of Canterbury. He feems to have arrived in England about the clofe of the year 601.† Few letters of the period are more interefting than that which Gregory wrote to Mellitus to inftruct him in his dealing with the Chriftian converts.‡ They were to be dealt with very tenderly. Heathen temples were not neceffarily to be deftroyed ; they might be purged and hallowed for the true worfhip. "You cannot cut off everything at once from rough natures. He who would climb to a height muft afcend ftep by ftep; he cannot jump the whole way." Outward enjoyments, and even feafts kept within due bounds, were by no means to be dif-

---

* Printed in *Documents*, etc., p. 58.

† This hiftory is excellently told in Bright's *Early Englifh Church Hiftory*, pp. 70 *et seq*.

‡ Bede, Book i. § 31.

couraged.   Humble country folk were not to be
deprived of their fimple pleafures, but rather taught
to ufe them moderately.   The letter teems with good
fenfe, and with abundant evidences of a kind and
liberal heart.

Mellitus had converted King Sigebert I., or Sabert,
who was Ethelbert's nephew, and Sabert took part
with Ethelbert in the erection of S. Paul's.   Some
fay that a Temple of Diana had once ftood upon
the fummit of the hill : but the ftory is doubtful, and
the evidence brought forward as to the bones of deer
and cattle found in deep excavations here, and as to
a building called *Camera Dianæ* or *Diana's Chamber*
at no great diftance, does not really throw light upon
the queftion.

The good Bifhop Mellitus did not always bafk in
the funfhine of royal favour ; for in due time, one-
and-twenty years after his converfion, the noble
Ethelbert died,* and was buried in S. Martin's porch
within the Church of the Bleffed Apoftles Peter
and Paul, befide the body of Bertha his Queen.
Eadbald, his fon, did not walk in his father's fteps ;
he refufed to embrace the faith of Chrift, and Bede
goes fo far as to fay that there were times when he
gave way to fits of madnefs, and was oppreffed with
an unclean fpirit.   Sabert alfo died, and left his
three fons, ftill pagans, to inherit his throne.   They
had fomewhat diffembled during their father's life-
time, and kept their attachment to heathenifm in the
background ; but now, left to themfelves, they openly

* Bede, ii. 5.

profeffed idolatry, and encouraged the people to ferve idols. Bede tells us a characteriftic ftory :* One day thefe impious fons of a godly father came to S. Paul's Church during the celebration of the Holy Euchariſt. They faw the Biſhop giving the Sacrament to the affembled people. "Puffed up with their barbarous folly, they faid to him, 'Why do you not give to us alfo that white bread, as you ufed to do to our father Saba' (for fo they were accuftomed to call him), 'and as you ſtill give it to the people in the church.' To whom the Biſhop anfwered, 'If ye will be waſhed in that life-giving fount in which your father was waſhed, then ye may become partakers of that holy bread of which he was wont to be a partaker. But if ye defpife the laver of life, ye are by no means able to receive the bread of life.' 'But,' faid they, 'we will not enter that fount, for we do not know that we have need of it, but neverthelefs we wiſh to be re-freſhed with that bread.' And when oftentimes and diligently they were admoniſhed by him that no one might by any means partake of the moſt holy Oblation without the moſt holy purging [of baptifm], they were moved to fury and faid, 'If you will not confent to us in this fo fmall a matter which we defire, you ſhall not remain in our province.' And accordingly they compelled him and his followers to depart from their kingdom." Mellitus being driven away from London, took counfel with his fellow-biſhops Laurentius and Juſtus as to the courfe which ſhould be adopted in this emergency. They decided that, for a

* Bede, ii. 5.

time at leaft, "until this tyranny was overpaft," it would be wife to withdraw from England. Mellitus and Juftus retreated to France. But Bede is careful to relate that the wicked kings did not go unpunifhed, for marching out to battle againft the nation of the Weft Saxons they were all flain and their army routed. The people, however, had relapfed into idolatry, and for forty years London was again plunged into heathen darknefs.

Mellitus is fent for, and returns: but the people of London would not receive him, nor could King Eadbald reftore to him his church. Idolatry was once more triumphant.

On the 2nd of February, 619, Archbifhop Laurence died, and Mellitus fuccceded him in the Archiepifcopal throne of Canterbury. And here we ought to leave him, as he no longer ruled over the See of London. A brief fpace, however, muft be devoted to the concluding chapter of his life, in which, once more, we will follow the guidance of the Venerable Bede.* Mellitus laboured under a phyfical infirmity; in fact, he was afflicted with the gout: but though his malady forely hindered his bodily activity, "his mind, with vigorous fteps, joyful leapt over worldly things, and flew to love, to feek celeftial things." There was a terrible conflagration in Canterbury; the whole city was in danger of being confumed by fire; water was thrown upon the flames, but all in vain; they continued to fpread with terrific power; the Church of the Four Crowned Martyrs, martyrs who had fallen

* Bede, Book ii. 7.

in the perſecution of Diocletian, ſtood in the place where the fire raged moſt fiercely : thither the Prelate, though weighed down by his infirmities and the pains of ſickneſs, bade his ſervants to carry him. Strong men had laboured to no purpoſe, to put out the flames—he would ſhow them the efficacy of prayer. He prayed fervently, and the wind which had been blowing from the ſouth now turned to the north ; the flames were beaten back, and preſently, the wind ceaſing altogether, were entirely extinguiſhed, and the city was ſaved.

This is the laſt recorded act of Mellitus. He ruled over the Church of Canterbury for five years, and departed to his reſt on the 24th day of April, 624 : a day long obſerved with honour in the Church of London, as may be ſeen in its ancient Calendar.

Foremoſt amongſt the early Biſhops of London, and towering above them both in hiſtory and legend, ſtands the ſainted Prelate Erkenwald. Mellitus had been gathered to his fathers ; Cedda, brother of S. Chad of Lichfield, had ſucceeded him ; he, in his turn, had been followed by Wina. Fourth in ſuc-ceſſion,* Theodore, Archbiſhop of Canterbury, con-ſecrated S. Erkenwald. He is ſaid to have been of royal deſcent, his father, Offa, being King of Eaſt England. When but a boy he had heard Mellitus preach in London, and, if the words of the *Golden Legend* are to be taken literally, had even liſtened to the preaching of S. Auguſtine himſelf. Before he was

* The dates of confecration are : Mellitus, 604 ; Cedda, 654 ; Wina, 662 ; Erkenwald, 675. Canon Stubbs' *Regiſtrum Sacrum.*

raifed to the epifcopate, he had founded two famous monafteries: one for himfelf, at Chertfey in Surrey; the other for his fifter Ethelburga, at Barking in Effex.

Chertfey became one of the mitred abbeys, but its abbots, though regarded as fpiritual barons, did not fit in Parliament. The Regifter of the Abbey is ftill preferved in the Britifh Mufeum, and contains a charter of privileges granted by Pope Agatho, which was brought from Rome by Erkenwald himfelf. During the Danifh wars in the latter part of the ninth century, the abbot, Beocca, a prieft named Ethor, and ninety monks were flain, the church and monaftery burnt, and the furrounding poffeffions laid wafte. It was reftored by Ethelwald, Bifhop of Winchefter. Many pages of Dugdale's *Monafticon** are filled with a record of the abbots of the houfe and with its charters. It fhared the fate of other religious houfes, was diffolved (at that time its grofs rental was valued at £744 18s. 6¾d.), and its fite was granted to Sir William FitzWilliam.

In 1673, when Aubrey wrote, fcarcely any of the old buildings of Chertfey Abbey remained. A few walls only were to be feen, and the ftreets of the town, he fays, were raifed by the ruins of the abbey. Even the Abbey Houfe, erected with part of its materials, has been demolifhed. The walls of a large barn, an arched gateway, and a wall nearly oppofite to it, are figured in the new edition of Brayley's *Surrey* (edited by Mr. Edward Walford), and in Mr. and Mrs.

* *Monafticon*, i. 422-435.

S. C. Hall's *Book of the Thames* as "The Remains of Chertfey Abbey ;" and thefe authorities add that the graveyard is now a rich garden, and that the old fifh-ponds, once fo important an appendage to a religious houfe, are even now not without water. In Stukeley's time, among the garden-ftuff one might "pick up handfuls of bits of bone at a time "—bones of abbots, great perfonages and monks, buried in numbers in the once famous church and cloifters of Chertfey.

Parts of the foundations of the old abbey church, which was about 270 feet in length, are yet to be feen, and there is a fmall fragment of pavement ftill *in fitu*. The teffelated pavements of Chertfey were of rare beauty, reprefenting fcenes in the life of Richard Cœur de Lion, paffages in the Story of Sir Triftram, the zodiacal figns, and the feafons or months. Portions of thefe are ftill preferved in private poffeffion.

A fmall relic from its treafury alfo remains, for the Britifh Mufeum contains an example of an offertory-difh of Northern manufacture, once belonging to the abbey, and dug up in its ruins at the beginning of this century. This veffel is a flat circular difh of nearly pure copper, with a very wide rim, bearing an infcription, which Mr. J. M. Kemble has rendered, "Offer, finner." A difcuffion as to the exact age of the alms-difh is epitomifed in the *Dictionary of Chriftian Antiquities* (Art., Offertory Plates). The dates affigned to it vary from the ninth to the eleventh century.

Barking Monaftery* is faid by fome writers to have

* Dugdale, *Monafticon,* i. 436-446.

been the earlieft and the richeft nunnery in England, but it can hardly maintain its claim to either of thefe defignations, as Folkeftone Nunnery was founded many years before it, and Shaftefbury and Sion were both wealthier. "It was a double foundation, like Whitby and others, having a feparate area for the monks apart from the nuns' building, and even a feparate chapel or oratory for each order."* The habit of the fifters, that of the Benedictines generally, is fhown in a plate in Dugdale ;† Lyfons engraves the feal of the monaftery and the ground-plan of the church. The nunnery was diffolved in 1539, and the fite with its buildings was granted by Edward VI. to Edward Lord Clinton. A mutilated flab at the eaft end of the north aifle of Barking Church commemorating the names of Ælfgiva, abbefs in the time of Edward the Confeffor, and of Maurice, Bifhop of London, was ftill extant in 1809, when an etching of it was publifhed. It cannot now be difcovered.‡ An ancient gateway, forming the principal entrance to the churchyard, ftill remains as a relic of the departed grandeur of this once ftately abbey. The chamber over the gateway was the Chapel of the Holy Rood : a very interefting carving reprefenting the Rood ftill, though it is much defaced, adorns the eaftern wall of the chapel, on the north fide of the fite of the altar. Some recent excavations in the garden of the adjacent

---

* Canon Bright, p. 257.   † *Monafticon*, i. 443.
‡ I have fearched carefully for it in the church, and have made many enquiries at Barking. Archdeacon Blomfield has moft kindly joined in the fearch ; but, as yet, without fuccefs.

fchool-houfe* have brought to light the foundations
of the Lady Chapel of the ancient church. The graves
of two abbeffes have been difcovered, together with
fome fragments of carved ftone (retaining traces of
the original colouring), which may probably have
formed part of a fhrine of S. Erkenwald once adorn-
ing the fanctuary.

Not far from Barking, at Ilford, was a lepers'
hofpital governed by the fociety at Barking. A certain
Mr. Agard gives a fomewhat remarkable account of
the mode of expulfion from this hofpital. " It was
my happe," he fays, "to fee once an abftracte out of
the lygyar-book of Barking Nonnery, in Effex, in a gentleman's hande, now dead, and who fhewed me, that
the abbeffe beinge accompanyed with the Bufhop of
London, the Abbot of Stratford, the Deane of Paule's,
and other great fpyrytuall perfonnes, went to Ilforde
to vifit the hofpytall theere founded for leepers . . .
The manner of his difgradinge was thus, as I remember: he came attyred in his lyvery, but bare-
footed and bareheaded, *tenâ depofitâ*, that is, without
a nightcap, and was fet on his knees uppon the ftayres,
benethe the altar, where he remained during all the
time of mafs. When mafs was ended, the priefte
difgraded him of orders, fcraped his hands and his
crown with a knife, took his booke from him, gave him
a boxe on the chiek with the end of his fingers, and
then thruft him out of the churche, where the officers

* Mr. King, the fchoolmafter of Barking, has taken a moft
intelligent intereft in thefe excavations, great part of which he
has made with his own hands.

and people receyved him, and putt him into a carte, cryinge *Ha rou! Ha rou! Ha rou!* after him."*

There is a letter extant† addreſſed by Sir Thomas Audley (afterwards Baron Audley of Walden in Eſſex, Lord Chancellor of England), to Secretary Cromwell, begging him to defer the viſitation of Barking till they ſhould meet and talk the matter over; "truſting," Sir Thomas ſays, that "for my ſake, and at my contemplation, ye will uſe the more favour to the houſe."

Sir Henry Spelman, in his *Hiſtory and Fate of Sacrilege*,‡ is careful to ſhow that it fared ill with the early intruders into the Abbey lands. He ſays that the property of Barking abbey, after the Diſſolution, had no leſs than ſix succeſſive poſſeſſors, belonging to four different families, in the ſhort ſpace of seventy-eight years, and that the barony of Edward Lord Clinton became extinct in the direct male line in 1692; and further, that when the abeyance of the barony was determined in favour of Hugh Forteſcue, Eſq., he died without iſſue. Nor were the intruded owners of Chertſey more fortunate.

Dugdale prints a curious document which throws ſome light upon the dietary of the convent. On "Seynt Alburgh's daye," the Cellareſſe of the House "muſt purvey for a pece of whete and iij gallons milke for frimete," that is for Frumenty, a dainty

---

* Thomas Hearne, *A Collection of Curious Diſcourſes on Antiquities*, vol. i. pp. 249, 250: edit. 1771.

† *Letters relating to the Suppreſſion of Monaſteries*, No. 32.

‡ Edition 1853, pp. 67, 319, 324, and pp. 265, 297.

dish which Halliwell says was made of hulled wheat boiled in milk, and seasoned with cinnamon and sugar. At Shrovetide my lady Abbess was to be supplied with "viij chekenes," and the convent was regaled with "bonnes" and "crum-cakes," that is pancakes. Some other little delicacies were provided at divers seasons, such as a "hoole hogg sowse" which "do serve four ladyes." Lest this dish over-exercise the reader's ingenuity, let him be told that a *souce* consists of the head, feet, and ears of swine boiled and pickled for eating; a toothsome meal it may be supposed, according to the taste of those days.

It was in Bishop Erkenwald's house in London that Archbishop Theodore was reconciled to Bishop Wilfrid, after their long estrangement. From this meeting may be dated the long series of negotiations which ended in Wilfrid's restoration to his cathedral church and to his minster.*

The saintly Erkenwald held the See of London from the year 675 to 693. He was canonised in due course. A cloud of legends surround him. Holy days were set apart in his honour; special religious offices were compiled to commemorate him ;† prayers were said and hymns were sung at his shrine ;‡ and thither flowed large crowds of pilgrims from all parts of the Diocese, and, indeed, from yet more distant places, to kneel before the bones of the sainted prelate.

* Canon Bright, p. 351.

† I have printed some of these Offices in my *Documents illustrating the History of S. Paul's Cathedral*.

‡ See *infra*, Chapter V.

The day of his death, April 30, and the day of his tranflation, November 14, were long obferved as feftival days in his own Cathedral of S. Paul.

Thofe who are curious in legendary lore will find the ftory of S. Erkenwald well told in Caxton's *Golden Legend.** The clofing fcene of his life—

> " Laft fcene of all,
> That ends this ftrange eventful hiftory "—

may beft be related in verfe.†

THE DEATH OF ERKENWALD.

And Erkenwald lay dying in his cell :
Afar the filver Thames, mift-robed and ftill,
Hufhed into filence at his paffing hour,
Stole on through emerald reaches toward the fea.
The waning Day moved by, and as he moved
Drew his dark cloak around, yet, ere he fled,
Turned one bright glance from out his golden eye
To that ftill cloifter-cell, and paufed awhile
And lit thofe noble features which in eve
Lay with a faintly glory moft divine ;
Thofe heavenward eyes, inftinct of deepeft love,
Were eloquent with prayer, and while the light
Grew brighter ere it faded, lo ! he flept.

Then, ftealing through the air in that deep hufh
Came rofeal perfume, foft as laden breezes
Pour out the golden gates of Paradife :
And long it lingered where the faint lay dead :
It feemed like the rich odour of good deeds
Wafted upon the mighty wings of Time.

---

* Reprinted in my *Documents*, pp. 186-190.
† The lines are by my fon, W. J. Sparrow Simpfon, Trinity College, Cambridge.

But deep gloom hung around the capital,
And chiefly through the arching nave of Paul ;
Then one faid weeping, " Erkenwald is dead ;"
And man to man remurmured, " He is dead ;"
And earth and air throbbed fighing, " He is dead."
Wherefore the priefts came forth from nave and aifle,
Came forth enrobed to bear the body thence,
Frail habitation that did erft contain
The pricelefs jewel of a faintly foul :
So, through the years, to lie in holy foil
Enfhrined amid a nation's reverence.

But Chertfey alfo claimed him for their own :
Then while they marked the long proceffion wind
Befide the rolling Lee, to bear away
That vacant temple of a faintly foul,
The monks wept bitter tears and fmote the gates
Of heaven with piteous prayer and lamentation,
Befeeching he might ever reft with them,
Praifed by their fong and bleffing all their need.
So they implored befide the rolling Lee.
And lo ! the ftream grew ftrong and terrible,
And whirled and fwelled in eddying fitfulnefs,
And black ftorms hung about the arching fky,
The torrent waters, and dark forefts deep.

And awful hands of might invifible
And wings of power feemed ever circling round :
Then ftood the priefts confounded, all the air
Seemed fraught with vivid energy and life,
And inftinct with ineffable Deity,
Moft dread and wonderful : and thence divining
The everlafting arm of Majefty
O'erfhadowing all, they ceafed in trembling fear.

Then rofe to God a mournful Litany
Upraifed of prieftly voices—grand and wild,
A De Profundis out of forrowing hearts.
And lo ! the tempeft ftayed, and wave on wave

Foamed backward and uprofe on either hand :
Then joyoufly the priefts arifing moved
And bore through floodlefs fpace their burden on
To fleep beneath the noble towers of Paul.

So there did they confign to wakelefs reft
Their well-beloved, their mafter Erkenwald,
Their God-fent light, their friend Saint Erkenwald,
And builded him anon a worthy fhrine,
Where lamps might burn for ever, and adorned it
With coftlieft gifts and nobleft offerings.
And lowly thoufands ofttimes knelt before it,
Befeeching him to bear their fervent prayers
Beyond the ftars of God, where feraphim
Bow down their radiant faces and adore.

And thus they chanted in the voice of prayer :

" O golden Lamp of Chrift, O Erkenwald,
Give prayer for us before the awful Throne,
Until we join with thee the joyous throng
In Heaven's high courts and ftarry palaces :
Where with the fong of feraphs may we fing
In jubilant praife to Chrift the Eternal King !
                                        Alleluia."*

---

* The laft fix lines are a tranflation of the *fequence* in the
Office of S. Erkenwald, printed in my *Documents,* etc., p. 23.

THE PERSONAL STAFF OF THE CATHEDRAL IN 1450.

CHAPTER II.

THE PERSONAL STAFF OF THE CATHEDRAL IN 1450.

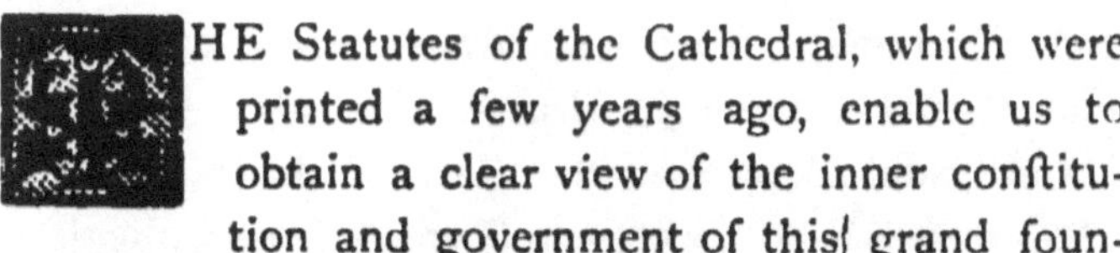

HE Statutes of the Cathedral, which were printed a few years ago, enable us to obtain a clear view of the inner conftitution and government of this grand foundation. Let us take our ftand at about the year 1450, the period at which Dean Lifieux compiled an important collection of ftatutes, many of which, however, had been gathered together by Dean Ralph de Baldock before the year 1305, and fome of which belong to a period far antecedent even to this.

In 1450, then, the Cathedral body confifted of the following perfons : The Bifhop, the Dean, the four Archdeacons, the Treafurer, the Precentor, and the Chancellor. To thefe we muft add a body of thirty Greater Canons, twelve Leffer Canons, a confiderable number of Chaplains, and thirty Vicars. A few words may be faid of thefe feveral perfons or claffes of perfons. The Subdean, Sacrift, Succentor, and many other officials, chiefly taken from the ranks of ſome of the ſeparate bodies already enumerated, will alſo require independent notice. Whoever will take the pains to remember the diſtribution of rank and office here ſet forth will have a fairly accurate view of the inner organiſation of a Cathedral of the Old Foundation.

It may be well to ſay in paſſing that the Cathedrals of the Old Foundation in England are nine in number. Theſe are Chicheſter, Exeter, Hereford, Lichfield, Lincoln, London, Saliſbury, Wells,* and York. There are eight Cathedrals of what is called the New Foundation, and theſe are Canterbury, Carliſle, Durham, Ely, Norwich, Rocheſter, Wincheſter, and Worceſter. Five Cathedrals were founded by Henry VIII., namely, Briſtol, Cheſter, Glouceſter, Oxford, and Peterborough. Two Cathedrals, Mancheſter and Ripon, were tranſformed from Collegiate into Cathedral Churches in 1847 and 1836 reſpectively; whilſt the Sees of Truro and of Liverpool are of ſtill more recent foundation.

The churches of the Old Foundation were churches of *Secular* Canons, the churches of the New Foundation were churches of *Regular* Canons. The Regular or Conventual churches were occupied by a religious community living under a certain rule (*regula*), generally the Benedictine Rule, though at Carliſle there were Canons of the Rule of S. Auguſtine. Of theſe churches the Abbot was the head, as in the churches

* The ſtudent of Cathedral Hiſtory ſhould read Mr. Freeman's admirable book on Wells Cathedral : a book whoſe value is not to be meaſured by its ſize.

of the Old Foundation the Dean prefided over the Chapter. The Welfh Cathedrals were of the Old Foundation.

At S. Paul's, then, the BISHOP held the moft honourable place. The ftatutes fupply very minute directions as to the manner in which he was to be received on the occafion of his firft vifit to the church after his confecration. It was the duty of the Dean, accompanied by the whole choir, wearing filken copes, to meet the Prelate at the weftern door and to lead him in proceffion to the high altar, the bells being rung and a fuitable office faïd. On the occafion of ordinary vifits the bells were to be rung, but there was to be no proceffion. It was the Bifhop's duty to be prefent in the Cathedral on the greater feafts, on Chriftmas Day, Eafter Day, Afcenfion Day, Whitfunday, the Feftivals of S. Paul and of S. Erkenwald, and alfo on Maundy Thurfday and Afh Wednefday. On thefe greater Feafts the Bifhop faid Mafs, the Dean and the *Sublimior Perfona* affifting, if they were prefent; in their abfence, two of the Greater Perfons (*Majores Perfonæ*) attended in their ftead. Thefe *Greater Perfons* were the Archdeacons, the Treafurer, Precentor, and Chancellor. When the Bifhop fat in his own ftall or in that of the Dean, the Dean himfelf and all other members of the church reverently bowed to the Prelate as they entered the choir. The Chancellor held before him with his own hands the book from which the chapter was to be read. In his gift were all the Prebendal Stalls, as indeed they ftill are, and the greater dignities except the Deanery. The

Epifcopal Palace ftood clofe to the Cathedral, at the weftern end of it, on the northern fide.

The DEAN was next in office to the Bifhop. When a vacancy occurred in the Deanery, the Chapter met together, and elected one of their own number to fill the vacancy ; and, if there were no canonical impediment, the Bifhop confirmed their appointment. At his inftallation, he was received at the weftern door with the fame honours as thofe accorded to the Bifhop himfelf. The Dean's authority was very great. He invefted the prebendaries, and he corrected all offenders of higher rank ; thofe of the lower grade he remitted for correction to the Chancellor. On the greater feafts he intoned the folemn antiphons. Benefices were to be conferred by the Dean and Chapter jointly : but in cafes where there were urgent reafons why a benefice fhould be at once conferred, left the King or fome other powerful perfon fhould afk that it might be beftowed upon a nominee of his own, then the Refidentiaries, with the Dean, or even, in the Dean's abfence, the Refidentiaries alone, were competent to fill the vacancy. A weekly Saturday Chapter was held, at which the fhortcomings of the week were reported and corrected : this excellent cuftom has been recently reftored. Once in three years the Dean made a vifitation of the Manors of the Chapter, and of the Houfes of the Canons in the City of London, carefully reporting their condition to the Chapter on his return, and eftimating the outlay required for repairs and dilapidations. The Manors belonging to the Dean were, in like manner, visited triennially by two of the Canons, appointed by the Chapter for that purpofe. During vacancies of the See of London the Dean and Chapter became guardians of the temporalities of the Bifhopric. Unlefs the Dean were alfo a Prebendary, he had no fhare in the Obits, nor in the Pittances, nor in the Common Fund.

In the Dean's abfence the SUBDEAN (then, as now, always one of the Minor Canons) fulfilled his duties in Choir, and exercifed fuch difcipline as belonged in right to the Dean over the Minor Canons, Chaplains, Vicars, and other minifters ; but he did not occupy the Dean's ftall. For his labours he received daily, befide his emoluments as a Minor Canon, a loaf of white bread fuch as was diftributed to the Canons, and a gallon of ale of a better quality than that which was fupplied to the inferior clergy. The Church of S. Giles, Cripplegate, was alfo granted to him in 1295.

Next in dignity to the Dean were the four ARCH-DEACONS, London, Effex, Middlefex, and Colchefter, who took precedence in the order in which their names have been enumerated. The Dean, of courfe, occupied the firft ftall on the fouth fide at the entrance of the choir ; the Archdeacon of London fat in the firft ftall on the north fide. The Archdeacon of St. Alban's was added to the number in the time of Henry VIII., but he had no ftall nor place in the Chapter.

To the TREASURER belonged the cuftody of all the goods of the church, such as the relics, books, facred veffels, veftments, altar-cloths, hangings, and the like. Twenty-fix folio pages, each page with two columns and a very moderate-sized type, in Dugdale's *Hiftory of S. Paul's*, are filled with an inventory of theſe precious things, taken in the year 1295. They were certainly of very great value. Rich ſtores of veſtments are there—copes, chaſubles, tunics, dalmatics ; altar-plate in great abundance, croſſes, chalices, patens ; proceſſional croſſes, reliquaries, cenſers. Still more precious than all theſe, great numbers of manuſcripts, early Texts of the Goſpels ; service-books of all kinds, miſſals, antiphonals, manuals, legends ; hiſtorical books, and chronicles: all lost, alas! with very few exceptions. The maker of the inventory gives us occaſional glimpſes of the illuminated pages, and tells us in a few pregnant words of the gorgeous binding, in gold and ſilver, enamel and precious ſtones.

The care of all theſe treaſures would, of courſe, be far too onerous for one man ; the Treaſurer, therefore, appointed the SACRIST as his deputy, and, under the Sacriſt, three VERGERS. The Sacriſt's duties were very multifarious. He muſt ſee that the elements for the Euchariſt were duly ſupplied ; that the linen and veſtments required in the Divine Offices were pure, ſound and clean; that they were replaced, without injury, when ſervice was ended ; that the ſervice-books were well bound, with competent claſps; that no one practiſed ſinging in the veſtibule ; that the doors of the veſtibule were opened at the firſt bell at matins, ſo that the rulers of the choir might enter in due time. In ſhort, his duties were ſo numerous, that they may be more " eaſily imagined than deſcribed."

The PRECENTOR was the director of the muſic of the Cathedral; and he, too, had his deputy, the SUC-

CENTOR, whom he appointed.   He alfo nominated the
MASTER of the Singing School.

The CHANCELLOR, or *Magifter Scholarum*, was the
perfon from whom the schoolmafters of the metropolis
received their licence to teach.   He compofed the
letters and deeds of the Chapter, and whatever was
read aloud in Chapter was read by him.   The feal
was in his cuftody, and for fealing any deed he
received one pound of pepper as his fee.*   He appointed the MASTER of the Grammar School of the
Cathedral, and repaired the houfe belonging to the
fchool at his own charges.   He prepared the Table in
which were fet down the names of the Prieft, Deacon,
and Subdeacon, who were to affift at High Mafs, and,
in general, he drew up what we fhould now call the
Rota of duty.   The punifhment of Clerks of the lower
grade was committed to him.

The CANONS or Prebendaries were thirty in number, and, with the Bifhop at their head, conftituted
the Chapter.   The Canons elected both the Bifhop and
the Dean.   Each Canon had an endowment or *corps*
attached to his ftall ; the names of the manors forming thefe endowments may ftill be read over the
ftalls of the Prebendaries in S. Paul's.   Of thefe
eftates, eight only were at fome diftance from the
Cathedral, two in Bedfordfhire, five in Effex, one in
Middlefex.   Of the other twenty-two, nine were in
Willefden ; the reft were in the immediate neighbour-
hood of London.   One of the ftalls ftill bears the
name of Confumpta per Mare ; the eftate was in

---

* *Pepper* probably ftands for any kind of fpice.

Walton-on-the-Naze, and the inundation which the name commemorates feems to have occurred about the time of the Conqueft.

Befide this feparate ftall property, a confiderable number of manors fupplied what was called the *Communa*, or *Common Fund* of the Chapter, and this was, for the moft part, allotted to the Residentiaries, of whom fomething will be faid by and by.

It was the duty of each Canon to recite daily, whether prefent in church or abfent, a portion of the Pfalter. The firft words of the fection to be recited by each ftill ftand, as of old they ftood, over the ftall of each of the Prebendaries. As there are thirty Prebendaries and one hundred and fifty Pfalms, the portion which each was bound to repeat was about five Pfalms. Dean Donne, when Prebendary of Chifwick, preached a feries of five fermons on "the Prebend of Chefwick's five Pfalms:" and in one of thefe fermons he fays, quaintly enough, "The Pfalmes are the manna of the Church. As the whole Book is manna, fo thefe five Pfalmes are my Gomer,* which I am to fill and empty every day of this manna." And in another place he fays, "Every day God receives from us [the Prebendaries], howfoever we be divided from one another in place, the Sacrifice of Praife in the whole Booke of Pfalmes. And though we may be abfent from this Quire, yet wherefoever difperfed, we make up a Quire in this fervice of faying over all the Pfalmes every day."

---

* Gomer, or Omer, as in our prefent Englifh verfion, in allufion to Exodus xvi. 32-36.

Of thefe thirty Canons a varying number, actually refident on the fpot, and taking their part in the daily offices, were called Refidentiaries. So clofely was he kept to his duties, that a Refidentiary in his firft year might not refide fo far from the Cathedral as *Hereford Houfe* in Old Dean's Lane, now called Warwick Lane; nor yet in the houfe called *Domus Dianæ* or *Rofamundæ* on Paul's Wharf Hill; thefe houfes were confidered too far diftant from the Cathedral, although either muft have been within four minutes' leifurely walk. He was to be prefent at all the Canonical Hours; to fhow large and coftly hofpitality, daily entertaining fome of the clergy, and from time to time inviting the Bifhop, and the Lord Mayor, Sheriffs, and Aldermen, for it was defirable to maintain kindly relations with the City. So late as 1843 the fhadow of the old hofpitality remained, for the Canon-in-refidence, up to the clofe of that year, ftill continued to entertain at dinner on Sundays the Clergy and Vicars-Choral of the Church who had attended the morning fervice. At that time the Sunday dinners were abandoned, and a money payment fubftituted in their ftead.

This is not the place in which to fpeak at length of the prolonged difputes about refidence; thofe who defire full information will find it in Dean Milman's *Annals*. Suffice it to fay that when the Common Fund was low, it was very difficult to find Refidentiaries, ftatutes were paffed to compel the Prebendaries to refide: when the Fund was large, the fame authority found it neceffary to limit the number.

Some Canons preferred to live upon their own eftates; others held their ftalls as one of many pluralities, for they were fometimes beftowed upon Bifhops, dignitaries, foreigners, and, it muft be added, even upon children.

As the Canons were bound to keep the Canonical Hours, and to ferve fucceffively at the High Altar, and as many were non-refident, each Canon had his Vicar. The thirty VICARS had their Common Hall. They took rank after the Chaplains, who, in their turn, were inferior to the Minor Canons. In Dean Colet's time the number of Vicars had dwindled down to fix, and that is the number of the Vicars-Choral at the prefent day. Twelve Affiftant-Vicars-Choral have recently been appointed to augment the ftrength of the Choir.

The MINOR CANONS, twelve in number, are a body as old as the Cathedral itfelf. They were incorporated as a College by Richard II. in 1394, and they ftill poffefs the Royal Charter granted to them by the King. A Statute iffued by the Dean and Chapter in 1364 ftates that they excel in honour and dignity all Chaplains in the Cathedral, that they officiate at the High Altar in the ftead of the Greater Canons, and that they are to wear almuces of fur after the manner of the Greater Canons, inftead of almuces of black cloth fuch as Chaplains wore. They poffeffed eftates of their own, and had a common feal. When a vacancy occurred in their body, they nominated to the Dean and Chapter two candidates, of whom the Dean and Chapter elected one. One of their own number was appointed by themfelves as *Cuftos* or

Warden ; two were called Cardinals, *Cardinales Chori*, an office not found in any other church in England ; another was called the *Pitantiary*, and it was his duty to collect and to diftribute the *pittances* and other payments due to the body. Their drefs confifted of a white furplice, black copes with cowls, and almuces of black fur.

The CHANTRY PRIESTS, a large body of men, were bound not only to fay mafs at the fpecial Altars to which they were attached, but alfo to attend in Choir, and there to perform fuch duties as were affigned to them.

Chaucer alludes to the eagernefs with which fome of the country clergy, to the negleft of their own benefices, fought for Chantries in S. Paul's. He con- trafts with them his model Parifh Prieft :

> " He fette not his benefice to hire,
>   And lette his fhepe accombred in the mire
>   And ran unto London, unto S. Poules,
>   To feken him a chanterie for foules,
>   Or with a Brotherhede to be withold ;
>   But dwelt at home, and keptē well his folde.
>   So that the wolf ne made it not mifcarry.
>   He was a fhepherd, and no mercenary."

The paffage will be found in the *Prologue* to the *Canterbury Tales*, vv. 509-516. In the *Canon's Yeoman's Tale* Chaucer refers to another fomewhat fimilar office, that of the *Annuallere* or Prieft who fang *Annuals* or Anniverfary Maffes for the dead :

> " In London was a Prieft, an Annuallere,
>   That therein dwelled haddē many a year."—Vv. 16, 480-1.

The time would fail to enumerate the leffer officers,

such as the Almoner, the four Vergers and their *Garciones* or Servitors, the Surveyor, the twelve Scribes or Writers who sat at certain places in the nave of the Cathedral for the service of the public, the Book Transcriber, the Book Binder, the Chamberlain, the Rent Collector, the Baker, the Brewer, and the hosts of minor persons who followed in their train.

It would be very interesting, were it possible, to form some accurate idea of the number of persons who lived within the Cathedral Close or near at hand, and who derived their sustenance from the Cathedral revenues. But the task is too difficult. The Bishop, with his Chaplains and household ; the Dean, with his household ; the Residentiaries, varying probably from two to eleven ; the twelve Minor Canons ; the thirty Vicars; the crowd of Chantry Priests (in the first year of Edward VI. there would appear to have been not less than fifty-two) ; the Choir boys, and the boys of the Grammar School ; the Minor Officials ; these must represent a very large number of persons actually resident under the shadow of the Cathedral. To these must be added the Bedesmen and poor folk who came hither for relief.

The care, labour, and forethought required to feed this multitude must have been very great and constant. Archdeacon Hale, in his *Domesday of S. Paul's*, has treated this subject very fully and minutely. Certainly the Brewer had no sinecure. The brewings for the use of the Cathedral took place nearly twice a week. " In 1286 there were one hundred brewings in the year. The quantity of grain consumed consisted of 175 quarters of barley, 175 quarters of wheat, 720 quarters of oats.   We learn from the *compotus* (or account) of 1286 that the whole number of bollæ (or gallons) brewed was 67,814." *

If the Brewer's labours were fo heavy, the Baker alfo was not idle ; Archdeacon Hale calculates, that the yearly iffue of bread amounted to no lefs than forty thoufand loaves. The weight and quality of the loaves, varying according to the rank of the perfons fupplied, were matters of fufficient importance to be regulated by ftatute.

To convey from the manors of the Cathedral the food furnifhed by the tenants, and to prepare and dif-tribute this food to the appointed recipients, muft have been a work requiring in itfelf no little organifation and the aid of a very confiderable ftaff. Roads were not always eafily paffable, ruts were deep, robberies were frequent; in times of fcarcity or of tumult a well-laden waggon on its way to the Cathedral muft have prefented a tempting bait to the fparfe population which occupied the fuburbs of the City. A ftrong efcort muft often have been neceffary to enfure that the food fhould reach the hungry mouths which eagerly expe&ted it.

* *Domefday of S. Paul's,* p. l.

*THE RITUAL AND RELIGIOUS SERVICES
OF THE CATHEDRAL.*

CHAPTER III.

THE RITUAL AND RELIGIOUS SERVICES OF THE CATHEDRAL.

HE previous chapter has exhibited the Cathedral only fo far as its ftaff was concerned. We have feen the Bifhop, Dean, Canons Refidentiary, Minor Canons, Vicars, and Chantry Priefts, a large army, with the fubordinate officers who were affociated with them. Let us now endeavour to obtain a glimpfe of the Religious Life of the Cathedral. The Statutes of S. Paul's are exceedingly full of matter illuftrating the ancient Ritual. Seven times a day the bells of the Cathedral founded for the Canonical Hours: Matins and Lauds, Prime, Tierce, Sexts, Nones, Vefpers, Compline. Various reafons have been affigned for the number of thefe Hours. Some fee the original of the number in David's words, " Seven times a day do I praife Thee, becaufe of Thy righteous judgments."*   Others fay that the Hours are a thankf-

* Pfalm cxix. 164.

giving for the completion of the Creation on the seventh day. Another theory connects them, and the idea is a very reverent one, with the Acts of our Lord in His Passion. "Evensong with His institution of the Eucharist, and washing the disciples' feet, and the going out to Gethsemane; Compline with His Agony and Bloody Sweat; Matins with His appearance before Caiaphas; Prime and Tierce with that in the presence of Pilate; Tierce with His Scourging, Crown of thorns, and Presentation to the people; Sext with His bearing the Cross, the Seven Words, and Crucifixion; Nones with His dismission of His spirit, and descent into hell; Vespers with the Deposition from the Cross, and Entombment; Compline with the setting of the Watch; Matins with His Resurrection."* A brief but excellent analysis of the several offices said at these Canonical Hours will be found in the recently published *Dictionary of Ecclesiastical Antiquities.*†

Nocturns or *Matins* was a service before daybreak; *Lauds*, a service at daybreak, quickly following, or even joining *Matins; Prime*, a late morning service, about six o'clock; *Tierce*, at nine o'clock; *Sexts*, at noon; *Nones*, at three o'clock in the afternoon; *Vespers*, an evening service; *Compline*, a late evening service at bed-time.‡ In 1263 it was ordered that Vespers and Compline should be said together.

---

* Mackenzie Walcott, *Sacred Archæology*, p. 317.

† Under the words, *Office, the Divine*, and *Hours of Prayer.*

‡ J. H. Blunt, *Annotated Book of Common Prayer*, p. xxviii.

The Apoftles' Mafs was faid at S. Paul's very early in the morning, " in prima pulfatione," by one of the Minor Canons.　The Mafs of the Bleffed Virgin followed.　The Cardinals celebrated the Capitular Mafs, at which the Minor Canons and Vicars attended, unlefs hindered by reafonable caufe.　Very many Mafses were faid by the Chantry Priefts, daily.

In 1456-7, Bifhop Kempe promulgated an important Statute.*　He had obferved, he fays, at his vifitation of the Cathedral, that the Copes and Veftments ufed in the Divine fervice were worn and well-nigh deftroyed with age.　Inftead of being an ornament and a glory to the Church, they were, in truth, a deformity and a difgrace.　He ordains that, in future, every Bifhop of the See fhould, within three years from the time of his confecration, prefent a filken Cope of not lefs value than twenty marks fterling, and he himfelf fets an excellent example by prefenting a Cope of that value.　Each Dean fhould prefent a Cope worth ten marks : and the Major Perfons and Canons were directed to pay to the Sacrift, within a year of their inftallation, fums varying in amount according to the value of their preferment, to be applied to the fame purpofe.　Thus a provifion was made for the conftant renewal of the Veftments.

Dugdale prints a very important document, a Vifitation of the Cathedral in 1295,† made by the Dean, Ralph de Baldock, which exhibits a minute and careful catalogue of the Veftments, facred veffels, relics, ornaments, and books belonging to S. Paul's.　Thofe

---

* *Statutes*, p. 204.　　　　　† Dugdale, pp. 310-335.

who deſire to underſtand this ſubject thoroughly,
ſhould carefully ſtudy ſuch a liſt as this. At preſent,
we will ſpeak only of the books. The greateſt treaſures were, probably, the *Textus*, or manuſcripts of
the Goſpels. Of theſe there were no leſs than eleven,
remarkable for their handwriting, ſome written in very
large letters, others in what was, even in 1295, an
ancient character, and all bound with great care with
ſilver covers richly ſculptured and enamelled. As
all the copies enumerated in this inventory are
gorgeouſly bound, there were no doubt many other
plainer copies, intended for everyday use. Of ritual
books there was a rich ſtore. There were four
Pſalters, eight Antiphonals ; of Books of Homilies
(including under this head Legenda, Martyrologies,
and Paſſionals) there were no leſs than twenty ; of
Miſſals there were eleven, beſide ſix others always
kept in the Church ; of Manuals, Graduals, Troperia,
Organ-books, Epiſtle-books, Goſpel-books, Collectaria
and Capitularia, an ample ſtore ; whilſt Pontificals and
Benedictionals were not wanting. Under the head of
Cronica are inſerted ſome Bibles and portions of the
Holy Scriptures, with gloſſes, and a Chronicle by the
hiſtorian Ralph de Diceto. Other books were found
at the ſeveral altars.

It cannot be ſaid, with abſolute certainty, that any
one of theſe books is now in exiſtence, except the
grand Chronicle of Ralph de Diceto, which has found
its way to the Archbiſhop's Library at Lambeth ; and
a manuſcript collection of the Miracles of the Bleſſed
Virgin, which has ſtrayed to King's College Aberdeen.

The plate, jewels, ornaments, and veſtments, not already
feized by Henry VIII., were furrendered to the King's
Commiſſioners in Edward VI., the Dean and Chapter
requeſting that (of all the magnificent treafures, in-
valuable to the hiſtory of art) they might be allowed
to retain three chalices, " two pair of Bafyns for to
bring the Communion Bread, and to receive the offerings for the poor, whereof one pair fylver for every
day, the other for Feſtivals, gilt ; a fylver Pot to put
the wine in for the Communion Table, weighing
xl. ounces ;" and the written Texts of the Gofpels and
Epiſtles ; together with a few linen cloths, fome Albs
to be made into furplices, upholſtery-work, and a
Paſtoral Staff for the Biſhop.   The faid Dean
and Chapter alfo afked an allowance of £18 6s. 3d.
" towards the charges of taking down the ſteps and
place of the High Altar," and for providing fome
neceſſaries.*

There is an exceedingly characteriſtic letter extant,
written by Dr. John Smythe, Canon Refidentiary of
S. Paul's, to Sir Edward Baynton, Knight, Vice-
Chamberlain to Queen Anne Boleyn,† which fpeaks
volumes as to the manner in which Henry VIII. dealt
with the choice Ornaments of the Church.   It appears
the King had feen in the Cathedral " a preſſyous lytle
croſſe, with a crufefyxe, all of pure gold, with a riche
rubye in the fyde, and garneſhed with foare greate
diamonds, iiij. greate emeraulds, and iiij. large bal-
laſſes, with xij. great orient perles, etc."   " Uppon the
Kings highe affectyone and plefure of the fyghte of

* Dugdale, p. 391.   † Dugdale, pp. 403-4.

the fam," Dr. Smythe and others of the Refidentiaries,
" had in comaundements by the mouthe of Mr. Secretary, in the King's name, to be with his Grace with
the fame croffe to-morrow." Dr. Smythe writes, little
thinking that his letter would ever fee the light, to fay
that by his own " efpeffyal inftruΣtyon, convayaunce,
and labores, his Grace fhall have highe plefure thearin
to the accomplefhemente of his affeΣtyon in and of
the fam of our fre gyfte;" and he concludes by putting
forth fome urgent requefts for his own private ends in
oppofition to the Dean, of whom he fpeaks evil
fecretly behind his back, but " of no mallys," as he hy-
pocritically puts it. An unfpeakably mean letter, Dr.
Smythe ! When Kings forget their duty, men of the
bafer fort are always ready to pander to their paffions.

The lofs of the rich art treafures of the Church is
much to be deplored, but far more fad, becaufe utterly
irreparable, is the lofs of the Service-books. S. Paul's,
as became its venerable age and dignity, had, like
Sarum, like York, like Hereford, a " Ufe " of its own.
And of this *Ufe* no example is certainly extant, unlefs
the two offices of SS. Peter and Paul and of S. Erkenwald, lately difcovered in the Britifh Mufeum, are
fragments of it.*   There is, indeed, a miffal preferved
in the National ColleΣtion, which is lettered, " according to the Ufe of S. Paul's Cathedral, London ;" but,
unfortunately, it is of too late a date to be of much
intereft to the Liturgiologift, for its rubrics are
according to the Ufe of Sarum. On OΣtober 15,

* I found thefe *Offices* in one of Cole's MSS., and have printed
them in *Documents*, etc., pp. 17-39.

1414, Bifhop Clifford, with the confent of the Dean and Chapter, decreed that, from the firft day of December following, the Divine Office in S. Paul's fhould henceforth be conformable to that of the Church of Salifbury for all Canonical Hours both night and day.* The original decree of Bifhop Clifford has recently been difcovered in the Chapter Houfe by Canon Stubbs. The miffal referred to has been a very beautiful volume, but its illuminations have been cut out, poffibly to adorn fome utterly recklefs collector's fcrap-book.

In the Statutes of the Cathedral, compiled by Ralph de Baldock (Dean of S. Paul's, 1294-1305, and Bifhop of London, 1305-1313), and carried down to his own time by Thomas Lisieux (Dean, 1441-1456), will be found an elaborate and minute claffification of the Feftivals of the year, arranged according to their dignity and importance.† The two Feafts of S. Erkenwald, the Depofition, April 30, and the Tranflation, November 14 ; and the two Feafts of S. Paul, the Converfion, January 25, and the Commemoration, June 30, are of courfe Feafts of the firft clafs. On fuch Feaft-days, before Vefpers and Matins, the bells gave fpecial fignal of the importance of the day : they were rung two and two before the peal was founded. On ordinary days the bells were founded fingly. Four Cantors were appointed to rule the Choir, to fing the Invitatory, and to fay the laft refponfe at Matins. To fing the Refponfe at Vefpers four of the Greater Perfons were felected by the Precentor, or, in

* Dugdale, p. 16.　　　† See *Statutes*, p. 51.

his abfence, by the Succentor. If the Bifhop, Dean, and Four *Perfons* were prefent, the latter, with the Dean, fang the Refponfe. At Vefpers, Matins, and other Hours, four boys in furplices faid the Verficles. Two priefts with cenfers incenfed the Altar at the *Magnificat* and *Benedictus*, and fang the Antiphons.

Thefe details, however, will hardly intereft any who have not made ritual a fpecial ftudy. Suffice it to fay that each day brought with it an unceafing round of fervices. The Canonical Hours were faid, the Maffes celebrated; care was taken for religious inftruction by preaching. As early as 1281, Richard de Swine-field, Archdeacon of London, afterwards Bifhop of Hereford, was appointed preacher in the Cathedral.* He was "learned in the facred page, and an excellent preacher:" "a moft approved theologian, and a gracious preacher;" beloved by Clergy and Laity of the City. A few years later, Bifhop Richard de Gravefend appointed a Divinity Lecturer, and Ralph de Baldock, his fucceffor, endowed the office in 2 Edward II.

Each officer had his fpecial work to do. The Precentor appointed what mufic fhould be fung, and nominated the perfons who were to fing it. The care of the finging fchool, and of the general inftruction of the chorifters, brought its daily round of duty. The Treafurer, with his pricelefs ftore of rich jewels, books, and veftments, found ample occupation for himfelf and his attendants. The Chancellor gave licenfes to fchoolmafters, and, it may well be fup-

* *Statutes*, p. 188.

grauat̄ infirmitaſ. q̄ri pſona debet de
colata monibꝫ ꝺ iuxta. q̄ curā aīmarū
gerere. q̄ causā ꝫ utilitates eiusdem
ecclie: ſalubri ualeat ordinatione
disponere.   beda libᵒ ij. capᵐ̄

A uo. ordinauit mellitum epm̄ in ciuita   tercio
te lundonia. iuſtum in ciuitate rofenſi.   Beð libro ii

Edelbertus rex   capᵐ̄ iii.

conſtruxit ecꝉiam ſꝗ pauli lund.   Beð lib· ii.

Augᷤ pro ſe ordinauit laurentiū epm̄.   capᵐ̄ iii.

ꝫ epos britannie cōuocauit ad collo
quium.

pofed, examined them and their fcholars. Two fchools only, in all the City of London, claimed exemption from his jurifdiction: the fchool of S. Mary-le-Bow, and that of S. Martin-le-Grand. The Scriptorium of the Cathedral was an important department, and was ably governed: the grand Pauline hand is well known to thofe who have worked in the archives. The *Statuta Majora*, and a noble folio copy of Ralph de Diceto's *Hiftory*—the former preferved at S. Paul's, the latter now at Lambeth Library—are very fine examples of the bold, clear hand, in which the Pauline Scribes excelled.* The inks, both red and black, retain their full luftre: the colours could fcarcely have been more beautiful on the day that the writing was executed. Thefe accomplifhed Scribes wrote the Church Service-books, and multiplied copies of rare manufcripts to enrich the Library. Every man had his work to do, when the fyftem was properly developed.

To the ordinary daily offices muft be added occafional fervices. Many pilgrims vifited the famous fhrines of the Cathedral. The devout people came in great numbers to kneel at the renowned fhrines of S. Erkenwald, and of Mellitus, and of Roger Niger. A fhort form of prayer, with a hymn, which may probably have been recited by pilgrims at the fhrine of S. Erkenwald has been lately printed.†

Occafionally irregular forms of devotion fprung up

* The accompanying plate gives a *fac fimile* of a few lines from Ralph de Diceto's *Hiftory*.
† *Documents*, p. 16.

in the Cathedral, like the ſtrange popular devotion to Thomas of Lancaſter. Thomas, Earl of Lancaſter, " was the ſon of Edmund, the ſecond ſon of Henry III., and titular King of Sicily, by Blanche of Artois, queen dowager of Navarre. Couſin to the King, uncle to the Queen, high ſteward of England, poſſeſſor of the Earldoms of Lancaſter, Leiceſter, and Derby, he ſtood at the head of a body of vaſſals who, under Montfort and the Ferrers, had long been in oppoſition to the Crown. He was married to the heireſs of Henry de Lacy, Earl of Lincoln and Saliſbury. A ſtrong, unſcrupulous, coarſe, and violent man, he was devoid of political foreſight, incapable of political ſelf-ſacrifice, and unable to uſe power when it fell into his hands. His cruel death and the later develop-ment of the Lancaſtrian power, by a ſort of reflex action, exalted him into a patriot, a martyr, and a ſaint."* His ſtory cannot even be epitomiſed here. Suffice it to ſay, that he was defeated at the battle of Boroughbridge, March 16, 1322, and taken captive by Sir Andrew Harclay. " Six days after his capture, the great earl, in his own caſtle of Pomfret, before a body of peers with Edward himſelf at their head, was tried, condemned, and beheaded, as a rebel taken in arms againſt the King, and convicted of dealing with the Scots. The haſte and cruelty of the proceeding were too ſadly juſtified by the earl's own conduct in the caſe of Gaveſton. Yet cruel, unſcrupulous, treacherous, and ſelfiſh as Thomas of

* Canon Stubbs' *Conſtitutional Hiſtory of England,* ii. pp. 349, 350.

Lancafter is fhown by every recorded act of his life to have been, there was fomething in fo fudden and fo great a fall that touches men's hearts. The caufe was better than the man or the principles on which he maintained it. A people, new as yet to political power, faw in the chief opponent of royal folly a champion of their own rights : rude, infolent, and unwarlike, an adulterer and a murderer, he was liberal of his gifts to the poor, and a bountiful patron of the clergy : his fame grew after his death."* By-and-by the commons prayed for the canonifation of Earl Thomas, a propofal which was revived from time to time. It is even faid by Walfingham to have been fuccefsful in 1390.† It was reported that miracles were wrought at his tomb. At Briftol alfo, Henry de Montfort and Henry Wylyngton, who had been hanged there, were faid to be working miracles. The earl's relics fweated blood, it was believed.‡ A tablet erected in S. Paul's to commemorate him was the fcene of fome of thefe alleged miracles. "The crooked were made ftraight, the blind received their fight, and the deaf their hearing, and other beneficial works of grace were there openly fhown," fays the *French Chronicle of London.*§ A fhort *Office* probably intended to be faid at his tomb, and a more elaborate Office, confifting of an Antiphon, Collect, Profe, Sequence, and two Hymns, will be found in

---

* Canon Stubbs' *Conftitutional Hiftory of England*, Library Edition, ii. p. 380.

† *Ibid.*, pp. 385, 401.   ‡ *Ibid.*, iii. p. 220.

§ Edited by H. T. Riley, pp. 257, 258.

*Documents illustrating the History of S. Paul's Cathe-dral.** Crowds of people thronged to the Cathedral to pay their devotion to this faint of their own making, for it is highly improbable that he was ever canonifed.   Lingard fays,† that the requeft for his canonifation was not even noticed by the Pope.

This new *culte* was exceedingly unpalatable to the King. On June 28, 1323, Edward II. iffued a peremptory letter addreffed to Stephen Gravefend, Bifhop of London, concerning this Tablet and thefe fpecial devotions.   The Tablet muft be removed ; upon it was pourtrayed the effigy of Thomas, formerly Earl of Lancafter, "a rebel and our enemy."   The devotion before it had not received the fanction of the Holy See.   The Bifhop had, neverthelefs, con-nived at it.   The King does not hefitate to infinuate that the Bifhop had been influenced by low and bafe motives, and that the love of "filthy lucre" had not been wanting.   The people are to be reftrained from thefe devotions, that the indignation of God and the King may be avoided.   Accordingly, on July 7, by virtue of the King's writ, iffued from the Chancery, the Tablet was taken down, and the wax taper which ftood before it was removed.   For fome little time, however, the people continued to make oblations at the pillar on which the Tablet had hung.‡

A relic of the devotion to Thomas of Lancafter was brought to light in 1824, when a richly-embroidered chafuble of the time of Henry VII. was difcovered in a walled-up crypt beneath the chancel of the parifh

---

* *Documents*, pp. 11-14.   † Lingard, iii. p. 34.
‡ *Documents*, pp. xviii., xix.

church at Warrington. On one of the orphreys of the
chafuble is the figure of a man fully armed, holding a
battle-axe in his left hand, which has been decided
by the late Dr. Rock to be the effigy of the Earl
of Lancafter. Leaden brooches, reprefenting a knight
holding a battle-axe, have been found in London, and
thefe, too, may poffibly be tokens given to pilgrims
who had vifited the tablet.

The meetings of the various Guilds for their own
appointed fervices, and the proceffions from parifhes in
the City to the Cathedral at ftated times, efpecially
at Pentecoft and at certain other Feafts, added greatly
to the multitude of worfhippers who thronged the
long-drawn aifles of the Cathedral.

The foolifh and profane rites of the Boy-Bifhop
found their place here, as in other cathedrals and very
many parifh churches. Holy Innocents' Day, Chil-
dermas, as the old name is, was his grand day of
office. On the eve of S. Nicholas, the fpecial patron
of children (December 6 is the faint's feftival), the
children of the choir elected one of their number to
be the boy-bifhop, and others who were to be his
clerks. A fet of Pontifical veftments was provided for
him. At S. Paul's thefe comprifed a white mitre embroidered with little flowers, a rich paftoral ftaff, and,
no doubt, all other veftments pertaining to his fuppofed dignity. His attendants were vefted in copes.
" Towards the end of evenfong on S. John's Day, the
boy-bifhop and his clerks, arrayed in their copes and
having burning tapers in their hands, and finging

thofe words of the Apocalypfe (ch. xiv.), *Centum quadraginta*, walked proceffionally from the Choir to the Altar of the Bleffed Trinity, which the boy-bifhop incenfed. Afterwards they all fang the anthem, and he recited the prayer commemorative of the Holy Innocents. Going back into the Choir, thefe boys took poffeffion of the upper Canons' ftalls, and thofe dignitaries themfelves had to ferve in the boys' places, and carry the candles, the thurible, the book, like acolytes, thurifers, and lower clerks. Standing on high, wearing his mitre, and holding his paftoral ftaff in his left hand, the boy-bifhop gave his folemn benediction to all prefent : and, while making the fign of the crofs over the kneeling crowd, he said :

> " Crucis figno vos configno ; veftra fit tuitio.
>   Quos nos emit et redemit fuæ carnis pretio."*

The next day, the feaft of Holy Innocents, the boy-bifhop preached a fermon. Two fuch fermons in Englifh delivered, the one at S. Paul's and the other at Gloucefter, have lately been printed.† Dean Colet ex-preffly ordered, in the Statutes of his School, that all the fcholars fhould attend at the Cathedral to hear this fermon, " with the maifters and ferveyors of the fcole," and that each of the children fhould offer one penny to the youthful Prelate. The boy-bifhop was even

* Dr. Rock, *Church of our Fathers*, vol. iii., pt. 2, pp. 215-219.

† *Two Sermons preached by the Boy-Bifhop, at S. Paul's, temp. Henry VII., and at Gloucefter, temp. Mary*. Edited by the late able antiquary, Mr. John Gough Nichols, for the *Camden Society Mifcellany*, vol. vii.

allowed to commence the mafs, and to go on "up to
the more folemn part of the offertory."*

In 1263 fome rules were drawn up for the regulation
of this function at S. Paul's. Care was to be taken
left the liberty of that day fhould degenerate into
licenfe. The boy-bifhop muft not, in future, felect
any of the Canons, Major or Minor, to bear the tapers
or the cenfer, but he muft felect his minifters from
thofe who fat on the fecond or third form. The Dean
fhould provide a horfe on which the boy-bifhop might
ride forth to give his benediction to the people, and
each Refidentiary fupplied a horfe for fome other
perfon in the proceffion. There was feafting throughout the Clofe. The boy-bifhop, attended by two
chaplains, two taper-bearers, five clerks, and two of
the Church fervants preceding him with wands, fupped
with one of the Canons Refidentiary.

Cranmer forbad thefe proceffions, Queen Mary
reftored them, and they were finally abolifhed by
Queen Elizabeth.

A few notes as to Poft Reformation ufages may not
be unacceptable.

Bifhop Bancroft's *Vifitation* in 1598† gives us fome
details about the Divine Offices. Prayers were faid
in the Jefus Chapel at five in the morning, and at fix
o'clock in the winter, by the Minor Canons. The Subdean and the two Cardinals were, by ancient cuftom,

* *Statutes* pp. 91-93.
† The returns, in manufcript, are ftill preferved at the Cathedral.

exempted from this duty. The Saturday Chapter was retained. In term-time there was a divinity lecture, with prayers. The Lord Mayor and Aldermen aſſembled in S. Dunſtan's Chapel " every Sondaye morninge before thei goe vnto the Sarmon." Sermons were preached and Pſalms were ſung at Paul's Croſs. The details are ſcanty—probably the *Returns* are very imperfect.

In 1636 Archbiſhop Laud viſited the Cathedral, as Metropolitan. The Dean and Chapter proteſted ſtrongly, but in vain, againſt this exerciſe of the Archbiſhop's juriſdiction, but the King, in a curt letter, required their ſubmiſſion. The Returns of the Dean and Chapter, and of the Minor Canons, to the Viſitation queſtions have lately been printed in the *Reports* of the Hiſtorical Manuſcripts Commiſſion.* " Divine ſervice is daylie vſed, and the ſacraments duly adminiſtered in due time by ſinging and note according to yᵉ vſuall cuſtome of yᵉ ſaid church." A ſermon was preached every Sunday afternoon by the Dean or Reſidentiaries, or ſome deputed by them : previouſly two lecturers had taken this duty, a payment of £6 13s. 4d. being aſſigned to each. On every holiday the morning ſermon was preached by the *Greater Perſons*, the afternoon ſermon by a lecturer. Thrice a week in term-time a lecturer preached, who received £60 a year for his pains, £20 from the Chancellor and £40 from " an addition given by Dr. White," the pious founder of Sion College. There were four Reſidentiaries, and ten choriſters, in theſe days. The Dean

* *Appendix to Fourth Report*, pp. 154-157.

and Chapter make return, with the greateſt *naïveté* that the conſtitutions of the Church were duly obſerved, "excepting that in the long vacacion *and times of dangerous infeƈtion* wee all repaire to our benefices, leaveing the ordering of the Choir and Divine Service to the Subdeane according to the cuſtome of the church."

But Biſhop Compton's *Viſitation* in 1696 * is the moſt important Poſt Reformational Viſitation extant. The minuteſt details of public worſhip are here, ſet forth. Daily prayers are to be ſaid at ten and three; on Sundays, morning prayer at nine. The firſt Leſſon was read by a Vicar-Choral. The Litany was ſung by two Minor Canons, in the midſt of the Choir. The *Venite* and the Pſalms for the day were to be ſung in alternate verſes, antiphonally, *et harmonice*, as often as it ſeemed good to the Dean or Residentiaries. Early Morning Prayer was ſaid at ſix from Lady Day to Michaelmas, and at ſeven from Michaelmas to Lady Day; Evening Prayer at ſix o'clock all the year round.

But probably the moſt important feature of Biſhop Compton's regulations was his Order for Preaching on all Feſtival Days. It is in ſubſtance the ſame as that now in uſe. Every one of the Greater Perſons and Canons, found himſelf reſponſible for one or two ſermons in the courſe of each year; and was thus brought into viſible aſſociation with the Cathedral. There was to be a celebration of Holy Communion

---

* *Statuta*, pp. 281-286.

on all Sundays and Feaſts, the *Triſagion* and the *Gloria in Excelſis* being ſung by the Choir.

At Biſhop Gibſon's Viſitation in 1742, the hours of the daily ſervice were altered to a quarter before ten, and a quarter paſt three.

In November, 1869, the daily morning ſervice was ordered to be ſaid at ten. The afternoon ſervice has, for many years, been ſaid at four. The Sunday ſervices were then at half paſt ten and a quarter paſt three, and the Sunday afternoon ſermon, which had been preached immediately after the Anthem, was at this time removed to the end of the ſervice. In 1872 an early celebration of the Holy Communion, at eight o'clock in the morning, on Sundays and Feſtivals was introduced : and ſince 1 January, 1877, there has been a *daily* celebration at the ſame hour.

A WALK ROUND OLD S. PAUL'S:
THE EXTERIOR.

CHAPTER IV.

S it is juſt poſſible that ſome of my readers may not be quite familiar with Old S. Paul's, its exterior and its interior, I will beg leave to act as their guide and will aſk them to accompany me on a ſhort excurſion. We will ſtart from the banks of the Fleet river, and imagine ourſelves to be walking up Ludgate Hill ſomewhere about the year 1510. At this time the Fleet, which took its origin at Hampſtead Hill, augmented by the waters of the Old Bourne (we have corrupted the name into Holborn), was beginning to acquire a ſomewhat evil reputation. The upper waters had been diverted and the once navigable ſtream was becoming choked and ſtagnant. Pope directs us in his *Dunciad* (Book II.):

> " To where Fleet-ditch, with diſemboguing ſtreams
> Rolls the large tribute of dead dogs to Thames,
> The king of dykes ! than whom no ſluice of mud
> With deeper ſable blots the ſilver flood.

And Swift, in his *City Shower*, in vigorous if not refined language, tells how

> " Drown'd puppies, ftinking fprats, all drown'd in mud ;
>   Dead cats, and turnip-tops, come tumbling down the flood."

Leaving the valley of the unfavoury Fleet, let us
turn our fteps eaftward, and afcend the Hill. We
foon arrive at the ancient wall (a fragment of it
ftill remains), and pafs under Lud Gate itfelf. [It
croffed the hill a little to the weft of S. Martin's
Church. Roman remains, a fragment of a ftatue of
Hercules, and a monument dedicated by Anencletus,
a Roman foldier, to Claudina Martina his wife, have
been difcovered near at hand.] The gate itfelf is
ufed as a prifon, and contains a chapel built by
Dame Agnes Fofter in the middle of the fifteenth
century.*

Paffing through this ftrongly fortified gate, which
is faid to have been " repaired or rather new-built " in
1215, when portions of the houfes of fome opulent Jews
were ufed in the reconftruction, we proceed along Ludgate Street, and foon arrive at the Great Weftern Gate
of the Clofe fpanning the ftreet towards the ends of
Creed Lane and Ave Maria Lane. The Cathedral
ftands within a fpacious walled enclofure. The wall,
erected about 1109, and by letters patent of Edward I.,
greatly ftrengthened in 1285, extends from the N.E.
corner of Ave Maria Lane, runs Eaftward along
Paternofter Row to the North end of Old Change in
Cheapfide ; thence Southward to Carter Lane, and on

* It was taken down in 1760-2.

the North of Carter Lane to Creed Lane, back to the Great Weftern Gate. There are fix entrances to the enclofure. The firft is the Great Weftern Gate, by which we have juft entered; the fecond, in Paul's Alley in Paternofter Row, leading to the poftern gate of the Cathedral; the third, at Canon Alley; the fourth or Little Gate, where S. Paul's Churchyard and Cheapfide now unite; the fifth, S. Auguftine's Gate, at the Weft end of Watling Street; the fixth, at Paul's Chain.

Entering beneath the Great Gate, we fee at once the Weftern front of the Cathedral. Perhaps, at firft fight, we may be a little difappointed, for it is a fimple Norman façade, and by no means ornate. Its broad fimplicity takes away from its real fize, and we fhould form no juft idea of its height were it not for the Church of S. Gregory neftling clofe to the Cathedral on its Southern fide, the Northern wall of the little fanctuary touching the Cathedral wall. The Church feems infignificant, and helps to fhow us how vaft the Cathedral is, juft as S. Margaret's Church helps to "fcale" Weftminfter Abbey. The Weftern elevation is flanked by two towers, the Northern of which is clofely attached to the Bifhop's Palace; the Southern, commonly called the Lollards' Tower,* is ufed by the Bifhop as a prifon for heretics.

But that which ftrikes us moft is the prodigious height of the fpire. The tower on which it ftands is 285 feet high, the fpire, of wood covered with lead, is

---

* Well known to the readers of Fox's *Acts and Monuments.*

208 feet more ; 493 feet in all.* Its height was pro-
verbial. In Lodge's *Wounds of Civil War*, a clown
talks of the " Paul's Steeple of honour," meaning by
that phraſe, the higheſt point that could be attained.

On our left, on the Northern ſide of the Nave, at
its Weſtern end, ſtands the Biſhop of London's
Palace. [The name of London Houſe Yard ſtill helps
to preſerve the memory of it.] A private door leads
from the Palace into the Nave of the Cathedral, ſo
that the Biſhop can paſs directly into the grand
Church. The Palace, the Deanery, and ſome of the
more important houſes in the Cloſe have private
Chapels of their own. The Chapel in the Palace has
a crypt or " lower Chapel " beneath it, like the ex-
quiſite Chapel and crypt of Lambeth Palace.

Paſſing beyond the Palace and its grounds, we
arrive at Pardon Church Haugh. Here is a large
and goodly cloiſter, wherein are buried ſundry perſons,
" ſome of worſhip, and ſome of honour," whoſe monuments, in number and curious workmanſhip, " paſſed
all other " in the Cathedral itſelf. Within the cloiſter
ſtands a Chapel, founded by Gilbert, father of the
ſainted Thomas à Becket, and rebuilt by Dean Moore
in the time of Henry V. But we ſhall turn away
even from the chapel and the monuments to ſtudy
the very ſtriking paintings on the wall of the cloiſter:
for here is pourtrayed in all its quaint horrors the
Dance of Death. And leſt we ſhould fail to underſtand the meaning of the ſymbolical paintings, verſes
tranſlated out of the French by John Lydgate, a

* I adopt throughout Mr. Ferrey's meaſurements.

monk of Bury S. Edmund's, are added to expound them to us.   But, indeed, the allegory needs little expofition.   Death, perfonified by a fkeleton, appears in each feveral picture, holding by the hand a Pope, an Emperor, a Cardinal, a King, a Patriarch, a Conftable, an Archbifhop, in fhort, all orders and degrees of men : for

> " To this complexion we must come at last."

Lydgate's verfes are a Dialogue between Death and the perfons whom he conducts.   We will tranffer a fingle example to our tablets.   Death leads along a merchant, and thus fpeaks to him :

> " Ye rich Marchant ye mot look hitherward,
>   That paffed have full many divers lond,
>   On horfe and foot, having moft regard
>   To lucre and winning as I underftond,
>   But now to dance you mot give me your hond,
>   For all your labour full litle avayleth now,
>   Adue vainglory. both of free and bond,
>   None more covet then thei that have ynough."

To whom the Merchant maketh anfwer :

> " By many a hill and many a ftrong vale
>   I have travailed with many marchandife,
>   Over the fea down carrie many a bale,
>   To fondry Iles more then I can devife :
>   Mine heart inward ay fretteth with covetife,
>   But all for nought now death doth me conftrein,
>   For which I fee by record of the wife,
>   Who all embraceth litle fhal conftrein." *

---

* Dugdale, p. 423.   Should we not read *contein* inftead of *conftrein* in the laft line : and, perhaps, *long* inftead of *ftrong* in the firft line?

You will think Dan Lydgate is very quaint, and indeed he apologifes for his rude fpeech, as you will fee if you will walk but a few fteps farther and read the lines with which he concludes his poem. He says :

> " Out of the French I drough it of intent,
>   Not word by word, but following in fubftance,
>   And froum Paris to England it fent
>   Only of purpofe you to do pleafance.
>   Have me excufed, my name is John Lidgate,
>   Rude of language, I was not borne in France,
>   Her curious miters in Englifh to tranflate,
>   Of other tong I have no fuffifance." *

Over the eaftern fide of the cloifter is a fair library built by Walter Sherington, Chancellor of the Duchy of Lancafter in King Henry VI.'s time, and Canon Refidentiary : and the Librarian can fpread before us countlefs and pricelefs manufcripts.† Here are books on the four parts of Grammar ; the never-failing Boethius ; books on Medicine by Galen, Hippocrates, Avicenna, and Egidius ; Ralph de Diceto's Chronicles, and his difcourfes on Ecclefiafticus and Wifdom ; a large number of manufcripts of portions of the Holy Scriptures, with gloffes and with fermons founded upon them ; the great commentary of Nicolas

---

* Perhaps it is hardly neceffary to add a note to thefe verfes to explain one or two forms unfamiliar to modern readers, fuch as *mot* for *muft*, *lond* and *hond* for *land* and *hand*, *adue* for *adieu*, *covetife* for *covetoufnefs*, *miters* for *metres*, *fuffifance* for *fufficiency*.

† The catalogue of thefe manufcripts fills fix clofely printed folio pages, Dugdale, pp. 393-399.

de Lyra; works of the illuftrious fathers of the Church, fuch as Chryfoftom, Auguftine, Gregory, Bernard, Jerome, Thomas Aquinas; fome writings of Jofephus; and, that claffical literature may not be entirely unreprefented, we find in this ancient catalogue, drawn up in 1458, works of Seneca, Cicero, Suetonius, and Virgil. Books of Decretals, and works on Civil Law, are, of courfe, not wanting. Perhaps from yonder prefs the Librarian will draw a few printed books, rare as they ftill are. In this quiet retreat we may fpend a long fummer's day, merely in turning over the richly emblazoned pages. We have not, however, made half the circuit of the Clofe, fo let us reluctantly fay *farewell* to the Librarian.

The College of the Minor Canons lies to the North of the Cathedral, and Canon Alley to the Eaft: between the two is Walter Sherington's Chapel, near to the North Door. To the Eaft, adjoining Canon Alley and ftill on the North fide of the Cathedral, is the Charnel Chapel, an early building, already ftanding in the reign of Edward I., containing fome monuments and alabafter figures. Beneath is a crypt in which are carefully piled together an enormous quantity of bones taken from the adjoining cemetery. [The Chapel was pulled down by the Duke of Somerfet in 1549, and the materials ufed in the building of Somerfet Houfe in the Strand. It is faid that the bones from the vault beneath amounted to a thoufand cart-loads, and that they were conveyed to Finfbury Fields, with fo much foil to cover

them as did raiſe the ground for three windmills to
ſtand on.]*

At the North-east angle of the Choir ſtands the
famous outdoor Pulpit, Paul's Croſs.†   Eaſtward of
this we come upon an excavation, and a large number
of labourers ; and amongſt them a grave eccleſiaſtic.
He is very ſimply dreſſed, his habit is of woollen cloth
and quite plain ; it is black in colour, though the
higher clergy are uſually clad in purple.   Yet there
is ſomething about him which beſpeaks the man of
learning : his bright eye, his refined and well-marked
features, his carriage and demeanour, his "handſome and well-grown " perſon, evidently mark him out
as a man of no common order.   We enquire his name.
It is Colet, the newly appointed Dean, and the building about to be erected is S. Paul's School.‡   Till
lately an "old ruined houſe " had cumbered the
ground.   It will ſoon be covered by new buildings.
We ſee the plans : it will be a "handſome fabric,"
with "houſes as handſome " for the reſidence of the
maſters.   A noble gift, and worthy of the man.

We paſs the Eaſtern end of the Church, and as we
do ſo, gaze with great admiration at its magnificent
roſe window, one of the very fineſt in all England.
We alſo obſerve the clochier or bell-tower, which

° The windmills are ſeen in Aggas' Map of London.   Wind-
mill Street, Finſbury, marks the ſite.

† Paul's Croſs muſt have ſpecial and ſeparate notice—Chapters VII. to X.

‡ It was founded, Grafton and Lily agree, in 1509.   Colet
became Dean in 1505.

ftands at the Eaft end of the Church.   The tower has
a fpire of wood covered with lead, and within it
hung of old time a bell which has often called the
citizens of London to a Folkmote, held clofe befide it.
It now contains four very great bells, known as the
Jefus Bells, becaufe they fpecially belong to the
Jefus Chapel in the crypt of the Cathedral.   On the
top of the fpire is an image of S. Paul.

[The bells, fays Dugdale, were won by Sir Miles
Partridge, Knight, from Henry VIII. at one caft of
the dice.   Sir Miles pulled them down, but Dugdale
adds, with fardonic fatiffaction, that the fame Sir
Miles afterwards, temp. Edward VI., fuffered death on
Tower Hill for matters relating to the Duke of Somerfet.   He was hanged, according to Fox, 26th February,
1552.]

Turning Weftward, along the fouth fide of the Clofe,
we are attracted by the high-pitched roof of the
Chapter Houfe, rifing above the lofty walls which enclofe it.   But we cannot pafs into this enclofure from
without; we muft wait patiently till we can enter the
Cathedral, and unfortunately the Dean and Chapter
have allowed "cutlers, budget-makers, and others, firft
to build low fheds, but now high houfes, which do hide
this beautiful fide of the Church, fave only the top and
fouth gate."   Near at hand is the houfe of the Chancellor, and turning afide, down Paul's Chain, we arrive
at a great gate, and fee within it many fair tenements.
One of thefe bears the name of Diana's Chamber,
Camera Dianæ.   The refidents tell us a ftrange ftory,
for they fay that here Henry II. kept Fair Rofamond,

and that as he had called her at Woodſtock *Rosa Mundi*, ſo here he called her *Diana*. And they point out to us " Teſtifications of tedious Turnings and Windings, as alſo of a Paſſage under Ground from this Houſe to Caſtle Baynard ;" and they ſay that this was, no doubt, " the King's way from thence to his *Camera Dianæ*, or the Chamber of his brighteſt Diana." But the ſtory is not very edifying, and ſo we leave them. We are going into the preſence of one who has little reliſh for ſuch tales, and we will not even ſay that we have turned aſide out of the ſafer precinĉts of the Cloſe.

Here, too, is Paul's Brewhouſe,* and near to this an ancient houſe built of ſtone, belonging to the Cathedral, and formerly let to the Blunts, Lords Mountjoy, and afterwards to the Doctors of the Civil Law and Arches. On the ſame ſide is another great houſe called Paul's Bakehouſe, employed in baking of bread for the Church of Paul's.

A maſſive chain, *Paul's Chain*, bars the way againſt carriages; but we are on foot, and we once more enter the encloſure, gaining a grand view of the ſpire from the Southern ſide. To the Weſt lies the Deanery, an ancient houſe, given to the Church by a very famous Dean, the hiſtorian, Ralph de Diceto. We are eſpecially privileged, and we will enter. The preſent Dean, John Colet, is a man temperate almoſt to auſterity. For many years he has eaten but one meal a day, that of dinner. It is juſt dinner-time, and we will go to

---

* Paul's Brewhouſe became at a later period the Paul's Head Tavern. Stow, p. 137.

the dining-hall. The Dean is feated at the head of the long table, his houfehold and a few chofen guefts form the company. Grace is faid, and a boy—probably he is one of the Cathedral choir, for he has a very frefh and pleafant voice—begins to read a leffon out of S. Paul's Epiftles: at other times the lection is taken from the Proverbs of Solomon. His fweet voice ceafes, and prefently the Dean begins to fpeak. He makes the chapter which has been read the fubject of his difcourfe. His talk is grave and ferious, but never wearifome. By-and-by he changes his tone, almoft before the company are "fatiffied rather than fatiated" with what he has faid. He rifes early from the table, for he has no delight in coarfe fenfual pleafures. He loves the fociety of congenial friends: he will fit with them till very late in the evening, difcourfing on religion or on learning. If he has no congenial friend, one of his fervants will read a portion of Holy Scripture to him, and the Dean will very likely prepare for fome fermon to be delivered in the Church or at the Crofs, or fome lecture to be addreffed to a learned audience. He never travels without a book, and all his talk is feafoned with religion.

It is time, however, that we left this pleafant company. There are divers houfes for the ufe of the Canons at the Weft end of the Church, and alfo refidences for the Vicars: but thefe, and the other dwellings fcattered round the Clofe, we have not time to vifit. Let us haften to the Weftern Portal. But ftay a moment; the Bifhop, Richard Fitz-James, is juft entering within the gates of the Palace. Let us follow him ; perhaps he may fay fomething about his neighbour the Dean.   It is rumoured that the Bifhop does not greatly love the Dean.

Colet has fpoken very boldly in fermons at the Crofs and before the King againft the vulgar fuperftitions and other errors of the time.   He has denounced the corruptions which were rampant in the Church. Even of his own clergy, and of the choir, fome have been ftrictly and fternly called to order for their irregular behaviour.   There are thofe who fmart under the lafh of his rebuke, and who do not love his almoft afcetic life, as that is a fharper rebuke than his words.   But let us hear Bifhop Fitz-James, as he fits in his ftudy with fome of his clergy in private conference.   They are talking about the Dean.   We juft catch the word *herefy*, half whifpered at prefent.   " He has taught," fays the Bifhop, " that images are not to be worfhipped.   That is rank herefy enough.   Shall the fhrine of S. Erkenwald be deferted? Shall rich gems and offerings no longer be laid upon its altar?   And the Great Crucifix at the North door, are men no longer to kneel before it?"   The Bifhop is very angry.

" But that is not all," fays one ; " he has preached againft the temporal poffeffions of the Bifhops.   He faid that the command, *Feed my fheep*, was not meant of hofpitality, becaufe the Apoftles were poor, and unable to give entertainments."   The Bifhop does not find this teaching very palatable.   " Why does not the Dean drefs as becomes his rank ?   Can he never forget that his father was a mercer ? Why does he veſt his ſchool, with its new-fangled learning, in the Mercer's Guild, and not in the hands of the Biſhop, or, at leaſt, of the Dean and Chapter ?"

But there is more to come. " He has preached againſt ſome men reading their ſermons in a cold manner." This was very cruel, for Biſhop Fitz-James was an old man, and " had taken up that idler way of preaching," as Eraſmus calls it. The Biſhop loves him not. He has preſented Articles againſt him to Archbiſhop Warham : but Warham knows the integrity and the worth of Colet, and has diſmiſſed the Articles without even calling on the Dean to reply. *Hinc illæ lachrymæ.* The Biſhop takes a dreary view of the ſituation, as he ſits alone in his ſtudy, when his courtiers are gone—for Biſhops have courtiers as well as Kings—he laments the degeneracy of the times, and he ſees heavy clouds gathering which he cannot diſpel.

And indeed heavy clouds had gathered, and the firſt big drops began to fall, and the diſtant roar of the coming tempeſt could be heard by thoſe who, like Colet, had ears to hear. The Reformation was at hand.

But we muſt leave Deanery and Palace alike, if we are ever to ſee the interior of the Church at all. Yet ſtay, the day is nearly ſpent. We will viſit the Cathedral itſelf to-morrow ; and we will come quite early, that we may ſee the riſing ſun ſtreaming in through the ſtoried eaſtern window ; and making the chequered pavement glorious **with** brilliant colours.*

* The authorities for this chapter are Dugdale, Knight's *Life of Colet*, Nichols' *Pilgrimages to Walfingham and to Canterbury*, Longman's *S. Paul's*, my own *Documents illustrating the Hiftory of S. Paul's*, Maitland's *London*. etc., and original documents.

CHAPTER V.

A WALK ROUND OLD ST. PAUL'S: THE INTERIOR.

E will now commence our propofed vifit to the interior of the Cathedral. Let us enter at the Weftern end. Here are three ftately gates or entries, curioufly wrought of ftone. Obferve efpecially the middle gate, with its maffive pillar of brafs, to which the leaves of the great door are faftened. We pafs in at the open wicket. What a ftriking profpect! The Cathedral is 596 feet in length ;* and the breadth, including the aifle walls, is 104 feet. The grand Nave has no lefs than twelve bays, and the Choir—we fhall fee it by-and-by—has an equal number. Juft where we are ftanding the roof is 93 feet in height ; the Choir is even loftier by fome eight feet—a ftriking feature. The ftyle is very grand and very fimple, as that of large Norman Naves is apt to be; the vaulted roof is so

* Longer by 66 feet than Winchefter. Dugdale says 690 feet, but this is probably an error.

far above us that we cannot tell its material. Some say that it is of wood, but others that it is of ſtone, as the great flying buttreſſes outſide would have prepared us to expeſt. The triforium alſo is Norman, but the clereſtory windows are Pointed. On our left, entered from the ſecond bay, is the Court of Convocation ; and not far from us is the font, near to which Sir John Montacute* deſired to be buried, ſaying, with touching ſimplicity and devotion, in his laſt will and teſtament, " If I die in London, then I deſire that my body may be buried in S. Paul's, near to the font wherein I was baptiſed." At the ſixth bay, right and left, are two ſmall doors through the outer walls, and you will obſerve that theſe doors offer dangerous facilities for making the Nave a thoroughfare. See, here is a notice againſt the little north door forbidding ſuch deſecration :

> " All thoſe that ſhall enter within the Church dore
>   With Burthen or Baſket muſt give to the Poore :
>   And if there be any aske what they muſt pay
>   To this Box, 'tis a Penny ere they paſſe away :"

and below the inſcription is an iron cheſt to receive the penny; and here is another notice, " Hic ſacer eſt locus." But ſtay, we will not read out the reſt of it. Surely we have ſeen ſomething like it in the Satires of Perſius ;† it offends our refined ears: but, alas ! ſuch inſcriptions are neceſſary.

Here is a ſtruſture well worth our notice, on our

---

* *Testamenta Vetusta*, p. 124. The will is dated 1388.
† Perſius, Sat. i. v.v. 113, 114.

left, filling up the whole fpace between the columns of
the tenth bay. It is the Chantry Chapel of Bifhop
Kempe, Bifhop of the diocefe from 1448 to 1489. If
you look through the grille you may fee upon an
altar-tomb the figure of the prelate wearing his epifcopal habit and his mitre. He was a great benefactor
to this Church, and rebuilt Paul's Crofs. You may fee
his coat of arms in many places of its leaded cover.
Clofe at hand is the Chapel of the Holy Trinity.

Obferve the large aperture in the roof of the Nave.
What can be its ufe? An able antiquary fhall tell us.
Lambarde, in his *Topographical Dictionary,** fays, " I
myfelf being a child once faw in Paul's Church at
London at a feaft of Whitfuntide, where the coming
down of the Holy Ghoft was fet forth by a white
pigeon that was let to fly out of a hole that is yet to
be feen in the midft of the roof of the great aifle, and
by a long cenfer which, defcending out of the fame
place almoft to the very ground, was fwung up and
down to fuch a length that it reached at one fweep
almoft to the Weft gate of the church, and with the
other to the choir ftairs of the fame, breathing out over
the whole Church and company a moft pleafant perfume of fuch fweet things as burned therein." The
cenfer ufed in this ftrange ceremony is " a great large
cenfer all filver with many windows and battlements
ufed to cenfe withal in the Pentecoft Week in the
body of the Church of Paul's at the Proceffion time ;"
it weighs no lefs than clviij. ounces, iii. quarters.†

* It is an anachronifm to quote Lambarde in this chapter, as
he lived 1536-1601.

† Bifhop Pilkington alludes to the practice : " In the midft

Thofe little tables in the Nave mark the places where the Twelve Scribes fit for the accommodation of the public.*   They have taken an oath of fidelity to the Dean and Chapter.   They will write a letter for you, or prepare a legal inftrument, if you need their aid : but they have fworn in all that they do to have regard to the interefts of the Cathedral. If therefore you defire to take proceedings againft any of the Clergy you muft go elfewhere for your Scribe.

Croffing the Nave, at the eleventh bay on the right hand is the tomb of Sir John Beauchamp, Knight of the Garter, fon of Guy Earl of Warwick.   There lies his recumbent figure clad in complete armour, and on the four panels at the fide of the altar-tomb, you may fee the armorial bearings of his noble family.   The common people call it Duke Humfrey's tomb, although Humfrey Duke of Gloucefter lies honourably buried at S. Alban's, twenty miles away.   On Mayday, tankard-bearers and watermen, and others of like quality, come to this tomb early in the morning, and ftrew herbs about it, and fprinkle it with fair water. And they have fome odd fayings of their own.   A man who goes without his dinner (walking during dinner-time in this Nave) is faid "to dine with Duke Humfrey :" and, in reference to this faying, they have

---

alley was a long cenfer, reaching from the roof to the ground, as though the Holy Ghoft came in there, cenfing down in likenefs of a dove."   Mackenzie Walcott, *Traditions and Cuftoms,* pp. 92, 93.

* *Statuta,* p. 78.

a proverb, "Trafh and trumpery is the way to Duke Humfrey," that is, is the way to go dinnerlefs.*

The fmall door on your right gives admiffion to the leffer cloifters. Thefe are really very beautiful and of a rare type. There are feven arches on each fide and, what is fingular, the cloifters are two ftories high, and the upper ftory, like the lower, is open to the air. How delicate and beautiful is the tracery! In the middle of the enclofure rifes up the lofty Chapter Houfe, erected nearly five hundred years ago,† of two ftories alfo. Its lofty pointed roof we faw as we re-entered the Churchyard at Paul's Chain.

Returning to the Nave, we notice the image of the Bleffed Virgin, at the foot of Sir John Beauchamp's tomb, before which a lamp is kept burning every night; and every morning, after matins, a fhort Office is faid at this very place before the image.‡ Another taper is alfo kept burning, as you fee, before yonder Great Crucifix. Hard beneath the North-west pillar of the fteeple is the Chapel of S. Paul, "built of timber, with ftairs mounting thereunto." On the South fide of the Nave is S. Catherine's Chapel, on the North is the Chapel of the Holy

---

* Allufions to this hungry promenade are by no means rare in the current literature. Thus in Mayne's *City Match*, 1658, we read :
> " You'd not doe
> Like your penurious father, who was wont
> To walke his dinner out in Paules."

† Dugdale fays that it was built in 1332.

‡ Dugdale, p. 14.

Trinity: nor muſt we omit to viſit the Altar of the Apoſtles.

A few ſteps more and we reach the very centre of the building. The long Nave ſtretches out behind us; right and left are the two Tranſepts, with large bold entrances from the Churchyard. The Central Tower, over our heads, is open to the baſe of the ſpire: ſee, what a dizzy height it ſeems! Looking Eaſtwards, however, our view is not quite ſo ſtriking: the Choir is hidden from view by a ſtone ſcreen, adorned with figures ſtanding under rich canopies; and the Aiſles of the Choir are ſhut off by cloſe walls and gates. Not till we paſs theſe barriers ſhall we be able to admire the full beauty of the ſanctuary.

Near the door of the South Tranſept is the Chapel of S. John the Evangeliſt. The flight of ſeven ſteps which you obſerve on the Weſtern ſide gives acceſs to the Chapter House. We will enter. Obſerve the eight lofty windows. Small as the building is (it is only 32 feet 6 inches in internal diameter),* its great height makes it very effective. It is built on the ſite of a garden which belonged to the Dean and Chapter. Ah! what diſcuſſions have been held beneath this vaulted roof. What grand men have ſat in theſe ſtalls, have here preſided over councils—Canons, Stateſmen, Deans, Biſhops, a goodly array!

We will not linger over the tombs, though there are many of them, in either Tranſept. In the North Tranſept, there is much which will call for ſpecial notice. Firſt of all, there is that grand Crucifix near

* Longman, p. 15.

the North door.   Old chronicles fay that it was difcovered by King Lucius, the firft Chriftian King of
England, in the year 140 A.D. ;* but you will ufe your
own judgment as to your acceptance of the ftory.
Large oblations are made here, whereof the Dean
and Canons have the benefit.   It is a favourite objeᶜᵗ
of devotion amongft the people who come, far and
near, to kneel before it.   That graveftone marks the
tomb of Richard Martin, Bifhop of S. David's, in the
reign of Edward IV. : he had a fpecial veneration
for this Crucifix, and left an annual gift to the
chorifters that they might fing before it *Sanᶜᵗe Deus
fortis.*†

You will remember how Archbifhop Arundel fpoke
about this Crofs to William Thorpe, in 1407, when he
was under examination as being fufpected of herefy.
Thorpe afferted that images are not to be worfhipped.   Archbifhop Arundel replied very fharply :
" Ungratious lofell! thou favoureft no more truth
than an hound.   Since at the Rood at the Northdore
at London, at our Ladie at Walfingham, and manie
other diuers places in England, are many great and
praifable miracles done, fhould not the images of fuch
holie faints and places at the reverence of God, and
our Ladie, and other faints, be more worfhipped then
other places and images, where no miracles are done."‡

° *Documents*, p. 58.

† The receipts at this Crucifix in May, 1344, amounted to no
less than £50.   Milman's *Latin Chriftianity*, 3rd ed. ix. p. 24 ;
and *Annals*, App. B.

‡ Fox, iii. p. 266.

Thorpe, however, was not to be convinced. Let us be careful what *we* say ; even now ſharp ears may be liſtening.

If the Dean continues to preach as he has lately done, the devotion at this famous Croſs will ſoon diminiſh : and yet we hear that he has ſaid that he wiſhes "to be buryed nyghe unto the image of seint Wilgeforte " in this Cathedral. Cloſe to the Great North Door is a group of Chapels dedicated to S. James, to S. Thomas, to the Holy Ghoſt, to S. John Baptiſt, to S. Margaret. The Chapel of S. John Bap-tiſt was built by Sir John Poultney, Mayor in 1348, and he endowed it for three chaplains.

Before entering the Choir we will firſt viſit its two aiſles, reſerving its central and grandeſt portion till the laſt. In theſe aiſles and in the Choir we have great wealth of tombs and monuments. If you care for monumental braſſes, you ſhould obſerve cloſely that of Biſhop Fitz-Hugh near the altar, depiĉted in full pontificals, with his paſtoral ſtaff in his left hand, and his right upraiſed in benediĉtion ; or that of Dean Evere, near the entrance of the Choir, wearing a cope richly embroidered with ſaints, and ſtanding beneath a canopy with figures of the twelve Apoſtles and a piĉture of the Annunciation ; or that of John Newcourt, Canon, who died in 1485, treated in a ſimilar manner; or that of Archdeacon Lichfeld, 1496, in the ſouth aiſle, who wears an embroidered cope, and his hands, uplifted but not claſped, are raiſed in prayer. Theſe are all fine examples of the graver's art, an art unhappily much decayed in thefe days, for the recently-erected braffes are far inferior.

In the fouth ambulatory I will point out to you the image of S. Wilgefort, on your left as you enter. Here Dean Colet is to be buried when he dies: that, at leaft, is his expreffed defire. A little farther on your right, you will obferve two altar-tombs under one common canopy. Upon each is a recumbent figure wearing a mitre. Who are thefe? They reprefent two early Bifhops of London, both of them eminent men. The one is Euftace de Fauconberge, Treafurer of the Exchequer, who died in 1228; the other is Henry de Wingham, Chancellor of England, who died in 1262. Quite at the Eaftern end of this aifle is S. Dunftan's Chapel. That ftriking monument reprefents Henry de Lacy, Earl of Lincoln, who died at his houfe, now called Lincoln's Inn, in 1310. The recumbent crofs-legged figure deferves attention, and fo do the carefully-wrought effigies around the altar-tomb.

The North Aifle of the Choir contains fome monuments of certainly not lefs importance than thefe. Entering at the Weftern end, we at once find two tombs of the higheft intereft, for thefe low fhrines, under deeply-receffed arches, beneath the fecond window on your left, are the refting-places of the bones of King Sebba and King Ethelred. Read the tablets over the fhrines. The one relates how Sebba, King of the Weft Saxons, was converted by S. Erkenwald; whilft the other records a prediction uttered by S. Dunftan, Archbifhop of Canterbury, to King

Ethelred on his Coronation Day: "Since thou haft afpired to the kingdom by the means of thy brother's death, againft whofe blood the Angli have confpired together with thy wicked mother, the fword fhall not depart from thine houfe, raging againft thee all the days of thy life, and flaying thy feed until thy kingdom fhall be tranfferred to a ftrange kingdom whofe religion and whofe language the nation which thou ruleft knoweth not. Nor fhall the fin of thyfelf, thy mother, and thy counfellors be expiated till a terrible vengeance has been taken." The tablet further records that S. Dunftan's words were fully accomplifhed, and that Ethelred, after many battles and defeats, was at length befieged in London, and met a miferable death.*

A few fteps farther, and another deeply receffed tomb attracts us: it is that of John de Chifhull, Dean of S. Paul's, and afterwards Bifhop of London, who died in 1279-80; the arcade in front of it is worth your notice. But I fee that you are turning to the right, and are afking whofe is that monument with a low canopy and an exquifite fcreen above it? It reminds us of that of William Rufus at Winchefter. And you afk, why is the pavement fo worn round about this fpot? Here is buried Roger Niger, Bifhop of London, who died in 1241. He was canonised after his death, and his fête is held on the 29th of September in every year. It is faid that great miracles have been wrought at this tomb, and the ftones are worn by the feet of countlefs

* Dugdale, p. 64.

pilgrims. In 1269, John le Breton, Bifhop of Hereford, granted an indulgence of twenty days to all who fhould devoutly vifit this fhrine ; and in the facrifty there is ftill preferved a cope which S. Roger wore, made of red famite, embroidered with ftars and rofes.

That is a fine canopied altar-tomb, on which lies an armed figure. The infcription above it bears the name of Sir Simon Burley ; but fome fay that the tablet is in error, and that the perfon really commemorated is his nephew, Sir Richard Burley, K.G. Notice the garter around two of the fhields on the canopy, or perhaps it is a collar of SS., like that which he wears about his neck.* You will foon turn from this memorial, however, to that which is one of the very fineft monuments in the Cathedral, the tomb of John of Gaunt, Duke of Lancafter. It occupies the fpace between two columns north of the High Altar. Here refts "time-honoured Lancafter," and there againft the lofty canopy is his fhield and lance ; there alfo is his effigy and that of his confort. I will tell you fome other time how he fupported Wiclif, and dared to oppofe the proud Courtenay in his own Cathedral.†

A few fteps farther will fhow you, on the left, the low altar-tomb of Ralph de Hengham, Canon of this Church, and Chief Juftice of the Common Pleas : you may fee him in his robes, as he is depicted on a monumental brafs, lying on the marble slab. At the Eaft end of this Aifle is S. George's Chapel.

And now we will return to the central tower, and

---

* Dingley's *Hiftory from Marble*, ii. Introd. p. 132.
† *Infra*, Chap. VI.

enter the very heart of the building. Immediately before us is a fair fcreen with a central archway : on each fide of the entrance are four canopies with figures beneath them. An afcent of twelve* fteps will take us to the level of the Choir pavement. Enter at once. What a noble Choir ! It is in very pure pointed Gothic with a triforium and clereftory. Obferve the ftalls of delicately carved woodwork : over each of the Canon's ftalls is the name of his Prebend, and the firft words of the fection of the Pfalter which he is bound to recite daily. On the North fide, over the ftalls, is the Organ with its folding-doors.   But the chief objeƈt which attraƈts us is the Reredos with the High Altar in the centre, dedicated to S. Paul ; an altar to the north, dedicated to S. Ethelbert, King and Confeffor ; and an altar on the fouth, dedicated to S. Mellitus. Thefe three altars were originally dedicated by Richard de Bynteworth, Bifhop of London, on March 24th, 1339. Notice, over the High Altar, the " beautiful tablet,"† adorned with many precious ftones and with enamelled work, and with divers images of metal. The tablet ftands between two columns, with a frame of wood to cover it, richly ornamented with curious piƈtures. It coft two hundred marks in 1309. On the right you will fee that tabernacle of wood, with a piƈture of S. Paul, richly painted, placed beneath it. The altars, the fcreen, and the canopied tomb of John of Gaunt form a ftriking *coup d'œil;* whilft above

* Hollar's *View* fhows 11 fteps, his *Plan* 12.
† Dugdale, pp. 11, 12.

the fcreen the magnificent rofe window with the feven long windows beneath it pours down a flood of many-coloured light. Afcending fix more fteps we reach the fanctuary, from which we will pass behind the Altar Screen. Juft eaftwards of the fcreen is the famous fhrine of S. Erkenwald. He died on April 30, 693, a day long kept in memory in the Cathedral by fpecial Offices of devotion. He was buried in the Nave. In the great fire of London in 1087-8 the Cathedral was deftroyed, and the legends fay that the Saint's refting-place alone remained unharmed. On November 14, 1148, his bones were tranflated and placed in a very precious tomb. In 1314, Gilbert de Segrave laid the firft ftone of a new and more magnificent fhrine, to which on February 1, 1326, the body of the faint was tranfferred. Canterbury has its world-famed fhrine of Thomas à Becket, Weftminfter its fhrine of Edward the Confeffor, Durham that of S. Cuthbert, Ely that of S. Etheldreda, S. Alban's its twin fhrines of the Englifh Proto-martyr and of S. Amphibalus, and fo, as you fee, S. Paul's poffeffes a treafure of fcarcely lefs importance. Clerics and laymen have vied with each other in defiring to enrich it. Walter de Thorpe, a Canon of this Church, gave to it all his gold rings and jewels; in 18 Edward II., the Dean and Chapter lavifhed upon it rich ftore of gold and filver and of precious ftones; in 31 Edward III., three goldfmiths were engaged to work upon it for a whole year;* King John of France, when he was a prifoner

---

* At the wages of 8s. a week for one of them, and of 5s. a week for each of the others.

in England, made here an oblation of twelve nobles ;
this remarkable ſapphire was preſented in 15 Richard II., by Richard de Preston, citizen and grocer, there
·to remain for curing of infirmities of the eyes, and the
donor directed proclamation to be made of its great
virtues. The ſhrine is adorned with many figures,
and eſpecially, you will note the gilded image of S.
Erkenwald himſelf. (I dare ſay you remember that
a ſtone figure of the ſainted Biſhop ſtands in a niche,
on the ſouth ſide of Biſhop's Gate.) This iron grate
encloſing the ſhrine coſt no leſs than £64. The
lights now burning before it are provided by an endowment left for that purpoſe by Dean Evere in
1407. It is really very magnificent. See the gilded
image of the ſaint, the leſſer images, the figures of
angels, that repreſentation of the Coronation of the
Virgin, the cryſtals, the beryls, the other jewels, the
ſumptuous painting. All London cannot ſhow you
anything more ſplendid.*

And now let us turn Eaſtward. The ſcreen running quite acroſs the Church encloſes three Chapels :
the Lady Chapel in the midſt, S. George's Chapel in
the North Aiſle, and S. Dunſtan's in the South. The
Choir was rebuilt early in the thirteenth century ; it
was completed in 1240 : a little later the eaſtern part,
in which we are now ſtanding, was added, for the

----

* The rough ſketch given by Dugdale evidently repreſents
one end only of the ſhrine, and that, after it had been deſpoiled
of its chief ornaments. Creſſy, in his *Church Hiſtory of
Brittany*, publiſhed in 1668, ſays that the body of S. Erkenwald
continued here " till about fourſcore years agoe, at which time
it diſappeared."

Choir was greatly extended then.   Before this period a ſtreet ran, cloſe to the Eaſt end of the Cathedral, from Watling Street to Cheapſide:* and here alſo ſtood the Church of S. Faith which was pulled down in order to lengthen the Choir.   The Pariſhioners, as we ſhall ſee preſently, have been provided with a Church in the Crypt beneath our feet.   In the Lady Chapel, the Guild of the Minſtrels ſtill meet; they poſſeſs a grant from Edward IV. which records that the brethren and ſiſters of the Guild aſſembled there for devotion.   As we leave the Chapel, we paſs by the grave of a notable man, Robert de Braybrooke, Biſhop of London, who died in 1404.   He held the Great Seal of England from 20th Sept., 1382 to 10th March, 1383 : a vigorous and vigilant biſhop, and one who laboured hard to reform the vices of the humbler people, and the corruption which he lamented in his own Chapter.   Obſerve his well-marked features as they are pourtrayed on yonder monumental braſs. He was certainly an earneſt reformer.

Even yet we have not exhauſted the wonders and the beauties of S. Paul's, for we have not viſited the famous Crypt.   We can enter it very conveniently from without.   About the middle of the North ſide of the Choir we ſhall find a low-arched door: ſome ſix and twenty ſteps will take us down to the lower Church.   This is the Church of S. Faith, but the eaſtern part is called the Jeſus Chapel.   Three rows of columns, there are eight columns in each row,

* Sir Chriſtopher Wren found nine wells in a row, marking the exaƈt ſite of theſe houſes, under the Choir.

divide the Crypt into four nearly equal aifles, and carry the great weight of the Choir floor and fuper-ftructure. At the South-weft is the little Chapel of S. John Baptift, and here too are the Chapels of S. Anne, S. Sebaftian, and S. Radegund : that figure, looming in the darknefs, pierced with arrows, is S. Sebaftian. Over the door leading into Jefus Chapel is "curioufly painted" the image of Jefus, and the figure, wearing her armorial mantle, with her children kneeling around her, is Margaret, Countefs of Shrewfbury, who lies buried before the image. You can read the couplet beneath it :

> "Jesus our God and Sauior,
>   To us and ours be Gouernour."

In this Chapel meets the wealthy Guild of Jefus. It was incorporated by Henry VI., and the prefent Dean, Dean Colet, has drawn up a very remarkable feries of Acts and Ordinances for the "weale, poletique guid-yng, and maintenaunce" of the Guild, of which he is himfelf the Rector.* They fpecially obferve the Feaft of the Tranffiguration, and that of the Name of Jefus, and here they meet in full number on thefe Holydays. Every Friday the Mafs of Jefus is faid at this Altar by one of the Cardinals of the Church ; and after that, on the fame day, is faid a Mafs of Requiem. On the Feaft of the Tranffiguration "lyveries of golde and filver" are "made and given to the Brothren and Suftren" of the Guild. At Mafs on the day of the

---

* I have printed thefe *Ordinances* and other Documents relating to the Guild in my *Regiftrum S. Pauli.*

Tranffiguration the Subdean is the celebrant.   It is a very wealthy fraternity, for their annual income fometimes amounts to £400.* Alms for the Guild are collected far and wide, even in Wales, and in the Northern Province.

There are feveral other Guilds in the Cathedral. The earlieft, I think, is that founded by Dean Ralph de Diceto in 1197, the members of which met four times a year to be prefent at the celebration of the Mafs of the Holy Ghoft.   We have already fpoken of the Minftrels' Guild ; and to this we may add the Guilds of S. Catherine, of the Annunciation of the Bleffed Virgin, and that of All Souls which affembled in the Charnel Chapel.

And here we muft bring our circuit to a clofe : but before we part, confefs that S. Paul's Cathedral is well worth a vifit, and can hold its own for fize, for majefty, for its monuments, its chapels, its fhrine, its guilds, its fpacious crypt, with any other Church that you have vifited in merry England.

The date which has been chofen for this imaginary vifit to the Cathedral, the year 1510, has compelled us to omit mention of many grand or interefting monuments.   Amongft thefe are the fhrouded figure of Dean Donne, 1631, the only perfect effigy now remaining, fince the Great Fire on the one hand, and wanton deftruction on the other, ruined thefe unique

---

* It was £406 os. 11½d. in 1534-5 ; although in 1514-15 it was only £144 6s. 8d.

memorials; Dean Colet's tomb, with his buſt above and a ſkeleton beneath, 1519; Sir William Hewit, 1599; Sir William Cokaine, with his wife and eleven children, two of them *Chriſoms*, 1626; Sir Nicolas Bacon, 1578; John King, Biſhop of London, 1621; the vaſt maſs of Sir Chriſtopher Hatton's monument, 1591, of which, as Stow records, "a merry poet wrote":

> " Philip and Francis have no tombe,
>   For great Chriſtopher takes all the roome,"

referring to Sir Philip Sidney and Sir Francis Walſingham, who reſt hard by; William Herbert, Earl of Pembroke, 1569; Sir John Maſon, 1566; William Aubrey, LL.D., 1595,; Sir John Wolly, 1595; Sir Thomas Heneage, 1594; Dean Nowell, 1601; and others. But the period was choſen adviſedly. It enabled us to ſee the altars and chapels undiſturbed, and the ſhrine of S. Erkenwald in all its beauty.

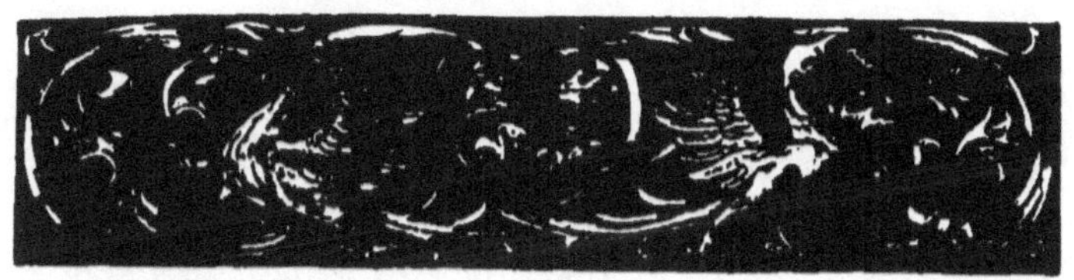

CHAPTER VI.

WYCLIF IN S. PAUL'S.

HE fun was fetting on the life of the Third Edward, when an incident occurred which is for ever memorable in the hiftory of S. Paul's: John Wyclif, the great Reformer, "the father of Englifh profe," ftood within its walls.   If he had no other claims upon our notice, his literary ability alone would place him amongft the firft rank of Englifh writers.   Mr. Shirley, the able editor of the *Fafciculi Zizaniorum*,* claffes him amongft the greateft of our countrymen, and fays that " in his original tracts, the exquifite pathos, the keen delicate irony, the manly paffion of his fhort nervous fentences, fairly overmafters the weaknefs of the unformed language, and gives us Englifh which cannot be read without a feeling of its beauty to this hour."   His

* *Fafciculi Zizaniorum Magiftri Johanni Wyclif cum tritico :* edited by the Rev. W. W. Shirley (in the Mafter of the Rolls' Series of Chronicles, 1858) pp. xlvi., xlvii.

tranſlation of the Bible into the mother tongue, his moſt holy life, his reſolute defence of the truth, cauſe him·to ſtand out from the times in which he lived, a ſtriking figure, a maſter in Iſrael.

Born at Lutterworth, about the year 1324, he was appointed Warden or Maſter of Balliol Hall, as it was then called, in the Univerſity of Oxford.* Here he oppoſed the Mendicant Friars who were drawing away ſtudents from the Colleges into their own convents : " Freres," to borrow Wyclif's words, "drawen children fro Christ's religion into their private Order by hypocriſie, leſings, and ſteling." In 1366 he oppoſed the Pope's demands for arrears in the payment of the tribute money granted by King John. He ſoon began to attack the abuſes of religion, and eſpecially the ſubſtitution of fabulous legends—legends differing only from thoſe of the ancient heathen poets in that they were more incredible and leſs elegant—for the pure faith of Chriſt. In 1374 he accompanied Simon Sudbury, Biſhop of London, and John of Gaunt, Duke of Lancaſter, on an important miſſion to Bruges, where, it may be ſuppoſed, he laid the foundation of a friendſhip which was ſoon to be of eminent ſervice to him. A ſtrange friendſhip enough, "between an aſcetic prieſt of deep piety and irreproachable morals, and an ambitious and ſomewhat diſſolute noble."†

---

* The authorities here uſed are the *Faſciculus Zizaniorum;* Thomas of Walſingham's *Hiſtoria Anglicana;* Hook's *Lives of the Archbiſhops;* Fox; Longman's *Life and Times of Edward III.,* etc.

† Longman, *ibid.,* p. 284.

Lancafter was the friend of Chaucer as well as of Wyclif. This ftrange intimacy has been explained " by attributing to the Duke a mind capable of appreciating, and indeed deeply loving, energy and intellect, but not untinged by a confcioufnefs that men poffeffed of thefe qualities might be ufeful to him in his oppofition to the clergy."

Wyclif, who had learned much about the ambition and faithleffnefs of the Pope, attacked him boldly in his public lectures, calling him, in no very meafured language, " Antichrift, the proud worldly prieft of Rome, and the moft curfed of clippers and purfekervers." The Pope retorted by iffuing bulls commanding the Archbifhop of Canterbury and the Bifhop of London to take proceedings againft Wyclif. His doctrine of the fupremacy of kings was moft unpalatable at Rome. Horrible herefics were attributed to him.*

Courtenay, the Bifhop of London, had been eagerly oppofed to the affumption by the Papacy of temporal power in England.† John of Gaunt had little love for the fecular power of the Pope, but he would have fided with him if the Roman Pontiff would but abet the Duke's defigns againft the clergy, whom he defired to expel from fecular offices altogether. The Pope was chiefly concerned that the Papal treafury fhould be replenifhed. Courtenay and John of Gaunt,

---

* See Harpffeld, *Hiftoria Wicliffiana; Hiftoria Anglicana Ecclefiaftica*, p. 724.

† Hook, *Lives of the Archbifhops*, iv. pp. 321-324.

agreed on fome points, found themfelves ftrongly oppofed on the queftion of the ftatus of the clergy. The clergy were the lawyers of the day; they held the high offices of ftate; great political power was in their hands, and a ftrong feeling was fpringing up amongft the people that fpiritual perfons fhould be limited to fpiritual work. On this point the Bifhop of London and the Duke ranged themfelves on oppofite fides. "Lancafter, feudal to the core, refented the official arrogance of the prelates, and the large fhare which they drew to themfelves of the temporal power. Wyclif dreamt of reftoring, by apoftolical poverty, its long-loft apoftolical purity to the clergy. From points fo oppofite, and with aims fo contradictory, were they united to reduce the wealth and humble the pride of the Englifh hierarchy."* But, as Canon Stubbs obferves, although "Apoftolic poverty for the clergy was the idea which they had in common, it was recommended to the two by very different reafons."† John of Gaunt looked upon Wyclif and his teaching as tools and weapons for the humiliation of the clergy, and particularly of the prelates.

Prefently Courtenay fummons Wyclif to appear before himfelf and before the Metropolitan on a charge of herefy. The accufations againft the great Reformer are of a political rather than of a doctrinal character. Nothing is faid of his opinions on the Incarnation, nothing as to his views concerning the imperifhability of matter, nothing about the tenets of

* Dr. Shirley, *Fafciculus Zizaniorum,* p. xxvi.
† Canon Stubbs, *Conftitutional Hiftory,* ii. pp. 474-477.

Bradwardine. "The object of the profecution was to proclaim to the world that fociety was endangered by the political principles which John of Gaunt was putting in practice againft the Church."*

On the 23rd of February, 1377,† Wyclif obeyed the fummons, and appeared before his judges in S. Paul's. Let us try to realife the fcene. At an early hour prelates and nobles had affembled in Our Lady's Chapel, eaftward of the High Altar. "Dukes and barons were fitting together with the Archbifhops and other Bifhops." ‡   A fhout is heard, a crowd rufhes in tumultuoufly, Wyclif has arrived. He comes, not unattended. John of Gaunt is by his fide, and fo is the newly-appointed Earl Marfhal, Lord Percy. Four bachelors of divinity, one from each order of friars, are alfo with him, as Fox affirms, to aid him with their advice. The Duke of Lancafter has felected them, for Wyclif will furely need fage counfel. There is a denfe crowd, "a main prefs of people," filling the church. "Such was there the frequency and throng of the multitude, that the lords, for all the puiffance of the High Marfhal, unneth with great difficulty could get way through." The Lord Percy had much ado to break through the crowd, and that not without noife and tumult and grave offence to the citizens. What right had the Earl Marfhal to iffue orders in the Cathedral at all? They would protect their Bifhop.

Courtenay was popular amongft the Londoners.

* *Fafciculus*, etc., p. xxvii.

† *Ibid.*, p. xxvii. Fox fays that the day was Thurfday, Feb. 19, ii. p. 800, and note, p. 919.

‡ Fox, *Acts and Monuments*, ii. p. 801.

He had gone fo far as to allow the Pope's bull excommunicating the Florentines to be publifhed at Paul's Crofs, and had himfelf fpoken imprudent words in a fermon there. The rabble had forthwith proceeded to plunder the houfes of the rich Florentines, and the Lord Mayor had come forward to defend them. Courtenay was fummoned to appear before the Court of Chancery, and was commanded to unfay his words. An official, in due time, declared from the Crofs, that the Bifhop had been mifunderftood.

Now the people throng in to defend the Bifhop. The Earl Marfhal and the Duke fhall not ride rough-fhod over him. There is a great uproar. The Bifhop is offended ; the fanctuary, he fays, is profaned, the fynod is difturbed. A fierce contention follows, and a dialogue enfues,* pitched in a fomewhat high key.

Bifhop Courtenay. Lord Percy, if I had known beforehand what mafteries you would have kept in the Church, I would have ftopped you out from coming hither.

Duke of Lancafter. He fhall keep fuch mafteries here though you fay nay.

Lord Percy. Wyclif, fit down, for you have many things to anfwer to, and you need to repofe yourfelf on a foft feat.

Bifhop Courtenay. It is unreafonable that one cited before his Ordinary fhould fit down during his anfwer. He muft and fhall ftand.

---

* The verfion in the text is that given by Fuller in his *Church Hiftory of Britain*, vol. ii. pp. 340, 341 : edit. J. S. Brewer. Fuller, however, cites Fox as his authority.

Duke of Lancaſter. The Lord Percy his motion for Wyclif is but reaſonable. And as for you, my lord Biſhop, who are grown ſo proud and arrogant, I will bring down the pride, not of you alone, but of all the prelacy in England.

Biſhop Courtenay. Do your worſt, ſir.

Duke of Lancaſter. Thou beareſt thyſelf ſo brag upon thy parents,* which ſhall not be able to help thee ; they ſhall have enough to do to help themſelves.

Biſhop Courtenay. My confidence is not in my parents, nor in any man elſe, but only in God in Whom I truſt, by Whoſe aſſiſtance I will be bold to ſpeak the truth.

Duke of Lancaſter. Rather than I will take thoſe words at his hands, I would pluck the Biſhop by the hair out of the church.

The laſt words were but whiſpered by the Duke, and that ſoftly, in a neighbour's ear ; but they were caught up by the Londoners, who were enraged at the affront offered to their Biſhop. They fell upon the lords who were preſent, and had not the Biſhop himſelf interpoſed and ſtayed them from their purpoſe, the ſanctity of the holy place itſelf would not have prevented them from avenging the inſult. It was yet but nine o'clock in the morning, for our anceſtors were early riſers, when the meeting was diſſolved.

The Duke had plotted againſt their liberties. In the Parliament he had attempted nothing leſs than to

---

* His father was Hugh Courtenay, Earl of Devon.

diffranchife the City of London, to annul its charter, to abolifh the office of Lord Mayor, to rule the city by a Captain. The Marfhal of England should have power to arreft in the City as in other places, contrary to the rights of the citizens.* They are highly incenfed with him, and the riotous conduct in the Cathedral fets the fpark to the powder. They attack the Marfhal's inn, and break open the gates and doors, and bring out a prifoner confined there, "gyves and all wherin his feet were faftned, intending to burne them in the midft of the citie." Fortunately for him, the Earl is abfent. He and the Duke were dining with a Flemifh merchant, one John of Ypres, in S. Thomas Apoftle, at Ypres Inn, weft of the Church ; a great meffuage, as Stow fays. Their hoft was a perfon of fome importance, and was appointed as one of the executors to King Edward.†

Inflamed by their fuccefs, the turbulent people rufh down to the Duke's Palace, the Savoy, hoping there to find their prey. On their way they encounter an unhappy prieft who fays that Sir Peter de la Mare,‡ whom they thought to be imprifoned in Lord Percy's Inn, was a traitor, and was worthy to be hanged. Whereupon they all cried out, " This is Percy ; this is the traytour of England. His fpeech bewrayeth him, though hee be difguifed in apparell."§ Then they all

---

* Stow's *Annales*, by Howes, p. 273.

† Fox, ii. p. 920.

‡ " Sir Peter de la Mare, one of the Knights who reprefented Herefordfhire," who had been elected foreman or Speaker by the Commons. Dr. Stubbs' *Conftitutional Hiftory*, ii. p. 467.

§ Stow, *Annales*, p. 274.

ran upon him, ſtriving who ſhould give him his death-
ſtroke; and they beat him ſo ſavagely that he died
of his wounds.

The Biſhop of London ſoon hears tidings of the
riot. He was juſt ſitting down to table. "The Epiſcopal palace was a place of conſiderable ſtrength;
but it was at this time more than uſually ſtrong, for
that the Biſhop himſelf lived in the affections of the
people. The ordinary routine was obſerved, and at
the uſual hour the large family of the Biſhop, chaplains, knights, clerks, and retainers aſſembled in the
vaſt and lofty hall. It was a gloomy, priſon-like
apartment, ſcantily furniſhed. It was lighted by two
large windows high in the wall, and looking into the
inner court. In the centre ſtood a long table on
treſſels, and beneath was a plentiful ſupply of freſh
ſtraw. Along the table were forms, until the daïs
was reached. On the daïs ſtools were arranged, and
in the centre, for the Biſhop, a ſtraight-backed,
wooden-ſeated arm-chair. There was a hatch on
either ſide of the door, and near it a large cupboard
or buffet, on which were arranged diſhes of earthen-
ware and braſs, with a few of ſilver for the high table;
ſilver goblets being intermixed with cups of horn, a
few drinking-glaſſes, and jacks."* Information is
brought that all London is in an uproar. The Biſhop
does what in him lies to quell the riot.

The people had commenced the attack upon the
ducal palace. The Biſhop addreſſes them. It is

* Hook, iv. p. 334. (Dean Hook muſt be held reſponſible
for theſe minute details.)

Lent; let them not profane the holy feafon.   At his bidding, at his nod,* they defift.   They would fain have burnt down the palace.   They reverfe the Duke's arms "in Foro publico," as if he were a traitor. And prefently, when a certain foldier of the Duke's called Thomas Wynton, a Scotchman born, came through the city with the Duke's arms hanging by a lace about his neck, the citizens, "not abiding the fight thereof, caft him from his horfe, and plucked the efcutcheon from him, and were about," as Fox oddly words it,† "to work the extremity againft him," had not my Lord Mayor delivered him out of their hands.

The Duke and Lord Percy alfo hear the ill-tidings. A knight of the Duke's houfehold hurries down into the City.   He arrives at the houfe where the feaft was being held.   He knocks at the gate and cannot get admittance, the houfehold are bufy at the banquet. At laft Haverland, the porter, comes: and the impatient knight cries out : " If thou love my lord and thy life, open the gate ;" with which words he gets entry.   He hurries into the hall and tells the Duke that without the gate were infinite numbers of armed men, and that unlefs he took good heed that day would be his laft.   The Duke fees the gravity of the fituation.   "He leapt fo haftily from his oyfters, that hee hurt both his legges againft the fourme.   Wine was offered to his oyfters, but hee would not drinke

* Walfingham, *Hiftoria Anglicana*, i. p. 325.
† Fox, ii. pp. 804, 920.

for hafte. Hee fledde with his fellow Sir Henry Percie, no manne following them, and entring the Thames, neuer ftinted rowing untill they came to a houfe neere the Manor of Kenington (befide Lambeth)."* Here they took refuge with the Princefs of Wales, who, as the widow of the Black Prince, had great influence with the Londoners, and fucceeded in pacifying them.

No word fpoken by the Archbifhop or by Wyclif on this occafion has been recorded. "The former," fays Fuller, "feeing the brawl happened in the Cathedral of London, left the Bifhop thereof to meddle, whofe ftout ftomach and high birth made him the meeter match to undertake fuch noble adverfaries. As for Wyclif, well might the client bee filent, whilft fuch counfel pleaded for him. And the bifhops found themfelves in a dangerous dilemma about him; it being no pity to permit, nor policy to punifh, one protected with fuch potent patrons. Yea, in the iffue of this fynod, they only commanded him to forbear hereafter from preaching or writing his doctrines; and how far he promifed conformity to their injunctions doth not appear."†

Thefe were troublous times. There was a dangerous difcord at Rome. Urban VI., and Clement VII.—the one at Rome, the other at Avignon—ftruggling for the maftery. "Peter's chair was like to be broken betwixt two fitting down at once;" as honeft Fuller puts it.

* Stow, *Annales.*
† Fuller, *Church Hiftory*, ii. p. 342.

A few days more, and Edward III. lay dead.
He was in the fixty-fixth year of his age, and the
fiftieth of his reign. On the 21ft of June he died, at
his palace at Shene, deferted by all, even by Alice
Perrers, who, before fhe fled, ftole the very rings from
the fingers of the dying man. A certain prieft alone,
of all the courtiers and attendants, ftood by that
folitary deathbed, and offered to the quivering lips
the figure of the Crucified. The dying King devoutly
kiffed the feet of the image, and fought for pardon
from his offended God and from all whom he had
wronged : and fo, alone, but for this faithful chaplain,
breathed out his foul.* Let us hope that he found
the pardon which he fought. His later fins may be
the more eafily forgiven, when it is remembered that
he was mentally and phyfically the mere wreck of his
former felf.

About one-and-forty years after Wyclif's death,
Richard Fleming, Bifhop of Lincoln, who in his early
years had adopted Wyclif's opinions but had afterwards
renounced them, fent his officers, "vultures with a quick
fight-fcent at a dead carcafe," to pull the remains of
the Reformer from the quiet grave at Lutterworth.
"To Lutterworth they come (Sumner, commiffary,
official, chancellor, proctors, doctors, and the fervants,
fo that the remnant of the body would not hold out
a bone amongft fo many hands), take what was left
out of the grave, and burnt them to afhes, and caft
them into Swift, a neighbouring brook running hard

* Walfingham, i. p. 327.

by. Thus this brook hath conveyed his afhes into Avon, Avon into Severn, Severn into the narrow feas, they into the main ocean; and thus the afhes of Wyclif are the emblem of his doctrine, which now is difperfed all the world over."* Which things, as Profeffor Blunt pointedly obferves, are an allegory.†

It was an eafy tafk to burn the bones of Wyclif. It was impoffible to root out his teaching, or to deftroy the loving memory in which the people held him. Let two fhort ftories fuffice to fhow that the great Reformer lived in the hearts of the people.

When Hufs appeared before the Emperor, a friend of his, one Stephen Paletz, faid‡ that a Bohemian "brought out of England a certain fmall piece of the ftone of Wyclif's fepulchre, which they that are the followers of his doctrine at this prefent do reverence and worfhip as a thing moft holy." This is in 1416.

George Bull, of Much Hadham, draper, fays§ "through the credence and report of Mafter Patmore, Parfon of Hadham, that where Wyclif's bones were burnt, fprang up a well or well-fpring." This is in 1531.

If the bones of Wyclif were to be facrilegioufly dif-turbed, thofe of Archbifhop Sudbury alfo were to have fome ftrange experiences.

On the 14th of June, 1381, the aged Archbifhop,

---

* Fuller, *Church Hiftory*, ii. p. 424.
† *Sketch of the Hiftory of the Reformation*, chapt. v.
‡ Fox, iii. p. 484.   § *Ibid.*, v. p. 34.

Simon Sudbury, was dragged from the Chapel within
the Tower by the infuriated rabble under Wat Tyler.
He had adminiftered the Bleffed Sacrament to the
King, and this was his laft act. A block was extem-
porifed—an executioner was found—eight times the
deadly axe fell upon the brave old man—firft it
flightly wounded his neck—then it amputated the
tips of his fingers—at length the butchery was ended.
His laft recorded words were thefe,* " *Ah! ah! manus
Domini eft.*"   His head is preferved in a niche in the
wall of the Veftry of S. Gregory's Church, Sudbury.†
He was a native of that town, and a great benefactor.
For fix days the head had been exhibited at London
Bridge. It was then taken down by Sir William
Walworth. In due time, by a juft retribution, Wat
Tyler's head was fubftituted for it. If Thomas of
Walfingham is to be believed, his executioner was
vifited with infanity and with blindnefs.‡ Had the
King himfelf been in the Tower at the moment when
the Archbifhop was feized, he, too, muft have fallen
into the hands of the rioters, for the men of Kent
entered his very bedchamber ;§ but he was hurried
away juft in time to efcape from the moft imminent
danger.

* Hook's *Lives of the Archbifhops*, iv. pp. 309-313.
† I have feen it feveral times. Dean Hook fays that it was
conveyed to Canterbury, p. 312, therein following Godwin, *De
Præfulibus.*
‡ *Hiftoria Anglicana*, :. p. 461.
§ Canon Stubbs, *Conftitutional Hiftory*, ii. p. 498.

LOLLARDS' TOWER.

CHAPTER VII.

LOLLARDS' TOWER.

VERY fchoolboy has heard of Lollards' Tower, but it is not quite fo certain that every one knows where this famous prifon really ftood. As the river fteamboats pafs under Weftminfter Bridge on their courfe up ftream, thofe who are on board are attracted by " a broken, irregular pile of buildings, at whofe angle looking out over the Thames is one grey, weather-beaten tower. The broken pile is the Archiepifcopal Palace of Lambeth ; the grey, weather-beaten building is called " its Lollards' Tower. " From this tower the manfion itfelf ftretches in a varied line, chapel, and guard-room, and gallery, and the ftately buildings of the new houfe looking out on the terrace and garden ; whilft the Great Hall, in which the Library has now found a home, is the low, picturefque building which reaches fouthward along the river to the gate." On the river face of the tower is a fmall vacant niche, once filled, it is faid, by a ftatue of

S. Thomas à Becket, to which the watermen were wont to uncover their heads as they paffed along the filent highway. At the bafe of the tower is a chamber, and in its centre " ftands a large oaken pillar, to which the room owes its name of the *Poft-Room*, and to which fomewhat mythical tradition afferts Lollards to have been tied when they were 'examined' by the whip." Is this really Lollards' Tower? No—it is not. " Dr. Maitland has fhown that the common name refts on a mere error, and that the Lollards' Tower which meets us fo grimly in the pages of Fox was really a Weftern Tower of S. Paul's. But, as in fo many other inftances, the popular voice fhowed a fingular hiftorical tact in its miftake: the tower which Chichele raifed marked more than any other, in the very date of its erection, the new age of perfecution on which England was to enter. . . . It is ftrange to think how foon England anfwered to the challenge that Lollards' Tower flung out over the Thames. The white mafonry had hardly grown grey under the buffetings of a hundred years ere Lollard was no longer a word of fhame, and the reformation that Wyclif had begun fat enthroned within the walls of the chapel where he had battled for his life."*

Dr. Maitland, the late learned Librarian at Lambeth Palace, is careful to correct the popular error on this fubject. Lollards' Tower, he fays, was "the Bifhop of London's prifon at S. Paul's ;" and he adds, " I mention this becaufe the name has been (only, I

---

* J. R. Green's fingularly graceful Effays on *Lambeth and the Archbifhops* in his *Stray Studies*, pp. 109, 114, 120.

believe, in recent times), and quite improperly, applied to one of the Towers of Lambeth Palace."* It is very difficult, however, to root out a popular error, and the miſtake is conſtantly repeated even at the preſent time.

No reader of Stow's *Survey* ought to have had any doubt about the matter. He ſays, in his account of the Cathedral, that "at either corner of this weſt end is, alſo of ancient building, a ſtrong tower of ſtone, made for bell towers: the one of them, to wit, next to the Palace, is at this preſent to the uſe of the ſame Palace; the other, towards the ſouth, is called the Lowlardes' Tower, and hath been uſed as the Biſhop's Priſon, for ſuch as were detected for opinions in religion, contrary to the faith of the Church. . . . Adjoining to this Lowlardes' Tower is the pariſh church of S. Gregory."†

Are there any views of Lollards' Tower ſtill extant? This is a queſtion ſomewhat difficult to anſwer. In Hollar's grand view of the weſtern façade of S. Paul's are two low towers flanking the weſt front, but they are "little more than turrets, of a baſtard Italian ſtyle."‡ Perhaps the Tower is exhibited in Aggas' *Map*, but one can hardly be ſure that what is ſeen is not the tower of S. Gregory's Church. Perhaps it is

---

* *Eſſays on Subjects connected with the Reformation in England.* Note on the *Examination of Thomas Green*, p. 24.

† Stow's *Survey*, edited by Thoms, p. 138; and Strype's *Stow*, i. p. 708.

‡ Mr. Edmund B. Ferrey in *Notes and Queries*, 4th Series, i. p. 509.

fhown in Van den Wyngaerde's drawing taken in 1540, but in a blrd's-eye view the outlines are apt to be vague. One Thomas Stilman appears to have faid, "that he, being in Lollards' Tower, did climb up the fteeple where the bells were, and there, cutting the bell-ropes, did tie two of them together, and fo by them flipped down into Paul's Churchyard, and efcaped."* From which we may infer that Lollards' Tower was certainly a bell-tower, and probably a clock-tower alfo ; and, in faɛt, a clock-face is fhown on the weftern front of the Tower in Hollar's view of Inigo Jones' Portico.

In Fox's *Aɛts and Monuments*† are two woodcuts which purport to reprefent the interior of this famous Prifon. The firft of thefe depiɛts the unfortunate Richard Hun, of whom more will be faid prefently, hanging from a beam in his cell. If the gaoler's height may be taken as fix feet, and if we then ufe him as a ftandard of meafurement, the dungeon would be about nine feet wide and eight feet high. The furniture confifts of a bed with a bolfter, a ftool, and the ftocks, which really ftood "about feven or eight foot from the place where Hun was hanged." The ftocks would hold four perfons. The fecond woodcut probably reprefents another cell. The inevitable ftocks ftill form a prominent feature, but this time they are large enough to hold fix perfons. It is quite poffible that both thefe woodcuts are purely works of the imagination ; for it is not likely that vifitors were ad-

* Fox, *Aɛts and Monuments*, vol. iv. p. 230, in 1518-21.
† In the edition printed in 1641, ii. p. 15 ; iii. p. 413.

mitted to take sketches in the prison : and it is certain that, as in the *Nuremberg Chronicle*, so in the *Acts and Monuments*, the same woodcut often represents individuals widely separated in date and in station. Trusting to the short memory or the uncritical temper of his readers, Fox is bold enough to employ the same woodcut at least a dozen times to depict different persons : but I do not observe that *these* two woodcuts are repeated, a circumstance which may be taken, perhaps, as a note of truth. No doubt many a poor captive, if he escaped alive from his prison house, would carry away with him an indelible image of the narrow walls that had echoed back his prayers and sighs. His descriptions would be vivid enough to guide the artist's pencil.

The contiguity of a Prison to the Church seems to modern ideas most incongruous ; but our forefathers do not appear to have shared this view. The famous prison in Lambeth Palace is reached by a rude stair, to which access is gained through a doorway hard by the graceful arch which gives entrance to the Chapel. The massive oak door studded with nails probably prevented the sweet sounds of choral hymns from reaching the ears of the wretched captives, and the seven iron rings bolted into the wall still remain to tell the sad tale of their miserable bondage.

The stocks in the dungeon at S. Paul's had a very evil reputation. In a rare tract entitled the *Lyfe and Death of John Story*, 1571, reprinted in the Somers' *Collection of Tracts*,* are some remarkable details about them. The writer says that Dr. Story

" was committed to the Lollardes tower in Powles
. . . . but he lacked there one thing, which was the
monſtrous and houge ſtockes, that he and Boner, his
old faithful friend, had uſed to turmoyle and perſecute
the poore and innocent Chriſtians in, hanging ſome
therin by the heles ſo high, that only their heads laye
on the ground. Some were ſtocked in both feet and
armes, ſome alſo were ſtocked by both their feet and
by both their thombes, and ſo did hang in the ſtockes.
And ſome also were ſtocked by both theyre fete, and
chyned by the necke wyth collars of iron made faſt
behynde theim to a poſt in the wall, and ſuch other
develiſhe and tyrannus engynes and devyſes by hym
practiſed. Theſe at his beinge in the Lollardes
tower he myſſed, and great pitie it was that he had
not taſted of theym ; but alack the good biſhop
Gryndall, late biſhop of London, had brent and conſumed theym with fire."

Certainly, if the writer repreſents the public opinion
of his day, there was little difference between the con-
tending parties as to their love for the dungeon and
the ſtocks. It is very likely that the ſtocks were conſumed in 1561, in the ſecond year of Grindal's epiſ-
copate, in the great fire which deſtroyed the lofty ſpire
of the Cathedral.

A very graphic account of this part of S. Paul's is
to be found in the *Examinations and Writings* of

* Vol. i. p. 477, edit. 1809. I am indebted to Mr. Solly for
this intereſting paſſage. *Notes and Queries*, 5th Series, x.
p. 474.

John Philpot;* he fhall tell his ftory in his own words: "And he [Bifhop Bonner] followed me, calling the keeper afide, commanding to keep all men from me, and narrowly to fearch me (as the fequel did declare), and brought me to his privy door that goeth into the church, and commanded two of his men to accompany the keeper, and to fee me placed. And afterwards I paffed through Pauls up to the Lollards' Tower, and after that turned along all the Weft fide of Pauls through the wall, and paffing through fix or feven doors came to my lodging through many ftraits: where I called to remembrance that *ftrait is the way to heaven.* And it is in a tower, right on the other fide of Lollards' Tower, as high almoft as the battlement of Pauls, eight feet of breadth and thirteen of length, and almoft over the prifon where I was before, having a window opening toward the eaft, by the which I may look over the tops of a great many houfes, but fee no man paffing into them: and whofo walketh in the bifhop's outer gallery going to his chapel may fee my window, and me ftanding in the fame." From this paffage it would appear that the Northern Tower as well as the Southern was ufed as a prifon: the Northern Tower clofely adjoined the Bifhop's Palace.

Thofe who had once tafted the rigours of this prifon retained an indelible recollection of its horrors. Honeft old Latimer fays, "I had rather be in purga-

* Parker Society, pp. 86, 87. Compare alfo Fox, *octavo* edition, vii. pp. 647, 648.

tory, than in the Bifhop of London's Prifon; for in
this I might die bodily for lack of meat, in that I
could not." And again, writing to Morice, he fays,
"I had rather be in it [*i.e.*, in purgatory] than in
Lollards' Tower, the Bifhop's Prifon, for divers fkills
and caufes."* In Bifhop Pilkington's *Burnynge of
Paules Church*, he does not omit to mention the fad
memories that hung about the walls: "in the top of
one of the pinacles is Lollers towre, where manye an
innocent foule hais bene by theym cruellye tormented
and murthered."

Nor were the two Weftern Towers the only places
of imprifonment near to the Palace. The *Bifhop's
Coal Houfe* at the back of the Palace in Paternofter
Row had alfo a very evil reputation. Thomas Whittle
dates a letter addreffed to his "Prifon fellows in
Lollards' Tower" from "the *Coal Houfe* this 4th day
of December," 1556.†

Here one Thomas Green remained for many days
(for twenty days, at leaft, it would appear), and here a
bolt and fetter were placed upon his right leg, and on
his left hand another, and fo he was fet "crofs-fettered"
in the ftocks, where he lay a day and a night. The
next day his hand was loofed out of the ftocks, and
his leg only was fhut in ; there he remained fix days.
He was then examined by Dr. Story, Queen Mary's
Commiffioner. More prifoners were brought in :
whereupon Miftrefs Story fell in a rage, and fware a

* Bifhop Latimer, *Sermons and Remains* (Parker Society),
pp. 237, 361.
† Fox, octavo edition, *Acts and Monuments*, vii. p. 725.

great oath, that it were a good deed to put a hundred or two of thefe heretic knaves in a houfe, "and I myfelf," faid fhe, "would fet it on fire." After this Thomas Green was committed to prifon again for fourteen days more. By-and-by we have a picture of Bifhop Bonner himfelf, "in his hofe and doublet," coming down a pair of ftairs by the fide of the *Coal-Houfe*, and looking in at the grate, as one might look at fome curious wild animal, and afking why and by whom he was imprifoned. His feet and hands were manacled, and fo he had continued ten days with nothing to lie upon but bare ftones or a board. Prefently he is removed from the Bifhop's *Salt-Houfe*, as he calls it, to the Lollards' Tower, where he was kept in the ftocks more than a month, both day and night.* It was thus that religious people tried to perfuade, convince, convert each other.

The cafe of Richard Hun, a prifoner in the Lollards' Tower, who, one unhappy morning (4th December, 1514) was found hanging from a beam in his dungeon, is familiar to all the readers of Fox.† It was charged againft the Chancellor of the diocefe that he had murdered Hun. Thus, in the *Supplication of Beggars*, it is faid :‡

"Did not alfo Dr. Horfey [the Bifhop's Chancellor] and his complices, moft heinoufly (as all the world knoweth) murder in prifon that honeft merchant,

---

* Fox, viii. pp. 521-523. It is only right, however, to refer thofe who wifh to ftudy this fubject, to Dr. Maitland's keen analyfis of the whole ftory in his *Reformation Effays*, pp. 18-27.
† Fox, iv. pp. 183-197. ‡ *Ibid.*, iv. p. 663.

Richard Hun, for that he fued a writ of *premunire* againft a prieft that wrongfully held him in plea in a fpiritual court, for a matter whereof the knowledge belongeth to your highnefs ?"

And again, in 1555, when Robert Smith is examined before Bifhop Bonner,* he fpeaks of—

"Mafter Hun, whom your predeceffor caufed to be thruft in at the nofe with hot burning needles, and then to be hanged, and faid the fame Hun to have hanged himfelf."

To whom Bonner fiercely replies :

"Ah ! ye are a generation of liars, there is not one true word that cometh out of your mouths."

Fox prints at confiderable length *The Verdict of the Inqueft* which was called to examine into the caufes of Hun's death, together with the depofitions of many witneffes. The jury, which confifted of twenty-four men, gave it as their verdict that the faid Richard Hun was "felonioufly killed and murdered " by the Chancellor, William Horfey, clerk, and one Charles Jofeph, fumner, and John Spalding, otherwife called John the Bellringer.

It is fcarcely poffible, at this diftance of time, to difentangle the truth from the perplexed ftories which have reached us. The death of Richard Hun, however, is referred to feveral times by Tyndale, and by Bifhop Bale in very ftrong terms.† Whether he was

* Fox, octavo edition, *Acts and Monuments*, vii. p. 351 ; and fee alfo Maitland, *Reformation*, p. 530.

† Tyndale, *Anfwer to Sir Thomas More's Dialogue* (Parker Society), pp. 146, 166, 167 ; Bale, *Image of both Churches* (Parker Society), p. 395.

murdered, or was *felo-de-se*, may be left to ftudents of Fox and Maitland : it is quite certain that very different views will be taken of the matter by different readers.

It is, of courfe, very eafy to utter the ufual commonplaces about the barbarity of the prelates and the horrors of thefe dungeons. Our hearts, heaven be praifed, revolt from the atrocious cruelties freely practifed by men of both parties under the holy name of religion. We muft remember, however, the cuftoms of the age in which they lived and the long-continued prevalence of judicial torture. When Damiens attempted the life of Louis XV., at Verfailles, 5th January, 1757, it is faid that M. de Machault, the Keeper of the Seals, tortured the miferable creature, " un pauvre fou," as Meffrs. Bordier and Charton call him,* with his own hands. " He thruft tongs into the fire, and, when they were red-hot, he began fingeing with his own hands the unfortunate Damiens'. legs, taking care never to pinch the fame part of the leg twice, fo that more acute fuffering might be inflicted." The torturer then caufed Damiens' legs " to be expofed to a fire until they were but one fore : and, as he was ftill filent, he threatened to throw him into the flames." The details of Damiens' execution are, fimply, too dreadful to be fet down on paper. This painful incident is cited, not becaufe our own hiftory does

* *Hiftoire de France*, ii. p. 379.

not supply horrors enough, but becaufe it would not be eafy to find a high Minifter of State fo late as 1757 fo utterly loft to all fenfe of humanity and even of perfonal dignity as with his own hands to torture *un pauvre fou.* Let us judge as harfhly as you will the atrocities of the period, but let us, in juftice to the men, whether Roman or Reformed, remember the time in which they lived, and the tedious and flow fteps by which we ourfelves have attained to our prefent light.   We, ourfelves, have yet much to learn.

It muft not be forgotten that our own Statute Book contained till the reign of George III. provifions for inflicting judicial torture.   " In the cafe of fuch as at their trial refufe to plead *guilty* or *not guilty*, the prifoner is laid upon his back, his arms and legs being extended with cords, and a confiderable weight laid upon his breaft ; he is allowed only three morfels of barley-bread, which is given him the next day without drink, after which he is allowed nothing but foul water until he expires.   This punifhment is, however, feldom inflicted ; but fome offenders have chofen it *in order to preferve their eftates for their children.*   Thofe guilty of this crime are not now fuffered to undergo fuch a length of torture, but have fo great a weight placed on them that they foon expire."*   This atrocious punifhment was inflicted fo late as 1741, when one Henry Cook, a fhoemaker of Stratford, was fentenced to death for highway robbery.   " On Cook's refufing to plead there was a new prefs made and

* *Notes and Queries*, 2nd Series, vol. i. p. 412.

fixed in the proper place in the prefs-yard, there having been no perfon preffed fince the famous (?) Spiggott the highwayman, which is about twenty years ago. Burnworth, *alias* Frafier, was preffed at Kingfton in Surrey, about fixteen years ago."* The law firft appears in the Statute Book, 8 Henry IV., and was not abolifhed till 12 George III. *c.* 20, which enacts that all perfons refufing to plead fhall be held to be guilty. It feems incredible that fuch cruelty could have been perpetrated under the facred name of Juftice at fo late a date as 1741, but the facts, it is to be feared, are indifputable. They will teach us to moderate our cenfures, or at leaft to apportion them with an equal hand.

The laft prifoner committed to Lollards' Tower was one Peter Burchet, gentleman, of the Middle Temple, who, in the year 1573, had defperately wounded and was minded to have murdered "a ferviceable gentleman named John Hawkings, Efquire, in the high ftreet near unto the Strand." Peter Burchet was taken and examined, and "was found to hold certain Opinions erroneous, and therefore committed thither and convicted ; but in the end, by perfuafion, he promifed to abjure his herefies, and was by the commandment of the Council, removed from thence to the Tower of London." So far Stow, in his *Survey.*† In

----

* *The Univerfal Spectator*, No. 674, quoted in *Notes and Queries*, 2nd Series, vol. i. p. 500.

† Stow's *Survey*, by Strype, i. p. 708.

his Annals * he gives a fuller account of the matter, and enables us to underftand what the " perfuafion " was under which Burchet recanted. It appears that fentence of death was about to be pronounced againft him " as an hereticke," and that then, " through the earneft perfwafions of diuers learned men, who tooke great paines in that matter, hee renounced, forfwore, and abiured his opinions." The attack on Hawkings took place on October 11th ; Burchet was committed to the Tower, where being examined he faid that the perfon whom he had intended to attack was Sir Chriftopher Hatton ; his heretical opinions having been detected he was fent to the Lollards' Tower, and examined in the Confiftory Court of S. Paul's ; fentence of death was to have been pronounced on November 4th, but he efcaped this by abjuration ; on November 9th he was remitted to the Tower, where the next day he murdered his keeper ; the following day he was arraigned and condemned at Weftminfter ; and on November 12th was hanged on a gibbet " nigh to the place where hee wounded mafter Hawkins. He had no fpeech, nor fhewed figne of repentance, but was by force and ftrength of men partly drawne, partly borne and thruft up to the gibbet, where, after his right hand being ftricken off and nayled to the gibbet, he was hanged." Such was the tragical end of this violent malefactor : the laft prifoner in Lollards' Tower.

* Stow's *Annals*, by Howes, pp. 677, 678.

THE GREAT FIRE OF 1561.

CHAPTER VIII.

THE GREAT FIRE OF 1561.

IRE has been always the implacable foe of S. Paul's Cathedral. The ancient Statutes ſtrictly enjoin the *Cuſtos Operis*, or *Surveyor*, not only to examine the roof of the Church with great care after heavy rains, but, eſpecially, to be very watchful when plumbers were at work upon it, leſt the fires which they employed to melt the lead ſhould attack the fabric itſelf. Reference has been already made * to the fire in 961, in which, according to the *Saxon Chronicle*, "the monaſtery of S. Paul's was burnt." On the 7th of July, 1087, according to the *Chroniculi S. Pauli*, "the Church of S. Paul, London, and all things which were therein, was conſumed by fire, in the time of Maurice, Biſhop of London, in the reign of William the firſt King of the Normans."† After this Biſhop Maurice laid the

---

* *Supra*, p. 8.

† See my *Documents*, p. 58; and *Statutes*, p. 477, for a ſimilar entry in one of the MSS. in the Cathedral Record Room.

foundation of a moſt magnificent pile of which William of Malmeſbury ſays, that it was "ſo ſtately and beautiful that it was worthily numbered amongſt the moſt famous buildings; the vaults or undercroft being of ſuch extent and the upper ſtructure ſo large that it was ſufficient to contain a great number of people."* But ere long this grand ſtructure ſhared the fate of its predeceſſor; in 1137 according to the *Chroniculi S. Pauli*, on December 22, 1136, according to Dugdale, "the Church of S. Paul was conſumed by a fire kindled at London Bridge, which burnt until it reached the church outſide the Bars of the New Temple," that is, the Church of S. Clement Danes.† "In ancient times the greater part of the City was built of wood, and the houſes were covered with ſtraw and ſtubble and the like. Hence it happened that when a ſingle houſe had caught fire, the greater part of the City was deſtroyed through ſuch conflagration." After this fire the citizens, deſiring to avoid ſuch a calamity in future, "built ſtone houſes upon their foundations, covered with thick tiles, and ſo protected againſt the fury of the flames: whence it has often been the caſe, that when a fire has broken out in the City and has deſtroyed many buildings, upon reaching ſuch houſes it has been unable to do further miſchief, and has been there extinguiſhed; ſo that, through ſuch a houſe as

---

* Dugdale, p. 4.

† *Documents*, p. 58; and Dugdale, p. 5: his words are, "on the xj. Cal. of January, in the very firſt year of King Stephen's reign."

this, many houfes of the neighbours have been faved from being burnt."*

Again, on February 1, 1445, as the *Grey Friars Chronicle* relates, ' Thys yere on Candelmas evyne was gret thunder and tempeft, that Powlles stepulle on the fowth-weft fyde mervelufly was fett a fyer, and the ftepull of Kyngftone up Temfe brent, and many men flayne." Stow's account, in his *Annals*, is more full and circumftantial : " On Candlemas eeuen, in diuers places of England, was great weathering of wind, hayle, fnow, raine, thunders with lightning, whereby the Church of Baldock in Hertfordfhire, and Church of Walden in Effex, and diuers others were fore fhaken, and the Steeple of S. Paul's in London, about two of the clocke in the afternoone was fet on fire in the middeft of the Shaft, firft on the Weft fide and then on the South, and the people efpying the fire, came to quench it in the Steeple which they did with vinegar, fo farre as they could find, fo that when the Maior with much people came to Pauls, to haue holpen if neede had beene, they returned againe euery man to his home, trufting to God all had beene well, but anon after between eight and nine of the clocke, the fire braft againe out of the Steeple, more feruent then before, and did much hurt to the Lead and Timber thereof, but the Maior and much people came thither, and with vinegar quenched the fire that was feruent, fo that no man was perifhed. The Steeple

* *Chronicles of the Mayors and Sheriffs*, edited by H. T. Riley, pp. 184, 185.

of Waltham in Effex and of Kingftone in Surrey was alfo fired by the fame lightning. The fire at Pauls being quenched, a Standard of tree* being fet up at Leaden Hall, in Cornehil of London, made faft in the midft of the pavement, and decked with Holme and Iuy for difport of Chriftmas to the people of the Citty, it was torne and caft downe with fuch violence that the ftones of the pavement were caft about in the ftreete and into diuers mens houfes, to the great ter-rour of the people that neuer had feene fo ftrange a tempeft." Dugdale adds that the fire, although " happily quenched by the morrow mafs prieft of Bow, did fuch harm therein that it was not fufficiently re-paired till the year 1462," when a coftly weathercock made of copper and gilt was fet up.†

The feat of putting out the fire with vinegar recalls irrefiftibly Hannibal's paffage of the Alps, when, as Livy fays, the foldiers of the advancing army having heated the rocks by great fires of wood, disin-tegrated them by pouring vinegar upon the heated ftone.‡

* That is, *of wood.*   † Dugdale, p. 95.

‡ The whole fentence runs thus :—" Inde ad rupem munien-dam, per quam unam via effe poterat, milites ducti, quum cæden-dum effet faxum, arboribus circa immanibus dejectis detrunca-tifque, ftruem ingentem lignorum faciunt : eanique (quum et vis venti apta faciendo igni coorta effet), fuccendunt ardentiaque faxa infuso aceto putrefaciunt," Livy, xxi. 37. A very curious difcuffion of this paffage will be found in *Notes and Queries*, 4th Series, vol. ii. pp. 289, 350, 443, 490, 534, vol. iii. p. 136 : where it is fuggefted that Livy may have been mifled by the fimilarity of the Latin word *acetum,* vinegar, to the Italian *accetta,* a pick-axe ; and very unexpected confirmation is given to this fanciful

Lightning-conductors had not then been difcovered, but the authorities of the Cathedral had done their beft, according to their knowledge, to avert "the flame of fier," for, in 1314, they had replaced in the bowl of the Crofs at the fummit of the fpire many relics of faints, "for the protection of the tower and of the whole building."* Amongft the relics were a piece of the True Crofs, a ftone from the Sepulchre of the Lord, a ftone from the Mount of the Afcenfion, and another ftone from Calvary. Some bones of the Eleven Thoufand Virgins of Cologne were alfo added, wrapped in a piece of red fendal. Thefe relics were exhibited to the people by the Chancellor of the Cathedral during his fermon on S. Botolph's Day, June 17, and were afterwards replaced in the Crofs, together with many other fimilar treafures. The Divines of the Reformation period were not flow to remember this day's proceedings. "We needed not to fear," fays one of them, "(if your opinion were true) the burning any more of Paul's. Make a crofs on the fteeple, and fo it fhall be fafe. But within thefe few years it had a crofs and reliques in the bowl, to boot : yet they prevailed not ; yea, the crofs itfelf was fired firft."†

---

fuggeftion by a communication from the well-known fcholar George Stephens, in which he quotes from King Alfred's Old-Englifh verfion of *Orofius* a paffage defcribing Hannibal's journey over the Alps, concluding thus: " So when he came to the feparate rock, he ordered it to be heated with fire, and then to be hewed with *mattocks*."

* *Documents*, p. 45.

† Calthill's *Anfwer to Marfhall*, p. 180 (Parker Society).

Amongſt all the conflagrations which have made havoc with the Cathedral, the Great Fire of 1561 holds a very prominent place. We will give a contemporary account of it, and we can ſcarcely do ſo in better faſhion than by printing *verbatim et literatim* a tract, extremely rare, if not unique, preſerved in the Britiſh Muſeum :

THE TRVE REPORT OF THE BURNYNG OF THE STEPLE AND CHURCHE OF POULES IN LONDON.

¶ Jeremy. xviii.

I wyll ſpeake ſuddenlye agaynſt a nation, or agaynſte a kyngedome, to plucke it vp, and to roote it out, and diſtroye it. But yf that nation, agaynſte whome I haue pronounced, turne from their wickednes, I wyll repent of the plage that I thought to brynge vppon them.

Imprynted at London, at the weſt ende of Paules Church, at the ſygne of the Hedghogge by Wyllyam Seres.

Cum priuilegio ad imprimendum solum. Anno. 1561. The x. of Iune.

¶ THE TRUE REPORTE OF THE BURNINGE OF THE STEPLE AND CHURCH OF PAULES IN LONDON.

On Wedneſday beinge the fourthe daye of June, in the yeare of our Lord. 1561. and in the thyrde yeare of the reigne of our ſoueraygne Ladye Elizabeth by the grace of God, Queene of England, Fraunce and

Ireland, defender of the faith, &c. betweene one and two of the clocke at after noone, was feene a marueilous great fyrie lightning, and immediately infued a moſt terrible hydeous cracke of thunder, fuche as feldom hath been heard, and that by eſtimacion of fenfe, directlyc ouer the Citie of London. At which inſtante the corner of a turret of yᵉ ſteple of faint Martins Churche within Ludgate was torne, and diuers great ſtones caften down, and a hole broken throughe the roofe & timber of the faid church, by the fall of the fame ſtones.

For diuers perfones in tyme of the faide tempeſt being on the riuer of Thamys, and others beyng in the fieldes nere adioyning to yᵉ Citie, affirmed that thei faw a long and a fpeare pointed flame of fier (as it were) runne through the toppe of the Broche or Shaft of Paules Steple, from the Eaſte Weſtwarde. And fome of the parifh of faint Martins then bcing in the ſtreate, dyd feele a marueylous ſtrong ayre or whorlewynd, with a fmel lyke brimſtone, comming from Paules Churche, and withal heard the rufhe of yᵉ ſtones which fell frō their ſteple into the churche. Betwene iiii. and fiue of the clocke a fmoke was efpied by diuers to breake oute vnder the bowle of the faid fhaf of Paules, & namely by Peter Johnfon principall Regiſtrer to the Bifhop of Londō, who immediatly brought worde to the Bifhops houfe. But fodeinly after, as it wer in a momente, the flame brake furth in a circle like a garlande rounde about the broche, about two yards to theſtimacion of fight vnder the bowle of the faid fhaft, & increafed in fuche wife, that

within a quarter of an howre, or little more, the croſſe
& the Egle on the toppe fell downe vpon the ſouth
croſſe Ile.   The Lord Maior being ſent for, & his
brethren, came with all ſpede poſſible, & had a ſhort
conſultaciō as in ſuch a caſe might be, with yᵉ Biſhop
of London and others, for yᵉ beſt way of remedy.
And thither came alſo yᵉ Lord Keper of yᵉ great
Seale, & the Lord Treaſorer, who by their wiſedom
and authoritie dyreƈted as good order, as in ſo great a
confuſiō could poſſible be.

Some there wer, pretēding experience in warres,
that coūceled the remanente of the ſteple to bee ſhot
down with Canons, whiche counſel was not liked, as
moſt perilous both for the diſperſing the fire, and de-
ſtruƈtiō of houſes and people, other perceiuing the
ſteple to be paſt al recouery, conſidering the hugenes
of the fier, & the dropping of the lead, thought beſte
to geat ladders & ſcale the churche, & with axes to
hew down a ſpace of the roofe of the Churche, to ſtay
the fier, at the leaſte to ſaue ſome part of the ſaide
churche, whiche was concluded.   But before yᵉ ladders
& buckets could be brought, & things put in any
order, and eſpecially becauſe the churche was of ſuch
height, that thei could not ſkale it, & no ſufficiente
nomber of axes could be had, yᵉ laborers alſo being
troubled with yᵉ multitude of ydle gaſers, the moſte
parte of the higheſte roofe of the Churche was on fier.

Fyrſt the fall of the Croſſe and Egle fired the ſouthe
croſſe Ile, whiche Ile was firſte conſumed, the beames
& brands of the ſteple fell down on euery ſide, & fired
the other thre partes, that is to ſaye, the Chauncel or

Quier, the north Ile, & the body of the church.   So
that in one howres fpace ye broch of the fteple was
brent downe to ye battlementes, and the moft part of
ye higheft roofe of the churche, likewife confumed.
The ftate of the fteple & churche feming both def-
perate : my Lord Mayor was aduifed by one Maifter
Winter of ye admiraltie, to conuerte the mofte part of
his care & prouifiō to preferue the Bifhops palace ad-
ioynyng to the Northweft end of the church : leaft frō
that houfe beinge large, the fier might fprede to the
ftretes adioyning.   Wherupon the ladders, buckets, &
laborers, were commaunded thither, & by greate labor
& diligence, a piece of ye roofe of the Northe Ile was
cut down, & the fier fo ftayed and by muche water,
that parte quenched, and ye faid Bifhops houfe pre-
ferued.   It pleafed god alfo at the fame tyme bothe
to turne & calme the winde, which afore was vehemēt,
& continued ftil high & greate in other partes without
ye citie.   There wer aboue v. c. perfons y^t laboured in
carying & fillīg water &c.   Diuers fubftantial Citizens
toke paynes as if thei had bene laborers, fo did alfo
diuers & fondrye gentlemen, whofe names wer not
knowen to the writer hereof, but amongft other, the
faid M. Winter, & one M. Stranguifh, did both take
notable paines in their own perfons, & alfo much
directed and encouraged other, and that not without
great daūger to thēfelves.   In ye euening came the
Lord Clinton, Lord admiral, frō ye court at Grene-
wiche, whō the Queenes maiefty affone as the rage of
the fier was efpied by her maieftye and others in the
court, of the pitifull inclinacion & loue that her gracious

highneffe dyd beare both to ye faid church & the citie, fente to affyft my Lorde Mayor for the fuppreffyng of the fyre, who with his wyfdome, authority & diligēt trauayl did very much good therein. About x. of the clocke the fyercenes of the fyre was paft, the tymbre being fallen and lyinge brenninge vppon the vaultes of ftone, the vaultes yet (god be thanked) ftandynge vnperifhed : fo as onelye the tymbre of the hole church was confumed, & the lead molten, fauyng the moft parte of the two lowe Iles of the Queare, and a piece of the north Ile, and an other fmal piece of ye fouthe Ile, in the bodye of the churche. Nowithftandynge all which, it pleafed the merciful god in his wrath to remēbre his mercie, and to enclofe the harme of this moft fyerce and terrible fyre, wythin the walles of thys one church, not extending any part of his wrath in this fyre vppon the reft of the Citie, whiche to all reafon and fence of man was fubiect to vtter diftruc- tion. For in the hole city without the churche no ftycke was kyndled furelye. Notwithftanding that in diuerfe partes, and ftretes, and within the houfes bothe adioyninge and of a good diftaunce, as in fleteftreete, & newgate market, by the violence of fyre, burninge coles of greate bigneffe, fell downe almooft as thicke as haylftones, and flawes of lead were blowen abrode into the gardins without ye Citie, like flawes of fnow in bredthe w^toute hurt, god be thanked, to any houfe or perfō. Many fond talkes goe abrode of the original caufe of this fier. Some fay, it was negligence of plumbers, whereas by due examinacion it is proued that no plumbers or other workemen labored in the

churche for fixe monethes before. Other fufpect it
was done by fom wicked practife of wildfyer or gun-
pouder, but no iuft fufpicions thereof by any examinacion can be founde hitherto. Some fufpect coniurers
& forcerers, wherof there is alfo no great likelyhode.
And if it hadde bene wrought y^t waie, yet could not
the deuil haue done it, without Gods permiſſiõ, & to
fome purpofe of his vnfercheable iudgemẽts, as appereth
in the ftory of Job. The true caufe as it femeth, was
the tẽpeft by gods fuffrance : for it cannot be otherwife gathered, but that at ye faid great & terrible
thunderclap, when fainte Martins fteple was torne, the
lightning which by natural order fmiteth ye higheft,
did firft fmite ye top of Paules fteple, and entring in
at the fmall holes which haue alwaies remained open
for building fkaffoldes to the workes, & finding the
timber very olde & drie, did kindle ye fame, & fo y^e
fier increafing grew to a flame & wrought ye effecte
which folowed, moft terrible then to behold, & now
moft lamentable to looke on.

On Sonday folowyng beynge the viii. day of June,
the reuerend in god, the Bifhop of Durefme, at Paules
croffe made a learned & fruitful fermon, exhorting the
auditory to a general repentance, & namely to humble
obediẽce of the lawes & fuperior powers, whiche vertue
is muche decayed in thefe our daies : feming to haue
intellygẽce from the Queenes highnes, that her
maieftie intendeth that more feueritie of lawes fhalbe
executed againft perfons difobedyent, afwell in caufes
of religiõ, as ciuil, to the great reioyfing of his audi-
tours. He exhorted alfo hys audiẽce to take this as a

generall warninge to the wholc realme, & namclye to the citie of London, of ſome greater plage to folow, if amendemente of lyfe in all States did not enſue: He much reproued thoſe perſons whiche woulde aſſigne the cauſe of this wrathc of god to any perticular ſtate of mē, or that were diligent to loke into other mens lyues, & coulde ſee no faultes in themſelfes: but wiſhed that euery man wold deſcend into himſelfe and ſay with Dauid *Ego ſum qui peccaui*, I am he that hathe ſinned, and ſo furth to that effeét verye godlye. He alſo not onely reproued the prophanatyon of the ſaid Churche of Paules of longe time hertofore abuſed by walkīg, iangling, brawling, fighting, bargaining. &c. namely in Sermons & ſcruice time: but alſo aūſwercd by the way to the obieétiōs of ſuch euil tunged perſōs, which do impute this token of gods deſerued ire, to alteraciō, or rather reformaciō of religiō, declaring out of aūcient records & hiſtorics, yᵉ like, yca & greater matcrs had befallen in yᵉ time of ſuperſticiō & ignor-ance. For in yᶜ firſt yerc of King Stephā not only yᵉ ſaid church of Paules was brēt, but alſo a great part of yᵉ city, yᵗ is to ſay, frō Londō bridge vnto S. Clemēts without Tēple bar was by fier cōſumed. And in yᵉ daies of King Hēry yᵉ VI. yᵉ ſteplc of Paules was alſo fired by lightning, although it was then ſtaide by diligēce of yᵉ Citizens, yᵉ fier being thē by likelyhode not ſo fierce. Many other ſuchc like cōmon calamities he reherſed, whiche had happened in other coūtrcis, both nigh to this realm & far of, where yᵉ church of Rome hath moſt auéthority, & therefore cōcluded yᵉ fureſt way to be, yᵗ euery man ſhould iudge, examin,

& amēd himfelfe, & embrace, beleue, and truely folow yᵉ word of god, & earneftly to pray to god to turn away frō vs his deferued wrath & indignaciō, whereof this his terrible work is a moft certein warning, if we repent not vnfeinedly. The whiche god grāt maye come to paffe in all eftates & degrees, to yᵉ glory of his name and to oure endleffe comforte in Chrift our fauiour. Amen.

God faue the Queene.

This pamphlet, which appears to have been taken from the official report of the Fire entered in Bifhop Grindal's Regifter,* made its appearance alfo in Latin and in French. It is exceedingly rare in all its forms. There is a copy of the Latin tract in the Public Record Office, and a copy of the French tract in the Cathedral Library.†

The ballad-writers were not flow to difcourfe of the calamity, after their fafhion. Mr. Payne Collier has printed in his *Regifters of the Stationers' Company* the following quaint verfes entituled:

THE BURNING OF PAULES.

Lament eche one the blazing fire
That downe from heaven came,
And burnt S. Powles his lofty fpyre
With lightnings furious flame.
Lament, I fay,
Both night and day,
Sith London's fins did caufe the fame.

---

* Printed for the firft time in my *Documents*, pp. 113-119.
† See *Documents*, pp. 203-206.

The fire came downe from heaven foone,
  But did not ftrike the croffe,
At fower in the afternoone,
  To our moft grevous loffe.
    Could nothing ftay
    The fad decay :
The lead was molten into droffe.

For five long howers the fire did burn
  The roof and timbers ftrong :
The bells fell downe, and we muft mourne,
  The wind it was fo ftrong,
    It made the fier
    To blaze the higher,
And doe the church ftill greater wrong.

O, London ! think on thine amiffe,
  Which brought this great mifhap ;
Remember how thou livde in bliffe,
  And layde in vices lap.
    O, now begin,
    Repent thy fin,
And fay it fhall no more entrap.

Mr. Chappell has difcovered the mufic to which the ballad was fung.*

No wonder that London fhould be called upon to "lament the blazing fire." It entirely deftroyed the beautiful fpire, whofe height far exceeded that of Salifbury ; great part of the roof was burnt ; the Chapter Houfe and the exquifite Cloifters were very ferioufly injured. Divine fervice was tranfferred to S. Gregory's. "The xxiij of June, was mydfomer evyn, the ferves at Sant Gregore chyrche be-fyd Powlles [by] the Powlles quer tyll Powlles be rede

<hr>

° *Documents*, p. 211.

mad," fays Machyn.   Not till November in the fame year "was begone the ferves at Powlles to fynge, and ther was a grett comunion ther begane, the byfhope and odur," as the fame annalift teftifies.   Huge fcaffolds were erected with a view to the repair of the ruined tower.

> " Have you not feen a Hench boy lac'd all o're
> So thick, you could not tell what cloth he wore?
> Have you heard not the oaths of country people,
> They could not for the fcaffolds fee Paul's fteeple."

So writes Edmund Gayton in 1654.   The ultimate fate of thefe fcaffolds will be told in a later chapter.

In fome *Memoranda* by John Stow lately printed for the firft time,* it is faid that the Crofs fell fouthward, "and fo the fphere byrnt downeward lyke as a candil confumyng, to ye ftone werke and ye bells, and fo ye rouffe of ye churche, and thorow ye rouffes of ye churche all fowre ways, eaft, weft, northe and fowthe.   With in ye qwiers or chawnfylls was brynt no thyng but only ye communion table, and in ye reft of ye churche was brynt nothing but a fartayn tymber werke† whiche ftode at ye northe-weft pyllar of ye ftepull, which was fyeryd with ye tymber that fell in to ye churche owt of ye fteple ; whiche was a lamentable fyghte and pytyfull remembraunce to all people that have ye feare of God before theyr eyes, confyderynge it was ye hous of owre Lord, erectyd to prays hym and pray to hym, ye beawty of ye fyte of

---

* By Mr. James Gairdner, in *Three Fifteenth Century Chroni-cles* (Camden Society), p. 116.

† This was the Chapel of S. Paul.   *Stow*, p. 126.

London, ye beawty of ye holle Reallme. A mynſter
of suche worthy, ſtronge, and coſtly buldynge, ſo
large, ſo pleaſant and delectable, it paſſyd all com-
paryſon, not only of mynſtyrs within thys realme but
ells where as ſure as travayll hathe taught ws in other
realmes ethar Criſtyn or hethyn. Wherfore feare we
God that ſo fore hathe chatyſyd us, and let ws well
know that he whiche hathe not ſpayrd his owne hous
wyll not ſpare owres, exſept we repent owr formor
wykyd lyffe and ſerve hym in holynys and newenys of
lyffe, with a parffyt faythe in God and parffyt charytye
to owr neyghbour, ye whyche our Lorde for his byttar
paſſyon grawnt. Amen."

"Within one month after the firing of the church
all the fower greate rooſes wer covered with a ſleight
rooſe of boordes and leade, onely to preſerve the
walles, floores and vaultes from the enjurie of the
rayne. And before the yeare was expired, all the
long rooffes wer rayſed of new and ſtrong timber, the
moſt part whereof was framed in Yorkſhire, and by
ſea conveyed to London ; the charges of which worke
amounted to the ſumme of 5,982^li 13^s 4^d *ob.* Soe the
receites wer fully expended ; and yett the two croſſe
rooſes which ſtand north and ſouth were not finiſhed,
but remayned ſtill covered with boardes untill the
yeare 1564. At which tyme they wer rayſed and per-
fected at the onely charge of Edmund Grindall, then
Biſhopp of London ; whoe expended out of his proper
eſtate 720^li in finiſhing that worke."*

* *Annals of the Firſt Four Years of the Reign of Queen Elizabeth,* by Sir John Hayward (Camden Society), pp. 87-91.

The ſtory of the Great Fire of 1666, which overwhelmed in one common deſtruction the grand Cathedral and the City of London, has been ſo well and ſo often told, that it needs no recital here.

10—2

CHAPTER IX.

PAUL'S CROSS: ITS EARLY HISTORY.

PULPIT Crofs, from which the Word of God might be preached to a congregation gathered in the open air, under the blue vault of heaven, was by no means an uncommon adjunct to a church. To mention two examples only, in the City of London: the Church of S. Michael, Cornhill, had on its fouth fide "a proper cloifter and a fair churchyard (not much unlike to that in Paule's churchyard"*) in which a crofs was built by Sir John Rudftone, mayor, who died in 1531 and was buried in a vault beneath it. The Hofpital called S. Mary Spital, without Bifhopfgate, had alfo its pulpit crofs, with "a fair built houfe of two ftories in height, for the Mayor and other honourable perfons, with the aldermen and fheriffs, to fit in, there to hear

* Stow, *Survey*, p. 75, edition 1603, reprinted by Mr. Thoms, 1876.

the fermons preached in the Eafter holidays. In the
loft over them ftood the Bifhop of London and other
prelates ; now," fays Stow,* "the ladies and aldermen's wives do there ftand at a fair window, or fit at
their pleafure. And here it is to be noted that time
out of mind it hath been a laudable cuftom that on
Good Friday, in the afternoon, fome efpecial learned
man, by appointment of the prelates, hath preached a
fermon at Paules Crofs, treating of Chrift's Paffion ;
and upon the three next Eafter holidays, Monday,
Tuefday, and Wednefday, the like learned men, by the
like appointment, have ufed to preach in the fore-
noons at the faid Spittle, to perfuade the Article of
Chrift's Refurection ; and then on Low Sunday, one
other learned man at Paules Crofs, to make rehearfal
of thofe four former fermons, either commending or
reproving them, as to him by judgement of the learned
divines was thought convenient. And that done, he
was to make a fermon of his own ftudy, which in all
were five fermons in one. At thefe fermons, fo fever-
ally preached, the Mayor, with his brethren the aldermen, were accuftomed to be prefent in their violets
at Paules on Good Friday, and in their fcarlets at the
Spittle in the holidays, except Wednefday in violet,
and the Mayor with his brethren on Low Sunday in
fcarlet at Paules Crofs, continued until this day."
The Edition of Stow's *Survey* here quoted is that of
1603. In our own time, the Lord Mayor and his
brethren ftill meet at Chrift Church, Newgate Street,

* Stow, *Survey,* p. 63.

on the Monday and Tuefday in Eafter Week, to hear what are called the Spital Sermons.

A ftory is told of Bifhop Warburton that, dining with the Lord Mayor after preaching one of thefe Spital Sermons, his hoft faid to him that "the Common Council were much obliged to his Lordfhip, for that this was the firft time he ever heard them prayed for." "I confidered them," faid Warburton, "as a body who much needed the prayers of the Church."*

But of all the Pulpit Croffes, in and near London, that which ftood in S. Paul's Churchyard, and was called Paul's Crofs, has by far the moft interefting hiftory. It is mentioned by Fabyan in his *New Chronicles of England and France*,† as early as the year 1256, when a roll, found in the King's wardrobe at Windfor, which contained divers articles againft the Mayor and rulers of the City of London, affirming that they had grievoufly tafked and wronged the commonalty of the City, was read aloud to the people. The King fent John Mancell "one of his iuftycys vnto London ; and there in yᵉ feeft of yᵉ conuerfyon of feynt Pawle, by the Kynges auctoryte, callyd at Pawlys croffe a folkmoot, beynge there prefent fyr Rycharde de Clare, erle of Glowcetyr, and dyuerfe other of the Kynges counceyll ; where the fayd John Mancell caufyd yᵉ fayd rolle to be redde, before the comynalty of the cytie, and after fhewyd to yᵉ people that yᵉ Kynges pleafure and mynde was, that they

* Note, by Mr. Thoms, to Stow's *Survey*, p. 63.
† Edited by Sir Henry Ellis, in 1811, pp. 339, 340.

ſhulde be rulyd with iuſtyce, and that the lybertyes of the cytie ſhuld be maynteyned in euery poynt: and if the Kynge myghte knowe thoſe parſonys, that ſo hadde wrongyd the comynaltye of the cytie, they ſhulde be greuouſlye punyſſhed, to the exaumple of other." The King was Henry III.*

Paul's Croſs, it will be ſeen, had its political and ſecular uſes, as well as its religious. Here folk-motes were gathered together, Bulls and Papal ediĉts were read, heretics were denounced, hereſies abjured, excommunications publiſhed, great political changes made known to the people, penances performed.

It may be convenient to tell, in the firſt inſtance, what is known of the ſtruĉture itſelf, and then to ſpeak more fully of the various uſes to which it was applied. The preciſe period when a Pulpit Croſs was firſt erĉted at S. Paul's has not been aſcertained. It was ſtanding in 1241,† and, probably, exiſted long before. In 1382, "the one and twentieth day of May, was a great Earthquake in England at nine of the clocke, fearing the hearts of many."‡ It was moſt vehement in Kent, "where it ſunke ſome Churches, and threw them downe to the earth." On the 24th of May was a ſecond earthquake, "before the Sunne riſing, but not ſo terrible as the firſt." About the Feaſt of S. Thomas Apoſtle, "great raynes and inondations of waters chanced, ſo that the water roſe foure times more in height then before." It was a

---

* See alſo Riley, *Chronicles of the Mayors*, etc., pp. 37, 38.
† See *infra*, p. 123.
‡ Stow, *Annales.*

very memorable year. " The earthquake happened at the very moment when a Council of the clergy was fitting in London to pronounce judgment upon Wyclif and his adherents." A very interefting allufion to the earthquake is found amongft the Political Songs and Poems relating to Englifh Hiftory edited by Thomas Wright (in the Series of Chronicles publifhed under the superintendence of the Mafter of the Rolls.*)

> " For fothe this was a Lord to drede,
>   So fodeynly mad mon agaft ;
> Of gold and felver thei tok non hede,
>   But out of ther houfes ful fone thei paft.
>   Chaumbres, chymeneys, al to-barft,
> Chirches and caftelles foule gon fare ;
>   Pinacles, steples, to grounde hit caft ;
> And al was for warnyng to be ware.
>
> *　　　*　　　*
>
> " The ryfyng of the comuynes in londe,
>   The peftilens, and the eorthe-qwake,
> Theofe threo thinges, I understonde,
>   Beoth tokenes the grete vengaunce and wrake
>   That fchulde falle for fynnes fake,
> As this clerkes conne declare.
>   Now may we chefe to leve or take,
> For warnyng have we to be ware."

Certainly these were very anxious days, and we cannot wonder if the poet faw figns of vengeance in the trembling earth and ftorm-rent fky. The days of Wyclif, of Sir John Ball, of the reftlefs Commons, of John Tylar of Dartford, of the Blackheath rifing, of the plunder of Lambeth Palace and of the Savoy, the breaking open of the Fleet Prifon, the fpoiling of the

---

* *Political Songs and Poems*, i. pp. lxiv. 251, 252.

Temple, the fires at Weftminfter, the breaking of the
Prifon at Newgate, the forcible entry into the Tower,
the murder of Archbifhop Sudbury, Wat Tyler's
infurrection, Jack Straw's confpiracy—thefe* were
ftirring times.

Paul's Crofs did not efcape. Storm, tempeft, and
earthquake had done their work. It was " frail and
injured," and ready to fall into utter ruin. The
Bifhops, however, beftirred themfelves, and with
Archbifhop Courtènay at their head iffued *Indulgences* to the faithful of their diocefes, granting to
thofe who fhould contribute to the repair of Paul's
Crofs forty days' Indulgence. The following is a
literal tranflation of the original document, ftill preferved in the Cathedral record-room :†

"To all the fons of our Holy Mother the Church
under whofe notice thefe prefent letters fhall come,
William, by Divine permiffion Archbifhop of Canterbury, Primate of all England, and Legate of the Apoftolic See, wifhes eternal health in the Lord. We
efteem it a fervice pleafant and acceptable to God
whenfoever, by the alluring gifts of Indulgences, we
ftir up the minds of the faithful to a greater readinefs
in contributing their gifts to fuch works as concern
the honour of the Divine Name. Since, then, the
High Crofs in the greater Churchyard of the Church
of London, (where the Word of God is habitually

---

* Thefe are but a few of the events of the preceding year 1381.

† The tranflation follows, almoft word for word, the original
text.　The object has been, not to produce an elegant verfion, but
a clofe verbal rendering.

preached both to Clergy and Laity, being a place very public and well known,) by ſtrong winds and tempeſts of the air and terrible earthquakes, hath become ſo frail and injured, that unleſs ſome means be quickly taken for its repair and reſtoration, it will fall utterly into ruin : therefore, by the mercy of the Almighty God, truſting in the merits and prayers of the moſt Bleſſed Virgin Mary His Mother, and of the Bleſſed Apoſtles Peter and Paul, and of all the Saints, We, by theſe preſents, mercifully grant in the Lord to all the ſervants of Chriſt throughout our Province of Canterbury whereſoever living, truly repenting and confeſſing their ſins, who, for the reſtoration and repair of the aforeſaid Croſs ſhall give, bequeath, or in any manner aſſign, of the goods committed to them gifts of charity, Forty Days of Indulgence. In teſtimony whereof we have to this preſent letter affixed our ſeal. Given at the Manor of Fulham, in the Dioceſe of London, on the 18th day of May, in the year of our Lord One thouſand, three hundred, and eighty-ſeven, and in the ſixth year of our tranſlation."

The Biſhops of London, Ely, Bath, Cheſter, Carliſle, Llandaff, and Bangor, lent their aid to circulate this document with their full approval, in their own dioceſes. Doubtleſs other biſhops followed their example. Unfortunately we do not know the proceeds of theſe *Indulgences.* It is certain, however, that Biſhop Kempe, Biſhop of London from 1450 to 1489, was able to rebuild the Croſs, "as his arms, in ſundry places of its leaded cover, doth manifeſt." So Dugdale, writing in 1658, affirms.* Stow, alſo, ſpeaks as an eye-witneſs, when he ſays that Biſhop Kempe, "new built it in form as it now ſtandeth."†

No drawing of the earlieſt Croſs has been handed down. But if, as Stow and Dugdale intimate, the Croſs ſtanding in their day was the ſame as that which Biſhop Kempe conſtrutted, then we are able to produce a fairly correct repreſentation of it, ſo far at leaſt, as its general outline is concerned.

One Henry Farley, "a pious, diſintereſted, and zealous perſon," cauſed to be painted in the year 1616, a very remarkable picture. It was executed by one John Gipkyn. The picture, or ſeries of pictures, is painted on two folding leaves of wood, forming a diptych.‡ Farley had for ſome eight years buſily importuned the King, James I., for the reparation of S. Paul's Cathedral. His painting may be regarded as a prediction of that which actually came to paſs about four years later, when, on Sunday, 26th March, 1620, King James I., with his Queen and Charles Prince of Wales, attended by the Archbiſhop of Canterbury, Biſhops, Officers of State, and others, heard a Sermon at Paul's Croſs, preached by Dr. John King, the "King of Preachers" as James uſed to call him. We will attempt a deſcription of this picture, but we muſt premiſe that it utterly defies all the rules of perſpective, and is utterly wanting in minute

---

* Dugdale, firſt edition, p. 125.

† Stow, *Survey*, p. 124.

‡ It is figured in Wilkinson's *Londina Illuſtrata*, vol. i. A reduced woodcut from the picture illuſtrates the preſent volume.

accuracy. When we mention that the Eaftern Window of the Choir and the great North door of the North Tranfept are both prefented, with admirable im-

PAUL'S CROSS.

partiality, to the fpectator—and that the Choir has but four windows inftead of twelve, whilft the Nave is curtailed of nearly all its length,—it will be perceived

that the precifion which modern critics would require
in an architectural view is abfent here. Paul's Crofs
ftands at a point equidiftant from the N.E. angle of
the Choir, and the N.E. angle of the North Tranfept.
(This was not, in fact, its true pofition.)   Immediately
oppofite to the fpectator is a building in two ftories :
in the lower of which fits the Lord Mayor, accompanied by the Aldermen and by the Sword Bearer ; and
in the upper ftory fits, in a fort of projecting box, the
King, with the Queen on his right, and the Prince of
Wales on his left.   Ladies and gentlemen of the court,
three Bifhops, and other lefs diftinctly indicated perfons
occupy the remainder of this gallery.   On the right is
the North Tranfept, and againft it are built two long
low houfes obfcuring the buttreffes and the lower parts
of the windows : four chimneys belonging to thefe
houfes are fmoking freely.   From thefe chimneys the
following lines iffue, addreffed to the royal gallery :

> " Viewe, O Kinge ; howe my walles-creepers
> Have made mee worke for chimney-fweepers."

Above is feen the tower of the Cathedral.   It had
loft its fpire in 1561.   Pigeons are flying about, then
as now.

The Crofs itfelf is an octagon.   It is entered from
the back, and is large enough to contain the preacher
and three attendants.   An hour-glafs ftands at the
preacher's right.   The pulpit-cloth is embroidered
with the royal arms.   Accefs to the pulpit is obtained
by a ftair of fome fix fteps, on the loweft of which,
effectually to prevent intrufion, ftands a verger with

his ſtaff.　The whole ſtructure, which was of wood, is furrounded by a low dwarf wall, within which are ſitting ſeven perſons, two of them women, probably the choir.　The building is ſurmounted by a ſlightly domed roof, crowned by a diſproportionately large croſs. Before the Croſs ſits on benches a numerous congregation of men, women, and children, nearly all wearing their hats, and ſome having open books ſpread out upon their knees.　It is ſaid that they paid a penny or a halfpenny a piece for the privilege of uſing theſe forms.*　On the left a well-dreſſed youth bows and accoſts a grave and reverend citizen with " I pray, Sir, what is the text?" who anſwers, "The 2nd of Chron. xxiv."　On the right another citizen in his well-furred gown drops a coin into a large money-cheſt placed outſide the Tranſept door.　Two led horſes, a dog-whipper flogging a dog, a horſe-block of three ſteps, a lady and her cavalier, and a few figures ſcattered in the background, complete the picture.†

This is Paul's Croſs.　A lofty ſtructure, probably of wood, upon a ſtone baſe, with a leaded roof bearing Biſhop Kempe's arms, and ſurmounted with a croſs.

Wilkinſon gives alſo a ſecond view of the Croſs,‡ " From an original Drawing in the Pepyſian Library, Cambridge."　It muſt be frankly confeſſed that it is a little difficult to reconcile the two.　Here are three octagonal ſteps, the dwarf wall ſurrounding the front

---

* Walcott's *Traditions and Cuſtoms*, p. 70.
† Many details are neceſſarily omitted in the woodcut.
‡ *Londina Illuſtrata*, p. 31.

of the pulpit, the structure itself, and its domed roof and crofs ; but the architectural beauties faintly indicated in Henry Farley's picture are wanting here.

The Crofs was the fcene of a great number of events intimately connected with the hiftory of the country.

In 1241 " his Lordfhip the King afked leave of the citizens of London, at Saint Paul's Crofs, that he might pafs over into Gafcoigne to aid the Count de la Marche againft the King of France, and foon after croffed over."*

In 1252, the King "gave orders that all perfons in the City fhould meet together on the Sunday following at Saint Paul's Crofs, in prefence of thofe whom he fhould fend thither, and there make oath of fealty to Sir Edward, his fon, and to his Queen, to whofe charge he was about to commit his Kingdom. Afterwards, this matter was poftponed until the Tuefday in Pentecoft, on which day the whole Commons of the City did fealty at the Crofs aforefaid to Sir Edward, and in his prefence faving their fealty to his lordfhip the King."†

In 1259, " on the day before the feaft of S. Leonard [November 6], his Lordfhip the King came to the Crofs of S. Paul's, a countlefs multitude of the City being there affembled in folkmote, and took leave of the people to crofs over, juft as he had done before at Weftminfter ; and promifed them that he would preferve all their liberties unimpaired. Upon the morrow

* Riley, *Chronicles of the Mayors and Sheriffs*, p. 9.
† *Ibid.*, p. 20.

of the fea∫t of S. Leonard, his Lord∫hip the King took his departure from London for the ∫ea-coa∫t. On the fea∫t of S. Brice [November 13], which at that time fell on a Friday, his Lord∫hip the King cro∫∫ed over."*

In 1260, "on the Sunday before the Fea∫t of S. Valentine," the King cau∫ed the Folkmote to be ∫ummoned at S. Paul's Cro∫s; "whither he him∫elf came, the King of Almaine, the Archbi∫hop of Canterbury, John Maun∫ell, and many others. The King al∫o commanded that all per∫ons of the age of twelve years and upwards ∫hould make oath before their Aldermen in every ward that they would be faithful unto him, ∫o long as he ∫hould live, and after his death to his heir, which was accordingly done. Then all the gates of the City were ∫hut, night and day, by the King's command, the Bridge Gate and the Gates of Ludgate and Aldgate excepted, which were open by day, and well-fortified with armed men."†

Such incidents occurred frequently, and it would be ea∫y to multiply references. But our next citation ∫hall refer to a more religious u∫e of the Cro∫s.

In October, 1261, the King and his Queen were ∫ojourning at S. Paul's, probably in the Palace of the Bi∫hop, Henry de Wengham, who was in great favour with Henry III. In this year, in Lent, "the King cau∫ed to be read at S. Paul's Cro∫s a certain Bull of Pope Urban,‡ who had been made Pope the ∫ame year, which confirmed the Bull of Pope Alexander,§ his predece∫∫or, who had previou∫ly ab∫olved the King

---

* Riley, *Chronicles of the Mayors and Sheriffs*, pp. 45, 46.
† *Ibid.*, pp. 48, 49. ‡ Urban IV. § Alexander IV.

and all the others of the oath which they had made in the Parliament at Oxford."*

A little later, March 17, 1264, the Mayor and Aldermen of London did fealty to the King in S. Paul's Cathedral. "Then," fays the Chronicler, "thofe who were prefent might fee a thing wondrous and unheard of in this age ; for this moft wretched Mayor [Thomas Fitz Thomas], when taking the oath, dared to utter words fo rafh as thefe, faying unto his lordfhip the King in prefence of the people, ' My lord, fo long as unto us you will be a good lord and King, we will be faithful and duteous unto you.' " †

In 1266, on the Monday following June 25, the Legate Ottoboni (he was Cardinal of S. Adrian, and Pope for about five weeks as Adrian V. in 1276 ‡) laid a general interdict upon the City, for harbouring the Earl of Gloucefter. The interdict was fpeedily removed. On the Vigil of S. John Baptift in the fame year, Sir Alan la Suche, or Zouche, " was made Conftable and Warden of the City by his lordfhip the King, in the prefence of all the people at Saint Paul's Crofs."§ The following year, about the Feaft of S. Mark, 1267, Ottoboni held a great Council in S. Paul's, at which were prefent, in perfon or by their proctors, the Archbifhops, Bifhops, Abbots and Priors, Deans, Provofts, and Archdeacons of England, Ireland, Scotland, and Wales.

* Riley, *Chronicles of the Mayors and Sheriffs*, pp. 52, 53.
† *Ibid.*, p. 77, *marginal note.*
‡ He died 18th Auguft, 1276. *Dictionnaire des Papes.*
§ Riley, *Chronicles*, pp. 97-106, 107.

In 1269, on May 13, nine Bifhops, arrayed in their pontificals, came to the Crofs, and caufed to be read " a certain Bull of Pope Innocent, confirmatory of the Charters of the Liberties of England and of the Foreft, which the King had executed unto the Barons of England in the 9th year of his reign ; and caufed to be read openly and diftinctly before all the people, the fentence which, in the year of our Lord 1253, had been pronounced in the Greater Hall at Weftminfter, before the King and many Nobles of England, by thirteen Bifhops arrayed in pontificals, againft all tranfgreffors of the faid Charters." The Bifhops then proceeded to excommunicate all perfons who had done anything in contravention of the aforefaid Charters, and all thofe who had laid violent hands upon the Clergy or plundered them. The parifh priefts of the City publifhed this fentence in every parifh church.*

In 1271, in the time of the tumults in the City in reference to the election of Walter Hervey as Mayor, a Folkmote was called together at the Crofs, and it was decided that he fhould be Mayor for that year " to whofe election the greater part of the citizens fhould agree."†

In 1311, 5 Edward II., the King held his Parliament at the Friars Preachers, or Black Friars, in the City of London. The Parliament lafted fifteen days and the Statutes ordained during its feffion were proclaimed at the Crofs, on the Tuefday next after

* Riley, *Chronicles*, p. 128.　　† *Ibid.*, pp. 158, 159.

S. Michael, in the preſence of the Earl of Glouceſter, the Chancellor, the Treaſurer, and other lords of the King's Council.*

In 1378 the Biſhop of London publicly excommunicated at Paul's Croſs the murderers of one Robert Hawle. The ſtory is ſufficiently tragical, and can hardly be ſo well told as in the words of Dean Stanley.† "During the campaign of the Black Prince in the North of Spain, two of his knights, Shackle and Hawle, had taken priſoner a Spaniſh Count. He returned home for his ranſom, leaving his ſon in his place. The ranſom never came, and the young Count continued in captivity. He had, however, a powerful friend at Court, John of Gaunt, who, in right of his wife, claimed the crown of Caſtile, and in virtue of this Spaniſh royalty demanded the liberty of the young Spaniard. The Engliſh captors refuſed to part with ſo valuable a prize. John of Gaunt, with a high hand, impriſoned them in the Tower, whence they eſcaped and took ſanctuary at Weſtminſter. They were purſued by Alan Boxhall, Conſtable of the Tower, and Sir Ralph Ferrers, with fifty armed men. It was a day long remembered in the Abbey—the 11th of Auguſt, the feſtival of S. Taurinus. The two knights, probably for greater ſecurity, had fled not merely into the Abbey, but into the Choir itſelf. It was the moment of the celebration of High Maſs. The Deacon had

* Riley, *Chronicles*, pp. 224, 225.
† *Weſtminſter Abbey*, third edition, pp. 407-409. See alſo a graphic account in Walſingham, *Hiſtoria Anglicana*, i. pp. 375-378.

juft reached the words of the Gofpel of the day, ' If the goodman of the houfe had known what time the thief would appear,' when the clafh of arms was heard, and the purfuers, regardlefs of time or place, burft in upon the fervice. Shackle efcaped, but Hawle was intercepted. Twice he fled round the Choir, with his enemies hacking at him as he ran, and pierced with twelve wounds, he fank dead in front of the Prior's Stall, that is, at the north fide of the entrance of the Choir. His fervant and one of the monks fell with him. He was regarded as a martyr to the injured rights of the Abbey, and obtained the honour (at that time unufual) of burial within its walls—the firft who was laid, fo far as we know, in the South Tranfept ; to be followed a few years later by Chaucer, who was interred at his feet. ᴠ . . The Abbey was fhut up for four months, and Parliament was fufpended, left its affembly fhould be polluted by fitting within the defecrated precincts." The Archbifhops and Bifhops excommunicated the two chief affailants, and the excommunication was repeated every Wednefday and Friday by the Bifhop of London at S. Paul's. No doubt there were grave reafons for fuch denunciations. If the ancient right of fanctuary of the Abbey had thus been violated, the rude hands of violent and wicked men might foon profane the fhrine of the fainted Erkenwald himfelf.

In 1483 the unhappy Jane Shore was accufed by the Lord Protector of going about to bewitch him, and " that fhe was of councell with the Lord Chamberlaine to deftroy him." She was fpoiled of all her

goods and caſt into priſon.   But Stow * may be left
to tell us the reſt of the ſad ſtory.   The Protector
"(as a good continent Prince, cleane and faultleſſe of
himſelfe, ſent out of heaven into the vicious world for
the amendment of men's manners) hee cauſed the
Biſhop of London to put her to open penance, going
before the Croſſe in proceſſion upon a Sunday with a
taper in her hand.   In which ſhe went, in countenance
and pace demure, ſo womanly ; and albeit ſhe were
out of all aray ſaue her Kirtle onely, yet went ſhe ſo
faire and louely, namely while the wondering of the
people caſt a comely red in her cheekes (of which ſhee
before had moſt miſſe) that her great ſhame wanne her
much praiſe, among thoſe that were more amorous of
her body then curious of her ſoule.   And many good
folke alſo that hated her liuing, and were glad to ſee
ſinne corrected : yet pittied they more her penance
then reioyced therein, when they conſidered that the
Protector procured it more of a corrupt intent then
any vertuous affection."   She was brought from the
Biſhop's Palace, clothed in a white ſheet, with a Croſs
carried before her, and a wax taper in her hand.†

> Submiſſive, ſad, and lowly was her look.
> A burning taper in her hand ſhe bore,
> And on her ſhoulders, careleſſly confuſ'd,
> With looſe neglect, her lovely treſſes hung.
> Upon her cheek a faintiſh fluſh was ſpread,
> Feeble ſhe ſeem'd, and ſorely ſmit with pain,
> While barefoot as ſhe trod the flinty pavement,

---

* Stow, *Annales*, p. 449.   Sir Thomas More (*Life of Edward
V.*), Holinſhed, and Stow give the ſame account.
† Moor, in Rapin's *History*, i. p. 635, n., edit. 1732.

Her footfteps all along were mark'd with blood.
Yet filent ftill fhe pafs'd, and unrepining,
Her ftreaming eyes bent ever on the earth,
Except when, in fome bitter pang of forrow,
To Heaven fhe feem'd in fervent zeal to raife,
And beg that mercy man denied her here.*

In the fame year, on Sunday, June the 19th, 1483, Dr. Ralph Shaw, the brother of the then Lord Mayor, preached his famous fermon at the Crofs. The young King, Edward V., had been brought to London and lodged in the Bifhop's Palace near S. Paul's from the 4th to the 19th of May. " The firft Sunday in May, the anniverfary of that Palm Sunday which had eftablifhed his father on the throne, had been originally fixed by the Council in London for his coronation,"† but the folemnity had been deferred. The King was removed to the Tower, and June 22nd was named as the coronation day. The Duke of Gloucefter had gathered together in London fome twenty thoufand armed men. He had held fecret conference with Dr. Shaw, "to whom he utteryd, that his father's inheritance ought to defcend to him by right, as the eldeft of all the foones which Richard his father, Duke of York, had begotten of Cecyly his wyfe." And he did not hefitate to declare "that Edward who had before raignyd, was a baftard, that ys, not begotten of a right and lawfull wyfe."‡ Such ftatements he urgently

* Nicholas Rowe, *Jane Shore, a Tragedy.*
+ *Grants of Edward V.* (Camden Society). Introduction by J. Gough Nichols, pp. vii., viii.
‡ Polydore Vergil (Camden Society), xxix. pp. 183-5.

defired that Dr. Shaw would make to the people at
the Crofs. On the day appointed, Duke Richard
"came in royal maner, with a great gard of men
armyd unto the churche of S. Paule, and ther was at-
tentyvely prefent at the fermon." The preacher did
not do his work by halves. He declared that the late
King "was nether in phyfnomy nor fhape of body
lyke unto Richard the father; for he was high of
ftature, thother very little, he of large face, thother
fhort and rownd." Prefently, as if by chance, the
Protector fhowed himfelf from a gallery; "the place
where the doctors commonly ftand in the upper ftory,
where hee ftood to hearken the fermon":* and the
preacher indicating him to the people, pointed out to
them the clear refemblance between the Duke of
Gloucefter and his father. The text had been fufficiently fuggeftive: "The multiplying brood of the
ungodly fhall not thrive, nor take deep rooting from
baftard flips, nor lay any faft foundation."† The
people, however, had no fympathy with the preacher.
He had hoped that when he pointed out the Duke
to their notice, they would have cried, "Long live
King Richard!" but they continued filent. You
might have feen fome, fays Polydore Vergil, "aftonyed
with the noveltie and ftrangenes of the thing ftand as
mad men in a maze; others, all agaft with thowt-
rageous crueltie of thorrible fact, to be in great feare
of themfelves becaufe the war frindes to the Kinges
children; others, fynally, to bewayle the misfortune of

* Stow, *Annales*, p. 454.   † *Wifdom*, iv. 3.

the chyldren, whom they adjudgyd now utterly un-doone." The difgraceful fact that Richard allowed his own mother to be openly flandered and defamed, he himfelf hearing the preacher's words without rebuke, was intolerable to all good men. And Poly-dore Vergil goes on to fay that "Raphe Sha, the publifher of thabhomynablenes of fo weightie a caufe (who, not long after, acknowledgyd his error, throwgh the grevous rebukes of his fryndes that wer afhamyd of his infamy) fo fore repentyd the doing thereof that, dying fhortly for very forow, he fuffered worthie punifhement for his lewdnes."

On Sunday, the 24th of February, 1538, "the Rood of Boxely in Kent, called the Rood of Grace, made with divers vices to mooue the eyes and lips, was fhewed at Pauls Croffe by the preacher, which was the Bifhop of Rochefter, and there it was broken and plucked to pieces."*   The famous image of Our Lady of Walfingham, an object of pilgrimage of the higheft repute ; and the image of Our Lady of Ipfwich, were brought to London with all the jewels that hung about them, and divers other images both in England and Wales to which pilgrims had reforted.   They were all burnt at Chelfea.†   It will be remembered that in one of Erafmus' moft interefting *Dialogues* an account is given of a vifit paid to the famous fhrine at Walfing-ham.

Fox is feldom more in earneft than when he is denouncing fome idolatrous fuperftition, and he has,

---

* Stow, *Annales*, p. 575.   . † *Ibid.*, p. 575.

accordingly, ſomething to ſay about this Rood of Boxley. The details, if true, are ſad enough, as the records of what are called 'religious' frauds always muſt be.

"What poſteritie will ever thinke the churche of the pope, pretending ſuch religion, to have beene ſo wicked, ſo long to abuſe the people's eyes with an olde rotten ſtocke, called the Roode of Grace, wherein a man ſhould ſtand incloſed, with an hundreth wyers within the Roode, to make the image goggle with the eies, to nod with his head, to hang the lip, to moove and ſhake his jawes, according as the valew was of the gift which was offered? If it were a ſmall piece of ſilver, he would hang a frowning lip; if it were a piece of golde, then ſhould his jawes go merily. Thus miſerably was the people of Chriſt abuſed, their ſoules ſeduced, their ſenſes beguiled, and their purſes ſpoyled, till this idolatrous forgerie at laſt, by Cromwel's meanes, was diſcloſed, and the image, with all his engines, ſhowed openly at Paules Croſſe, and there torne in pieces by the people. The like was done by the blood of Hayles, which in like maner by Cromwell was brought to Paules Croſſe, and there proved to be the blood of a ducke. Who would have judged but that the mayd of Kent had beene an holy woman and a propheteſſe inſpired, had not Cromwell and Cranmer tried her at Paules Croſſe, to be a ſtrong and lewd impoſtor. What ſhould I ſpeak of Darvel Gatheren,*

* The image called Darvell Gatheren was brought from Wales to London in May, 1538, and burned in Smithfield: at the ſame time Friar Forreſt was burned.

of the rood of Chefter, of Thomas Becket, of Our Lady
of Walfingham, with an infinite multitude more of the
like affinitie?   All which ftockes and blockes of curfed
idolatrie, Cromwell, ftirred up by the providence of
God, remooved them out of the people's way, that
they might walke more fafely in the fincere fervice of
Almightie God."*

Fox tells a ftory of the Rood of Dover Court, which
may well be inferted here, although the Rood was not
brought to London.   One Thomas Rofe, a preacher
in that diftrict, had preached fo warmly againft idolatry in general and this Rood in particular that fome
of his audience determined to deftroy it.   The people
of Dover Court believed that the power of the image
was fo great that no man could fhut the door of the
Church in which it ftood.   The iconoclafts finding the
door open, took the image from its fhrine, and carried
it a quarter of a mile, "without any refiftance of the
faid idol.   Whereupon they ftrake fire with a flint-
ftone, and fuddenly fet him on fire : who burned out
fo brim, that he lighted them homeward one good

For further details about the Rood of Grace, fee Lambarde's
Perambulation of Kent, edition 1576, pp. 182-185.

Hayles Abbey was in Gloucefterfhire.   The relic of the Holy
Blood was prefented to the Abbey by Edmund Earl of Cornwall.
The Commiffioners appointed at the Diffolution of Monafteries
faid that the blood was clarified honey, "which, being in a
glaffe, appeared to be of a gliftering redde, refemblyng partly
the color of blod."—Fox, iv. p. 824.

* Fox, v. p. 397.   Compare the form in which this matter
appears in Wordfworth's *Ecclefiaftical Biography*, ii. pp. 281-4,
where are fome very full and inftructive notes.

mile."* This was in 1532. The enterprife coft three
of Mr. Rofe's difciples their lives : they fuffered and
were hanged in chains. " The faid Thomas Rofe had
the coat of the faid Rood brought unto him afterward ;
.who burnt it. The Rood was faid to have done many
great miracles, and great wonders wrought by him,
and yet being in the fire could not help himfelf, but
burned like a block, as in very deed he was."†

* Fox, iv. pp. 706, 707.   † *Ibid.*, viii. p. 581.

CHAPTER X.

HUGH LATIMER, the famous Bifhop of Worcefter, was a frequent preacher at the Crofs. He was releafed from his imprifonment in the Tower at the acceffion of Edward VI.; and on the 1ft of January, 1548, his voice was heard at Paul's Crofs. It was "the firft fermon by him preached in almoft eight yeeres before, for at the making of the Sixe Articles, he being Bifhop of Worcefter, would not confent vnto them, and therfore was commanded to filence, and gaue vp his bifhoprike."* It would be interefting to know what were the firft words which flowed from his lips after this long filence. He preached again at the Crofs on the 8th, 15th, and 29th of the fame month. He affirmed, in the firft of thefe fermons, "that whatfoeuer the cleargie commanded ought to be obeyed, but he alfo declared that the cleargie are fuch as fit in

---

* Stow, *Annales*, p. 1002, edit. 1603.

Moyſes chaire, and breake not their maſter's commiſſion, adding nothing thereto, nor taking any thing
there from ; and ſuch a cleargie muſt be obeied of all
men, both high and lowe."*　On the ſeventh of March,
a pulpit was "ſet vp in the King's priuie garden at
Weſtminſter, and therein doctor Latimer preached
before the King, where he mought be heard of more
then foure times ſo manie people as could have ſtood
in the King's chappell : and this was the firſt ſermon
preached there."†　In January, 1549, he preached at
S. Paul's three Sermons on *The Plough*, not now extant : and on the 18th of the month he delivered at
the ſame place the famous Sermon on *The Ploughers*,
in continuation of the former ſeries.　In Lent of the
ſame year he preached at Whitehall his Friday
Sermons before Edward VI., then only eleven years
of age.　The Sermon on *The Ploughers* has been
lately very carefully reprinted by Mr. Edward Arber,‡
with a brief but pithy Introduction.　Let us liſten to
a few ſentences.

Latimer comes from Lambeth Palace, he is reſiding
there with Cranmer as the gueſt of the Archbiſhop.
Great crowds are aſſembled to hear the famous
preacher.　He had always been popular, for he had
ſpoken from heart to heart.　Whilſt a Roman Catholic,
and the Croſs-Bearer of the Univerſity of Cambridge,
he had declaimed earneſtly againſt the new teaching :
now, he vigorouſly defended it.　Eleven years before,

---

* Stow, *Annales*, p. 1002, edit. 1603.　　　† *Ibid.*
‡ From whoſe Introduction the two previous citations and
much of the following matter have been taken.

March 10th, 1538, he had preached at the Crofs, and had fpoken out right boldly. Though himfelf a Bifhop, he had faid that the clergy were ftrong thieves: and had added that there was not enough hemp grown in the kingdom to hang all the thieves in England. In another Sermon,* he gave fome curious autobiographical details. "In my tyme," faid he, "my poore father was as diligent to teach me to fhote as to learne anye other thynge, and fo I thynke other menne dyd theyr children. He taught me how to drawe, how to laye my bodye in my bowe, and not to drawe wyth ftrength of armes as other nacions do, but with ftrength of the bodye. I had bowes boughte me accordyng to my age and ftrength; as I encreafed in them, fo my bowes were made bigger and bigger, for men fhal neuer fhot well, excepte they be broughte vp in it. It is a goodly art, a holfome kind of exercife, and much commended in phifike."

To-day, we may be fure, this archer will not draw his bow at a venture. He comes, "a fore brufed man," as his Swifs fervant and faithful friend, Auguftine Bernher writes. He is about fifty-fix years of age.† Winter and fummer, "about two of the clocke in the morning," he is at his book moft diligently. He preaches twice every Sunday, for the moft part, "to the great fhame, confufion, and damnation of a great number of our fatbellied vnpreachyng prelates," fays Bernher, who had learned his mafter's habit of plain fpeaking. It is winter time, Friday, 18th January,

* Sixth Sermon before Edward VI., 12th April, 1549.
† He was born about 1491. See Mr. Arber's *Introduction*.

1549: he is to preach at Paul's Crofs Sermon, but the weather is fo cold that, for the fake of the congregation, the Sermon will be preached under the fhelter of the "Shrouds."* We will enter, and ftanding under the arches of the crypt, we will lean againft this maffive pillar, and liften to the outfpoken preacher.

His text is this: "Whatfoever things were written aforetime were written for our learning."† He recapitulates, very briefly, what he had faid in previous fermons as to the feed which ought to be fown in God's field, in God's plough-land: that is to fay, what doctrine fhould be taught in the Chriftian Church. To-day, his fubject is to be not the feed, nor the plough, but the ploughers, that is, the preachers. Some perfons had objected to his homely fimilitudes. They had faid, "Oh Latimer, nay as for hym, I wil neuer beleue hym whyle I lyue, nor neuer trufte hym, for he lykened our bleffed Ladye to a faffrone bagge." In truth, he had never ufed that fimilitude: but if he had, there was a fenfe in which it was not untrue. Chrift had compared the Gofpel to a muftard feed and to leaven, and had faid that He Himfelf will come like a thief.

But to his fubject. A Plougher has always fome work to do. "In my countrey in Leceftre Shire, the ploughe man hath a tyme to fet furth and to affaie hys plough, and other tymes for other neceffari workes to be done." The preacher, too, muft never be idle amongft his people: "nowe caftynge them downe with the lawe and with threateninges of God for

* That is, in the crypt of the Cathedral. See *Statutes*, p. 435.
† *Romans* xv. 4.

fynne; nowe ridgynge them vp agayne with the gofpel and with the promifes of God's fauoure. Nowe weedinge them, by tellinge them their faultes, and makynge them forfake fynne. Nowe clottinge them, by breakynge their ftonie hertes, and by making them fupple herted, and makyng them to haue hertes of flefhe, that is foft hertes, and apte for doctrine to enter in." The preacher muft labour diligently. The preaching of the Word is likened to meat: "not ftrauberies, that come but once a yeare and tary not longe, but are fone gone. . . Many make a ftrauberie of it, miniftringe it but once a yeare, but fuch do not thoffice of good prelates."

Alas! there were many fuch. "Howe manye fuch prelates, how manye fuch byfhops, Lorde for Thy mercie, are there nowe in England."

The lay hearers are delighted with this plain fpeaking: but liften, their turn is come. "Nowe what fhall we faye of thefe ryche citizens of London? What fhall I faye of them? Shal I cal them proude men of London, malicious men of London, mercyleffe men of London? No, no, I may not faie fo, they wil be offended wyth me than. Yet muft I fpeake. For is there not reygning in London, as much pride, as much couetoufnefs, as much crueltie, as much oppriffion, as much fuperfticion, as was in Nebo? Yes, I thynke, and muche more to. Therfore I faye, repente, O London. Repent, repente." They could not endure to be told of their faults. "What a do was there made in London at a certein man becaufe he fayd, and in dede at that time on a

iuſt cauſe, ' Burgeſſes,' quod he, ' nay, Butterflies.'
Lorde, what a do there was for yat worde. And yet
would God they were no worſe than butterflies.
Butterflyes do but theyre nature, the butterflye is not
couetouſe, is not gredye of other mens goodes, is not
ful of enuy and hatered, is not malicious, is not cruel,
is not mercileſſe."

" London can not abyde to be rebuked, ſuche is the
nature of man. If they be prycked, they wyll kycke.
. . . London was neuer ſo yll as it is now. In tymes
paſt men were full of pytie and compaſſion, but nowe
there is no pitie, for in London their brother ſhall die
in the ſtreetes for colde, he ſhall lye ſycke at theyr
doore betwene ſtocke and ſtocke. . . . In tymes paſte
when any ryche man dyed in London, they were
wonte to healp the pore ſcholers of the Vniuerſitye
wyth exhibition. When any man dyed, they woulde
bequeth greate ſummes of money towarde the releue
of the pore. When I was a ſcholer in Cambrydge
my ſelfe, I harde verye good reporte of London, and
knewe manie that had releue of the rytche men of
London, but nowe I can heare no ſuch good reporte,
and yet I inquyre of it, and herken for it, but nowe
charitie is waxed colde, none helpeth the ſcholer nor
yet the pore." The plougher in ſuch ſoil will have
hard work. " Thys land is not for me to ploughe, it
is to ſtonye, to thorni, to harde for me to plough.
. . . What ſhall I loke for amonge thornes but prick-
yng and ſcrachinge ? What among ſtones but ſtum-
blyng ? What (I had almoſt ſayed) among ſerpenttes
but ſtingyng ?"

The Laity have had fharp meafure meted out to them, and now the Clergy fhall have their turn again. "Euer fence the Prelates were made Loordes and nobles, the ploughe ftandeth, there is no worke done, the people fteruc. Thei hauke, thei hunt, thei card, they dyce, they paftyme in theyr prelacies with galaunte gentlemen, with theyr daunfinge minyons, and with theyr frefhe companions, fo that ploughinge is fet a fyde. And by the lordinge and loytryng, preachynge and ploughinge is cleane gone." This is ftrong language from a Bifhop, but there is more to come. Thefe unpreaching Prelates are his abhorrence. "They are fo troubeled wyth Lordelye lyuynge, they be fo placed in palacies, couched in courtes, ruffelynge in theyr rentes, daunceynge in theyr dominions, burdened with ambaffages, pamperynge of theyr panches lyke a monke that maketh his Jubilie, mounchynge in their maungers, and moylynge in their gaye manoures and manfions, and fo troubeled wyth loyterynge in theyr Lordefhyppes, that they canne not attende it. They are otherwyfe occupyed, fomme in the Kynges matters, fome are ambaffadoures, fome of the pryuie counfell, fome to furnyfhe the courte, fome are Lordes of the Parliamente, fome are prefidentes, and fome comptroleres of myntes. Well, well, is thys theyr duetye? . . . I would fayne knowe who comptrolleth the deuyll at home at his parifhe, whyle he comptrolleth the mynte? If the Apoftles mighte not leaue the office of preaching to be deacons, fhall one leaue it for myntyng? I can not tell you, but the fayinge is, that fince priefts haue bene minters, money hath bene wourfe then it was before. And they faye that the euylnes of money hath made all thinges dearer.* And in thys behalfe I muft fpeake to England. . . . Paule was no fittynge bifhoppe, but a walkinge and a preachynge byfhop."

No clafs efcapes his fharp fatire. " The onely caufe, why noble men be not made Lord prefidentes, is becaufe they haue not bene brought vp in learninge. Therefore for the loue of God, appoynte teachers and fcholemaifters, you that haue charge of youth, and giue the teachers ftipendes worthy their paynes, that they maye brynge them vp in grammer, in Logike, in rethorike, in Philofophe, in the ciuile lawe, and in that whiche I can not leaue vnfpoken of, the Word of God." Then noblemen could take high offices of ftate, and Bifhops might become purely fpiritual perfons, and diligent preachers. "And nowe I would afke a ftraung queftion. Who is the moft diligent bifhoppe and prelate in al England, that paffeth al the refte in doinge his office? I can tel, for I knowe him, who it is I knowe hym well. But nowe I thynke I fe you lyfting and hearkening, that I fhoulde name him. There is one that paffeth al the other, and is the moft diligent prelate and preacher in al England. And wyl ye knowe who it is? I wyl tel you. It is the Deuyl. He is the mofte dyligent preacher of al other, he is neuer out of his dioces, he is neuer from his cure, ye fhal neuer fynde hym vnoccupyed, he is euer in

* Such charges were frequently brought againft the authorities of the Mint, whether clerical or lay. See Strype's Stow, i. pp. 101-109.

his parifhe, he keepeth refidence at al tymes, ye fhal neuer fynde hym out of the waye, cal for him when you wyl, he is euer at home, the diligentefte preacher in all the Realme, he is euer at his ploughe . . . Where the Deuyl is refidente and hath his plough goinge, there awaye with bokes and vp with candelles, awaye wyth Bibles and vp with beades, awaye with the lyghte of the Gofpel and vp with the lyghte of candlles, yea at noonedayes . . . Downe with Chriftes croffe, vp with purgatory picke purfe, vp with hym, the popifh pourgatorie, I mean . . . He goeth on vifitacion daylye. He leaueth no place of hys cure vnuifited. There was neuer fhuch a preacher in England as he is."

Then follows a long attack upon the doctrine of the Mafs: concluding with a vigorous onflaught upon the Pope himfelf. "The Deuyl by the healpe of that Italian Bifhop yonder, his chaplayne, hath labored by al meanes that he myghte, to fruftrate the death of Chrifte and the merites of His paffion. And they haue deuifed for that purpofe to make vs beleue in other vayne thynges by his pardons, as to haue re-miffion of finnes for praiynge on hallowed beades, for drynkyng of the bake-houfe bole, as a channon of Waltam Abbey once tolde me, that when foeuer they putte theyr loues of breade into the ouen, as manie as drancke of the pardon boll fhould haue pardon for drynckynge of it. A madde thynge to geue pardon to a bolle. Then to Pope Alexanders holie water, to hallowed belles, palmes, candelles, affhes, and what not? . . . Yea, and Alexanders holie water yet at thys day remayneth in Englande, and is vſed for a remedye againſt ſpirites, and to chaſe awaye deuylles."

This leads the preacher on to ſpeak of images and of the worſhip offered to them. They are to be deſtroyed even as Hezekiah deſtroyed the brazen ſerpent.

The peroration is now near at hand. The lordly Prelates are again rebuked. " The Deuill is diligente at his ploughe. He is no vnpreachynge prelate. He is no Lordelic loyterer from his cure, but a buſie ploughe man, ſo that amonge all the prelates, and amonge al the packe of them that haue cure the Deuil ſhall go for my money. For he ſtyl applyeth his buſynes. Therfore ye vnpreachynge prelates, learne of the deuill to be diligent in doing of your office. Learne of the deuill. And if you wyl not learne of God nor good man, for ſhame learne of the deuill. *Ad erubeſcentiam veſtram dico.** I ſpeake it for your ſhame. If you wyll not learne of God nor good man to be diligent in your office, learne of the deuill. Howe be it there is nowe verie good hoope that the Kynges maieſtie beinge by the healpe of good gouernaunce of his mooſte honourable counſaylours, he is trayned and broughte vp in learnynge and knowledge of Goddes word, wil ſhortly prouide a remedye and ſet an ordre here in, which thyng that it may ſo be, lette vs praye for hym. Praye for hym, good people, praye for hym ; ye haue great cauſe and neede to praye for hym."

And ſo the preacher ends, and his congregation

---

* " I ſpeak to your ſhame." (1 *Cor.* vi. 5),

difperfe, faying, "We have heard ftrange things to-day."*

Who does not underftand the prodigious power of this rude, uncultivated eloquence? Coarfe, very often, and to our modern taftes, profane, there was a force and a directnefs in it, which carried home the preacher's leffons. Latimer was effentially a preacher to the people. His language was their language, the plain mother tongue. He fpoke of that which was uppermoft in their thoughts, and lafhed, with unfparing hand, the follies, the abufes, the fins, the corruptions of the day. But he was laying up in ftore for himfelf retributions; the day was coming when the "lordly prelates" would have the pre-eminence, and his violent words would be remembered. Thofe who know only the bitter phrafes of the Roman Prelates as they find them plentifully recorded in the *Acts and Monuments* of John Fox, fhould certainly, in common fairnefs, read the equally ftrong language of the reforming Bifhops. If Bifhop Bonner is to be felected as the reprefentative of the one, Bifhop Bale is to be taken as the reprefentative of the other. In truth, the atrocious coarfenefs of the latter renders many of his utterances incapable of reproduction in the nineteenth century. In thefe troubled days of fierce debate men on both fides ufed the weapon which firft came to hand, regardlefs whether it were a fword,

---

* The edition ufed in the text has been Mr. Arber's reprint of that " Imprinted at London, by Jhon Daye, dwellinge at Alderf-gate, and William Seres, dwellinge in Peter Colledge."

a battle-axe, a bible, a ſpear, or a bucket of dirty water.

When Latimer was at the climax of denunciation, his words were certainly not meaſured. It muſt be remembered, however, that there was much to ſtir up his juſt wrath. Let us take one or two examples.

He denounces the holy water of Pope Alexander. In the Breviary, on May 3, the day of the Invention of the Holy Croſs, in the ninth lection for the day we read, that "Alexander was a Roman who ruled the Church during the reign of the Emperor Hadrian. . . . He ordained that bleſſed water mingled with ſalt, ſhould be kept always in churches, and ſhould be uſed in private houſes to ſcare away devils." The Breviary itſelf may be quoted as an authority on the fact.

He denounces the Pardon-bowl at Waltham. He might readily have found other examples. At Bury S. Edmunds, in the monaſtery there, was a "holye relique which was called the *pardon-boule;* whoſoever dronk of this boule in the worſhippe of God and Saynt Edmund, he had fiue hundred dayes of pardon, *toties quoties.."** Biſhop Bale, in his *Image of both Churches*, enumerates ſeveral other "pardon maſers or drinking diſhes, as S. Benet's bowl, S. Edmond's bowl, S. Giles' bowl, S. Blyth's bowl, and Weſtminſter bowl."† To theſe Calfhill adds S. Leonard's bowl.‡

A collection of ſome of the chief Indulgences in

---

* Becon's Works, iii. fol. 187, quoted in Corrie's edition of Latimer, *Sermons*, p. 75.
† Parker Soc. edition, p. 526.
‡ Calfhill, anſwer to Martiall, p. 287.

the Sarum *Book of Hours* will be found in Bifhop Burnet's *Hiftory of the Reformation.** thefe will fhow how deeply engrained into the popular thought the whole fyftem of indulgences and pardons had become.

The wonder-working images and pictures excited Latimer's vehement animadverfions. The Cathedral itfelf had its fhare of fhrines, and images, and pictures. The melancholy expofures of " roods with rolling eyes and fweating brows, with fpeaking mouth and walking feet "† were only too frefh in the minds of the people. It was time to fpeak out ; and no one can fay that Latimer was not outfpoken. In fuch ftirring times much muft be pardoned to earneft true-hearted men.

* Bifhop Burnet, *Records*, Book i. fect. 26. Edition 1841, iv. p. 280.

† Calfhill, p. 274.

CHAPTER XI.

THOMAS LEVER AT PAUL'S CROSS.

HOMAS LEVER may very well be taken as a typical example of another great preacher of the reign of Edward VI. In this cafe alfo we are indebted to Mr. Edward Arber for a careful reprint of three fermons, the firft preached in the Shrouds of S. Paul's on Septuagefima Sunday, 2nd February, 1550; the fecond preached before the King at Court on Mid-Lent Sunday; and the third preached at Paul's Crofs on the fecond Sunday in Advent in the fame year.*

Thomas Lever was fucceffively Fellow, Preacher, and Mafter of S. John's College, Cambridge; he was Paftor in exile of the Englifh Church at Aaran; Prebendary of Durham Cathedral, and Mafter of Sherborne Hofpital. Strype fays,† that on June 24,

---

* Mr. Arber's brief notes on the Life and Writings of Thomas Lever have been freely ufed in the following notice.

† *Eccles. Mem.*, edit. 1822, vol. ii. pt. i. pp. 402-3.

1550, Bifhop Ridley ordained twenty-five deacons before the high Altar of S. Paul's, and that amongft them were Thomas Lever, and John Fox the Martyr-ologift; and he adds that, on Auguft 10, Bifhop Ridley held an ordination at Fulham, when his chaplain, John Bradford, was ordained deacon, and Thomas Lever received prieft's orders.   It is difficult to reconcile thefe dates with the fact of his preaching at S. Paul's on February 2, 1550.   During the reign of Queen Mary we find him, with other exiles, at Zurich, at Geneva.   Upon the acceffion of Elizabeth, he marries, he returns to England, he is a more eager Proteftant than ever.   He died at Ware whilft journey-ing back to his Hofpital, and was buried at Sherborne, "under a blue marble ftone, whereon is cut a crofs flory with a bible and chalice, and on a brass plate,"

THOMAS LEAVER PREACHER

TO KING EDWARD THE SIXTE

HE DIED IN IVLY 1577.

The firft of thefe three fermons is an urgent exhor-tation to the religious performance of civil duties. The Preachers of the Reformation period were bold fpeakers, manful pleaders of the caufe of the poor, denouncing corruption even in the higheft places.   It muft be remembered that there were no newfpapers in thofe days.   At Paul's Crofs the laity often learned, for the firft time, what events were being tranfacted, far and near.   England was recovering from the long anarchy of the Wars of the Rofes, but whilft the rich had become richer, the poor had become poorer. Wool, the great ftaple of the country, had rifen fo greatly in price, "that poore folkes, which were wonte to worke it and make cloth therof, be nowe hable to bye none at all," fays Sir Thomas More in his *Utopia.** England had its "land queftion," and the enclofure of lands was one of the great caufes of Kett's rebellion. The Impropriation of Ecclefiaftical Benefices was another " burning queftion " : corporations, non-refident clergy, and even laymen held rich benefices, delegating the fpiritual duties to a half-ftarved curate, whilft the temporal duties, hofpitality and the like, were practically left undone. " Is it nat great pitye to fe a man to haue thre or foure bene-fyces : yea, paraduenture, halfe a fcore or a dofyn, whiche he neuer cometh at," afks Sir Francis Bygod, who joined the *Pilgrimage of Grace*, and was hanged at Tyburn in June, 1537.† He proceeds : " whiche [benefices] he neuer cometh at, but fetteth in euery one of them a Syr Iohn lacke laten that can fcarce rede his porteus,‡ orels fuche a rauenynge wolfe as canne do nothynge but deuoure the fely fhepe with his falfe doctryne, and fucke their fubftaunce from them. . . . I haue knowen fuche that whan they hauen rydden by a benefyce whereof they haue ben perfone they coulde natte tell that it was their bene-fyce. This is a wonderfull blyndneffe."

The Roman party charged many of thefe evils to the

* Mr. Arber, *Introduction to Lever's Sermons*, p. 11.
† *Ibid.*, pp. 12-14.
‡ An unlearned prieft who could not read his Breviary.

change of religion : the Reforming party indignantly
refuted and hurled back the charge.   Among all the
preachers of the period " none more bravely fought the
battle of the loyal poor ; none more vigorouſly, even
to perſonal hazard and danger, expoſed the cruelty,
covetouſneſs, and craft, of the rich and of the clergy,
than Thomas Lever, the Cambridge Fellow, and the
Boanerges of the Reformation."*   No wonder that
his Sermons were popular.   No leſs than five editions
of theſe three diſcourſes were publiſhed in 1550.

Let us turn to the firſt of theſe : " A fruitfull Sermon
made in Poules churche at London in the Shroudes
the ſeconde daye of Februari by Thomas Leuer.
Anno MD and fiftie."   He begins at once with words
of warning. " Alas England, God, whom thou mayeſt
beleue for his truthe, hathe ſayd playnly thou ſhalt
be deſtroyed, and all thyne ennemyes, bothe Scots,
Frenchmen, Papiſtes, and Turkes, I do not meane the
men in whome is ſome mercye, but the moſt cruell
vices of theſe thy enemyes beynge wythout all pitie,
as the couetouſenes of Scotland, the pryde of Fraunce,
the hipocryſy of Rome, and the Idolatrye of the
Turkes. A hundred thouſande of theſe enemies are
landed at thy hauens, haue entred thy fortes, and do
procede to ſpoyle, murther, and vtterly deſtroy : and
yet ſor all this thou wretched Englande beleueſt not
gods worde, regardeſt not hys threatninge, calleſt not
for mercye, ne feareſte not gods vengeaunce. Wherfore God beinge true of hys word and righteous in hys

---

* Edward Arber, *Introduction*, pp. 16-17.

dedes, thou Englande whyche wylt haue no mercye, fhalt haue vengeaunce; whyche wylte not be faued, fhalte be deftroyed. For God hath fpoken, and it is wrytten."

God had faid that every kingdom divided againft itfelf fhould be defolate and deftroyed. England "is not onelye diuyded, but alfo rente, torne, and plucked cleane in pieces."

Covetoufnefs is a fearful evil. "Every couetoufe man is proude, thynkynge hymfelfe more worthy a pounde then a nother man a penye, more fitte to haue chaunge of fylkes and veluettes then other to haue bare frife cloth, and more conueniente for hym to haue aboundaunce of diuerfe dilicates for hys daintye toth then for other to haue plenty of biefes and muttons for theyr hongry bellyes: and finnally that he is more worthye to haue gorgeoufe houfes to take his pleafure in, in bankettynge, then laborynge men to haue poore cotages to take reft in, in flepynge." The judgment of God will fall on all thefe.

This is but a fort of preamble to the Sermon. The text is, "Everye foule be fubiecte vnto the hygher powers," and the following verfes.* All ought to be under obedience, and to give to one another what is due: "howbeit experience declareth howe that here in Englande pore men haue been rebels, and ryche men haue not done their duetie."

The Apoftles had all things common, and now "ryche menne fhoulde kepe to theym felues no more

Romans xiii. 1-7.

13—2

then they nede, and geue vnto the poore fo muche as
they nede."   In this fenfe " chriften mens goodes fhuld
be comen vnto euery mans nede, and priuat to no
mans lufte."   There muft be rich men and rulers, but
the rich muft ufe their wealth as became Chriftians.
Alas, men did not fo.

"As for example of ryche men, loke at the mer-
chauntes of London, and ye fhall fe, when as by their
honeft vocacion, and trade of marchandife god hath
endowed them with great abundaunce of ryches, then
can they not be content with the profperous welth of
that vocacion to fatiffye theym felues and to helpe
other, but their riches mufte abrode in the countrey to
bie fermes * out of the handes of worfhypfull gentlemen, honefte yeomen, and pore laborynge hufbandes.
Yea nowe alfo to bye perfonages† and benefices, where
as they do not onelye bye landes and goodes but alfo
lyues and foules of men, from God and the comen
wealth, vnto the deuyll and theim felues.   A myf-
cheuoufe marte of merchandrie is this, and yet nowe
fo comenly vfed, that therby fhepeheardes be turned
to theues, dogges into wolues, and the poore flocke
of Chrift, redemed wyth his precious bloud, mofte
miferablye pylled and fpoyled, yea cruelly deuoured.
Be thou marchaunt of the citye, or be thou gentleman
in the contrey, be thou lawer, be you courtear, or what
maner of man foeuer thou be, that can not, yea yf
thou be mafter doctor of diuinitie, that wyl not do thy
duety, it is not lawfull for the to haue perfonage, bene-

---

* Fermes, *that is*, farms.   † Perfonages, parfonages.

fice, or any fuche liuying, excepte thou do fede the flocke fpiritually wyth goddes worde, and bodelye wyth honefte hofpitalitye. I wyll touch diuerfe kyndes of ryche men and rulers, that ye maye fe what harme fome of theim do wyth theyr ryches and authoritye. And efpeciallye I wyll begynne wyth theym that be beft learned, for they feme belyke to do mofte good wyth ryches and authoritie vnto theim committed. If I therefore beynge a yonge fimple fcholer myghte be fo bolde, I wolde afke an auncient, wyfe, and well-learned doctor of diuinitie, whych cometh not at hys benefice, whether he were bounde to fede hys flocke in teachynge of goddes worde, and kepyng hofpitalitie, or no? He wold anfwere and faye: Syr, my curate fupplieth my roume in teachynge, and my farmer in kepynge of houfe. Yea, but mafter doctor, by your leaue, both thefe more for your vauntage then for the paryfhe conforte: and therfore the mo fuche feruauntes that ye kepe there, the more harme is it for your paryfhe, and the more fynne and fhame for you. Ye may thynke that I am fumwhat faucye to laye fynne and fhame to a doctor of diuinitie in thys folemne audience, for fome of theim vfe to excufe the matter and faye: Thofe whych I leaue in myne abfence do farre better then I fhoulde do, yf I taryed there my felfe. Nowe good mafter doctor ye faye the verye truthe, and therfore be they more worthye to haue the benefice then you your felfe, and yet neyther of you bothe fufficient mete or able: they for lacke of habilitye, and you for lacke of good wyll. Good wyll, quod he? Naye, I wolde wyth all my harte, but I am

called to ſerue the Kynge in other places, and to take
other offices in the comen wealthe.   Heare then what
I ſhall aunſwere yet once agayne : There is lyuynges
and rewardes due and belongyng to theim that labour
in thoſe offyces, and ſo oughte you to be contente
wyth the lyuyng and reward of that office onelye, and
take no more, the duetye of the whyche office by your
labour and diligence ye can diſcharge onlye, and do
no more."

Let it be remembered that theſe words were ſpoken
at S. Paul's itſelf, in the very heart of the City of
London.   He was a bold man who ſpoke of pluralities
to the Clergy, and of the luſt for land to rich and
powerful merchants.

He proceeds to ſpeak of the ſuppreſſion of Abbeys,
Cloiſters, Colleges, and Chantries. The intention of the
late King had been good in this matter. "Suche abundaunce of goodes as was ſuperſticiouſly ſpente vpon
vayne ceremonies, or voluptuouſly vpon idle bellies"
might be more uſefully expended for the better relief
of the poor, the maintenance of learning, and the ſetting
forth of God's word.   Covetous officers had fruſtrated
this deſign.   " At the fyrſte the intente was verie godly,
the pretence wonderouſe goodly, but nowe the vſe, or
rather the abuſe and myſorder of theſe thynges is
worldlye, is wyscked, is deuilyſhe, is abhominable."
He attacks the evil-doers. " You whych haue gotten
theſe goodes into your own handes, to turne them
rom euyll to worſe, and other goodes mo frome good
vnto euyll, be ye ſure it is euen you that haue
offended God; begyled the kynge, robbed the ryche,

fpoyled the pore, and brought a comen wealth into a comen miferye. It is euen you that muft eyther be plaged with gods vengeaunce as wer the Sodomytes, or amende by repentaunce as did the Nineuites." Not that abbeys and cloifters were to be founded again, but that charitable alms and honeft hofpitality were to be beftowed, and fchools founded " for the brynngyng vp of yougth."

This is good contemporary evidence, if any were needed, as to the grievous abufes of the times. Greedy courtiers had fwallowed up the church lands, and fpent that which had been given for holy ufes upon their own lufts. How did the courtiers like this preaching ?

The people were groaning under heavy yokes, let them pray to God and He would deliver them. The rulers knew their duty to the people, let them forbear to load them with burdens that ought not to be borne.

He draws near to the end of the difcourfe, and gives a kind of parable to his hearers. " Harcke a lytle, and I fhal tell you of an abhomynable robbery done in the Citye, knowen to the officers of the City, and as yet not punyfhed, but rather mayntayned in the city. There is a greate fumme of monye fente from an honorable Lord by hys feruaunte vnto thofe whome he is indetted vnto in the citye. The officers knowynge that they to whom thys monye is fente haue great nede of it, knowe alfo in what places, at what tymes, thefe vnthryftye feruauntes by whome it is fente, at gamnynge, banckettyng, and riot, do fpende it. If thys be an euell dede, why is it not punyſhed? Bycauſe it is not knowen, ſome faye. But whyther they meane that it is not knowen to be done, or not knowen to be euyll, I doubte. And therefore here now wyll I make it openlye knowen boeth to be done, and alſo to be euell done, and worſe ſuffered. But doeth not manye of you knowe? Sure I am that all you that be officers oughte to know that all that ryches and treaſures whyche rych men, and rufflers, waſte at gredye gamning, glotonous bancketting, and ſuche riote, is not theyr owne, but ſente by theym· from the honorable Lord of heauen, vnto other that be honeſt, pore, and nedye: vnto whome God by hys promyſe is indetted."

Theſe are plain manly words, and muſt have gone home to many a heart. That they did ſo is quite certain, for in his ſecond ſermon, before the King, Thomas Lever ſets forth the facts of the plunder of Sedburgh School in Yorkſhire; in April 1551, that is within little more than a year after the ſermon was delivered, King Edward VI. refounded the School. His bold words had angered many a hearer. In the very outſet of this ſermon, Lever ſays that there were not wanting men who ſaid of a true preacher that he had "learned his leſſon in Jackanapes court": but idle jeſts would not turn him from his earneſt purpoſe. He could not endure that the rich ſhould waſte their money in riotous living whilſt "olde Fathers, poore Wydowes, and yong Chyldren lye beggyng in the myrie ſtretes." We have loſt, in theſe poliſhed days, the roughneſs, the occaſional coarſeneſs, of theſe

earneft old preachers : and we have loft, too, what is
of the higheft value, the dauntlefs courage which
enables men to denounce the crying evils of the time.
We fee them and are filent. Time is wafted on queftions of infinitely fmall importance, whilft great fins
and crying wickedneffes pafs unrebuked. Paul's Crofs
was not filent.

Lever's third fermon, at Paul's Crofs, is not inferior
in ability or in earneftnefs to thofe which preceded it.
He lafhes once more the covetoufnefs of the times,
and the prevailing corruptions. High places in the
ftate are bought and fold ; not merit nor ability, but
money, is the ftepping-ftone to power. Every fecular
office is in truth a religious office, every Chriftian
commonwealth is the fold of Chrift's fheep : yet a
man would take fuch office only that he might enrich
himfelf. "O that no man in thys faute wer gilty,
then myght I be fure yat no man wold be offended."
Thofe who held feveral offices or benefices are again
cenfured : a fmall portion only of the revenues " doth
ferue two honeft menne whyche ye leaue in your
abfence."

" Herke you that haue three or foure benefyces. I
wyll fay the beft for you that can be fpoken. Thou
lyeft al wayes at one of thy benefyces, thou arte
abfente alwayes from three of thy benefyces. Thou
kepeft a good houfe at one of thy benefyces, thou
kepeft no houfe at three of thy benefyces. Thou
doeft thy deutye at one of thy benefyces, thou doeft no
dutye at thre of thy benefices. Thou femeft to be a
good manne in one place, and in dede thou arte

founde noughte in thre places. Wo be vntoo you worfe then Scrybes and Pharifeis, Hypocrytes, whyche fhut vp the kyngedome of heauen afore menne, kepynge the paryfhe fo that neyther you enter in your felfe, neyther fuffer them that would enter in and do theyr dewtye, to haue your roumes and commodities. Woo be vnto you, dumme Dogges, choked wyth benefyces, fo that ye be not able to open your mouthes to barcke agaynfte pluralytyes, improperacions, bying of voufons,* nor againft anye euyll abufe of the cleargies lyuynges."

Great and rich men took to themfelves the advantage and the profit of benefices, and gave unto their very children, " being ignoraunte babes, the names and tytles of Perfonnages, Prebendes, Archedeaconryes, and of all manner of offyces." Plain fpeaking was moft neceffary, the whole fabric of fociety feemed corrupt.

But, left the laity fhould be boaftful, they fhall have a Parthian fhot before the preacher ends. " You of the laytye, when ye fee thefe fmall motes in the eyes of the clargye, take heede too the greate beames that be in your owne eyes. But alas I feare leaft yat ye haue no eyes at all. For as hypocrify and fuperfticion dooeth bleare the eyes : So couetoufneffe and ambycyon doeth putte the eyes cleane out. For yf ye were not ftarke blynd ye would fe and be afhamed that where as fyfty tunne belyed Monckes, geuen to glottony, fylled theyr pawnches, kept vp theyr houfe,

---

* Buying of advowfons.

and relyued the whol country round about them, ther
one of your gredye guttes deuowrynge the whole
houfe and makyng great pyllage throughoute the
countrye, cannot be fatiffyed." The Sermon has a
prefatory Epiftle, and this Epiftle is dedicated " unto
the right honorrable Lordes, and others of the Kynges
Mageftie hys Priuye Counfell," wifhing them " in-
creafe of Grace and godly honoure." There muft
have been fome amongft them who felt that the
preacher's arrow found its way through the joints of
the harnefs.

He proceeds to plead the caufe of the Univerfity
of Cambridge. Henry VIII. had made liberal gifts
to it for " the exibition and fyndynge of fiue learned
menne to reade and teache dyuynitye, lawe, Phyfycke,
Greke, and Ebrue." Thofe around the King had
defeated his good intentions. We " haue jufte occafion to fufpecte that you haue decyued boeth the
kynge and vniuerfitie, to enryche youre felues." The
funds had been alienated, the number of the ftudents
was confequently reduced. He gives a fketch of the
lives of fome of the " poore, godly, dylygent ftu-
dentes." " There be dyuers ther whych ryfe dayly
betwixte foure and fyue of the clocke in the mor-
nynge, and from fyue vntyll fyxe of the clocke, vfe
common prayer wyth an exhortacion of gods worde
in a commune chappell, and from fixe vnto ten of the
clocke vfe euer eyther pryuate ftudy or commune
lectures. At ten of the clocke they go to dynner,
whereas they be content with a penye pyece of byefe*

* Bifhop Fleetwood in his *Chronicon Preciofum* (pp. 116, 117).

amongeſt iiij. hauying a ſewe porage made of the brothe of the ſame byefe, wyth ſalte and otemell, and nothynge els.   After thys ſlender dinner they be either teachynge or learnynge vntyll v. of the clocke in the euenyng, when as they haue a ſupper not much better then theyr dyner.   Immedyatelye after the whyche, they go eyther to reaſonyng in problemes, or vnto ſome other ſtudye, vntyll it be nyne or tenne of the clocke, and there beyng wythout fyre are fayne to walk or runne vp and downe halfe an houre, to gette a heate on their feete whan they go to bed. Theſe be menne not werye of theyr paynes, but very ſorye to leue theyr ſtudye : and ſure they be not able ſome of theym to contynue for lacke of neceſ-ſarye exibicion and releſe.   Theſe be the lyuyng ſayntes whyche ſerue god takyng greate paynes in abſtinence, ſtudye, laboure and dylygence, wyth watching and prayer."   A collection ſhould be made among the rich merchants of the City to ſupport theſe poor laborious ſtudents.

The Grammar Schools, too, had been grievouſly plundered "by reaſon of the gredye couetouſnes of you that were put in truſt by God and the kynge to erecte and make grammer ſcholes in manye places."

Impropriations are, once more, vigorouſly de-

---

edit. 1707), ſays, quoting Stow, that in 1533 it was enacted "that Butchers ſhould ſell their Beef and Mutton *by weight*—Beef for a *Half Penny* the Pound, and Mutton for *Three Farthings*. . . . The Butchers of *London* ſold *Penny-Pieces* of beef, for the relief of the Poor ; every Piece two pound and an half ; ſometimes 3 Pound for a Penny."   Did the Cambridge Butchers in 1550 ſell as cheaply ?

nounced, in language of the ſtrongeſt. The greedy covetouſneſs of officers had devoured fair lands and goodly incomes. One man had ſwallowed up a whole Abbey, houſe, lands, and goods. If ſuch men had the power, they would ſeize upon whole countries too.

Wicked ſervants of Mammon made the fruits of the earth dear. "I haue heard howe that euen this laſt yere, ther was certayn Acres of corne growyng on the ground bought for viii. poundes : he that bought it for viii. ſold it for x. He that gaue x. pounds, ſold it to an other aboue xii. poundes : and at laſt, he that caryed it of the ground payde xiiii. poundes. Lyke-wyſe I hearde, that certayne quarters of malte were boughte after the pryce of iii. ſhyllynges iiii. pence a quarter to be delyuered in a certayn markette towne vpon a certayne daye. Thys bargayne was ſo oft bought and ſolde before the daye of delyueraunce came, that the ſame Malte was ſolde to hym that ſhoulde receyue it there and carrye it awaye, after vj. s. a quarter." Theſe unjuſt profits cauſed the poor to ſuffer, "the craftes man payinge ſo muche, and the huſbandman takynge ſo lytle."

Land was dealt with in the ſame manner. Within a few miles of London, an honeſt gentleman did let his land unto poor honeſt men after ii. s. iiii. d. an acre : "Then commeth a leſemounger, a theſe, an extorcioner, decceiuyng ye tenaunts, bieth theyr leaſes, put theim from the groundes, and cauſeth them yat haue it at hym nowe, to paye after ix. s. or as I harde ſaye, xix. s., but I am aſhamed to name ſo muche."

Thefe "Marchauntes of mifchiefe commynge betwixte the barke and the tree, do make all thinges
dere to the byers." They alfo carried away lead,
wool, leather, and fuch fubftantial wares as would fet
many Englifhmen to work, and do every man good
fervice : and brought back, in their place, from foreign
parts, filks, and fables, and foolifh feathers, to fill the
land full of fuch baggage as will never do rich or poor
good and neceffary fervice. God gave plenty, and
man made dearnefs and fcarcity.

He concludes with an appeal to all orders and
degrees. He would fhow each clafs its fins. "Vnto
the clergy, the finnes of ye clergy ; vnto the laitye,
the fynnes of the layte ; and vnto euery degre, ye
finnes yat be of that degre vfed." The Clergy fed
themfelves, and neglected the flock. They could not
teach others, becaufe they would not amend themfelves. The nobility oppreffed the commonalty. The
commonalty were traitors and rebels ; they hurt, and
troubled, ate up and devoured, one another. They
oppreffed each other, they made corn and land dear.
All muft repent and amend.

The Preacher's political economy may be received
with fcant favour nowadays ; but no one can rife from
the perufal of thefe Sermons without feeling that the
fpeaker is a bold, courageous, honeft man. He fpeaks
to the higheft and to the loweft fearleffly. He attacks
the actual fins of the day, and he does not fpare the
finners. If there be comparatively little of the fpiritual
element in his teaching, it muft be remembered that
he was trying to lay the foundations of religion. It

is worfe than idle to talk of high fpiritual privileges to men who are fteeped up to the eyes in fraud, oppref-fion, and injuftice. Thomas Lever was an Englifhman to the backbone, a lover of liberty, a friend of the poor. It would have been well if all Paul's Crofs Sermons had been filled with fuch found doctrine.

An interefting parallel to Thomas Lever's remarks upon the coft of Univerfity education is found in a letter written from London in 1550 by Chriftopher Hales, and addreffed to Henry Bullinger.* " I would rather recommend Oxford," he writes, " on account of the greater falubrity of the air. Cambridge, by reafon of the neighbouring fen, is much expofed to fever, as I have experienced more frequently than I could wifh. With refpect to expenfe, my friend informed me, that thirty French crowns would fuffice tolerably well for a year ; to which, if other ten could be added, a man might expect to live very comfortably. In my time, ten years fince, twenty crowns were a fufficient allowance ; but in thefe latter days, when avarice is everywhere increafing, and charity growing cold, and this by a divine fcourge, everything has become almoft twice as dear as it was. And this I attribute to no other caufe than our proud and Pharaoh-like rejection of the fpiritual food of our fouls fo liberally and abundantly offered."

* *Original Letters relative to the Englifh Reformation* (Parker Society), vol. i. p. 190, Letter CI.

CHAPTER XII.

FULL hiftory of Paul's Crofs would be a hiftory of religion in England. Every great event, political and religious, whilft the Crofs was ftanding, found here its eloquent defender or denouncer. Here, as in fome great panorama, the moft illuftrious forms pafs before our eyes ; Kings, Queens, Prelates, Preachers, in their habit as they lived, as they were figured in the grim *Dance of Death* upon the cloifter walls hard by. Papift denounced Proteftant, and Proteftant denounced Papift, with equal impartiality, as the ebb and flow of the tide brought either party to the front.

Let us take one or two examples.

Now the Reformers are in favour :

"The firft of Nouember, [1552,] being the Feaft of All Saints, the new Service Booke called Of Common Prayer, began in Paules Church, and the like through the whole Cittie, the Bifhop of London, Doctor Ridley,

executing the feruice in Paules Church in the fore-
noone in his rochet onely, without coape or veftment,
preached in the quier ; and at afternoone hee preached
at Pauls Crofse, the Lord Maior, Aldermen, and Crafts
in their beft Liveries being prefent : which Sermon,
tending to the fetting forth the faid late made Booke
of Common Prayer, continued till almoft fiue of the
clocke at night."*

Only two months before † Ridley had vifited the
Princefs Mary at Hunfden, and had offered to preach
before her.   She had declined to hear him.

"Ye may preach if you lift, but neither I nor any of
mine fhall hear you."

"Madam," faid Ridley, "I truft you will not refufe
God's Word."

"I cannot tell what ye call God's Word," replied
Mary, "that is not God's Word now, that was God's
Word in my father's days."

"God's Word is one at all times, but hath been
better underftood and practifed in fome ages than in
other."

Mary. "You durft not for your ears have avouched
that for God's Word in my father's days that now you
do : and as for your new books, I thank God, I never
read any of them, I never did nor ever will do."

At the clofe of the interview, the Bifhop accepted
Sir Thomas Wharton's offer of refrefhment ; but when
he had eaten, fuddenly exclaimed :

* Stow, *Annales*, p. 608.
† Fox, *Acts and Monuments*.   About Sept. 8, 1552.

" Surely I have done amifs."

" Why fo ?" quoth Sir Thomas.

" For I have drunk," faid he, "in that place where God's Word offered hath been refufed, whereas if I had remembered my duty, I ought to have departed immediately, and to have fhaken off the duft of my fhoes for a teftimony againft this houfe."

" Thefe words were by the faid bifhop fpoken with fuch a vehemency, that fome of the hearers afterward confeffed their hair to ftand upright on their heads." Had Mary been prefent, one would have liked to hear her rejoinder : it is poffible that fhe, too, would have fpoken with " fuch a vehemency."

In the like earneft fpirit, no doubt, Ridley came to Paul's Crofs. It was not the only time that he ftood there. In the *Second Conference between Ridley and Latimer in prifon*,* Ridley fays, in anfwer to the queftion, " Have not you ufed in times paft to fay maffes yourfelf?"—"I confefs unto you my fault and ignorance ; but know you that for thefe matters I have done open penance long ago both at Paul's Crofs, and alfo openly in the pulpit at Cambridge. And I truft God hath forgiven me this mine offence, for I did it upon ignorance." In his *Conference with Secretary Bourn*, at the Lieutenant's table in the Tower,† he refers to the doctrine which he had maintained at Paul's Crofs on the fubject of the Euchariit.

A fhort time only has elapfed, but the fcene is

---

* Parker Society, *Works of Bifhop Ridley*, p. 119.

† *Ibid.*, pp. 162, 163.

changed. Edward is gathered to his fathers, and Mary reigns in his ftead. The Roman party is triumphant, at leaft in high places.

On Sunday, Auguft 13th, 1553, Bourne, whom Queen Mary had appointed her chaplain, preached at Paul's Crofs. There had been a riot at S. Bartholomew's on Auguft 11th, when a prieft had attempted to fay mafs. The Queen removed to Richmond on Saturday, Auguft 12th. On the following day another prieft was attacked at the altar, the veftments were torn from his back, and the chalice fnatched from his hands. Bourne was fet to preach at the Crofs. "A crowd of refugees and Englifh fanatics had collected round the pulpit. He fpoke in praife of Bonner, and faid that he had been unjuftly imprifoned. At thefe words, fays Renard, the popular exafperation broke out. Yells arofe: 'Papift! Papift! tear him down!' A dagger was hurled at the preacher, fwords were drawn, the mayor attempted to interfere, but he could not make his way through the denfe mafs of the rioters; and Bourne would have paid for his rafhnefs with his life, had not Courtenay, who was a popular favourite, with his mother, the Marchionefs of Exeter, thrown themfelves on the pulpit fteps, while Bradford fprung to his fide and kept the people back till he could be carried off."*

In Wriothefley's *Chronicle*† it is faid that Bifhop Bonner himfelf was prefent, and that "the Lord

---

* Froude, *Hiftory of England*, vi. pp. 60, 61.
† *Chronicle*, ii. pp. 97, 98.

Courtney and the Lady Marques of Execeter had as much adoe by their meanes to fee the fayd Bifhop conveyed in fafetye through the Church, the people were fo rude."

Machyn,* in his wildeft fpelling, as if the tumult had difturbed his thoughts, records the riot in his own quaint manner. " The xiii day Auguft dyd pryche at Powlles Croffe doctur [Bourne] parfun of Hehnger [that is, of High Ongar] in Effex, the qwen chaplen : and ther gret up-rore and fhowtyng at ys fermon, as yt [were] lyke mad pepull, watt yonge pepell and woman [as] ever was hard, as herle-borle, and caft-yng up of capes. [If] my Lord Mer and my lord Cortenay ad not ben ther, ther had bene grett Myf-cheyff done." It is clearly the account of an eye-witnefs.

Gilbert Bourne was one of the Prebendaries of S. Paul's, and in his fermon he had prayed for the fouls departed, and had not only praifed Bonner, but had fpoken ill of Ridley. He certainly had a narrow efcape, for the dagger ftruck one of the fide-pofts of the pulpit.† Mafter Bradford came into the pulpit, fays Fox,‡ and " fpake fo mildly, chriftianly, and effectuoufly, that with few words he appeafed all: and afterward he and Mafter Rogers conducted the preacher betwixt them from the pulpit to the gram-mar-fchool door, where they left him fafe, as further, in the ftory of Mafter Bradford, is declared." Fox does

---

* Machyn's *Diary*, p. 41.
† Notes to Machyn's *Diary*, p. 332.
‡ Fox's *Acts and Monuments*, vi. p. 392.

not mention Courtenay's intervention; he was
anxious, it would feem, " to point a moral and adorn
a tale," for he goes on to fay that, fhortly after, Bradford and Rogers " were both rewarded with long imprifonment, and, laft of all, with fire in Smithfield."
Bourne was confecrated Bifhop of Bath and Wells on
April 1ft, 1554, but was deprived by Elizabeth in the
firft year of her reign, on his refufing to take the oath
of fupremacy.

On the following Sunday, Auguft 20th, Mr.
Watfon,* " a bachelor of divinity and chaplain to the
Bifhop of Winchefter," preached at Paul's Crofs, under
a guard of two hundred foldiers, " with their hal-
berdes." The companies ftood around " in their
liueries and hoodes all the fermon tyme, to herken yf
any leude or fedicious perfons made any rumors or
miforder." The preacher declared " the obedience of
fubiectes, and what erronious fectes are raigninge in
this realme by falfe preachers and teachers; to the
godly edyfyinge of the audience there prefent:" and,
thanks to the guard, there was no tumult. Thomas
Watfon was a young man. He was thirty-three years
of age in 1551, when he gave evidence on behalf of
Bifhop Gardiner.† Cranmer, long ago, had fet him in
the ftocks at Canterbury :‡ fo, no doubt, he fpoke
very earneftly. Thofe who are curious as to his
fermon may find fome account of it, written by an

---

* Wriothefley's *Chronicle*, ii. pp. 99, 100.
† Froude, *Hiftory*, vi. p. 68.
‡ Fox, vi. p. 151. At page 205, however, he is faid to have
been "of the age of 34 or 35 years," ftill under the fame date, 1551.

unfriendly hand, in Fox.* He had a goodly audience: the Marquis of Winchefter, the Earl of Bedford, the Earl of Pembroke, the Lord Rich, amongft them.

The time was near at hand when Roman doctrine would be heard without proteft, if not with approval. The dominant party knew how to filence gainfayers. That is a leffon which dominant parties foon learn.

On Monday, Auguft 21ft, the Duke of Northumberland, the Marquis of Northampton, Sir Andrew Dudley, Sir Henry Gates, Sir Thomas Palmer, recanted, and abjured the Proteftant faith, in the Chapel of the Tower, certain of the citizens of London being prefent. The Duke prayed earneftly for life—"Oh that it would pleafe her good Grace to give me life, yea, the life of a dog, if I might but live and kifs her feet, and fpend both life and all in her honourable fervice!" The next morning, at nine o'clock, Mafs was faid in the Tower Chapel. Northumberland repeated his abjuration on the fcaffold: it was foon red with the blood of the Duke, Sir John Gates, and Sir Thomas Palmer. "On the 24th, two days after the fcene on Tower Hill,† fo little was a guard neceffary, that Mafs was faid in S. Paul's in Latin, with matins and vefpers. The crucifix was replaced in the rood-loft, the high altar was re-decorated, the real prefence was defended from the pulpit, and except from the refugees not a murmur was heard."

And now it was eafy to re-introduce the images which had been deftroyed. "In the fecond year of Mary,

---

* Fox, vi. p. 768.   † Froude, *Hiftory*, vi. pp. 66-75.

Bonner in his royalty and all his prebendaries about him in Paul's Choir, the Rood laid along upon the pavements, and also, the doors of Paul's being ſhut—the Biſhop with others ſaid and ſung divers prayers by the Rood. That being done, they anointed the Rood with oil in divers places; and, after the anointing, crept unto it, and kiſſed it. After that, they took the ſaid Rood, and weighed him up, and ſet him in his old accuſtomed place; and all the while they were doing thereof, the whole Choir ſang *Te Deum;* and when that was ended, they rang the bells, not only for joy, but alſo for the notable and great part they had done therein.

" Not long after this, a merry fellow came into Paul's, and ſpied the Rood with Mary and John new ſet up; whereto, among a great ſort of people, he made low courteſy, and ſaid : ' Sir, your maſterſhip is welcome to town. I had thought to have talked further with your maſterſhip, but that ye be here clothed in the Queen's colours. I hope that ye but a ſummer's bird, in that ye be dreſſed in white and green.' "*

Once more the ebb and flow. Mary is dead, and Elizabeth reigns in her ſtead. The newly erected images are expelled. " On the euen of S. Bartholomew, the day and the morrow after, &c., were burned in Paules Churchyard, Cheape, and diuers other places of the City of London, all the roodes and other Images of the Churches, in ſome places the Coapes, veſtments, altar-clothes, books, banners, ſepulchres, and rood-lofts were burned." †

* Fox, vi. pp. 558-559.   † Stow, *Annales*, 1559, p. 640.

In Wriothesley's *Chronicle*[*] the significant addition
is made that these Roods and vestments had cost
about £2,000 when they were renewed in Queen
Mary's time. He seems to imply that the objects
then consumed were the roods and images "that
stoode in the parishe churches." The Reformers were
triumphant.

On Ash-Wednesday, 1565, a very different company
assembled at S. Paul's. The Queen, Elizabeth, came in
person to the Cross, de Silva, the Spanish Ambassador,
at her side. Alexander Nowell, the Dean of S. Paul's,
was the preacher. "A vast crowd had assembled—
more, the Queen thought, to see her than to hear the
sermon. The Dean began, and had not proceeded far
when he came on the subject of images 'which he
handled roughly.'

"'Leave that alone,' Elizabeth called from her seat.

"The preacher did not hear, and went on with his
invectives.

"'To your text, Mr. Dean,' she shouted, raising her
voice: 'To your text! leave that; we have heard
enough of that! To your subject.'

"The unfortunate Doctor Nowell coloured, stammered
out a few incoherent words, and was unable to go on.
Elizabeth went off in a rage with the ambassador.
The congregation—the Protestant part of it—were in
tears. Archbishop Parker, seeing the Dean 'utterly
dismayed,' took him 'for pity home to Lambeth to

* Wriothesley's *Chronicle*, ii. p. 146.

dinner,' and wrote to Cecil a refpectful but firm re-
monftrance."*

Nowell himfelf could fpeak ftrongly when he pleafed.
On the 12th of January, 1563, he and Day, the provoft
of Eton, had preached, Nowell at Weftminfter, Day
at S. Paul's. The occafion was the opening of Parliament and of Convocation. The fubject of both
fermons, fays Mr. Froude,† was the fame: "the pro-
priety of 'killing the caged wolves'—that is to fay the
Catholic bifhops in the Tower—with the leaft poffible
delay." The ftatement does not reft only upon the
authority of a letter from De Quadra to Philip in the
archives of Simancas, a fource which might be thought
open to fufpicion; but is fupported by an extract from
Dean Nowell's own Sermon, taken from a manufcript in the library of Caius College, Cambridge,
printed at the end of the feventh volume of Mr.
Froude's *Hiftory.*

Nowell had fallen under Elizabeth's difpleafure
before this occafion. He preached at S. Paul's on
New Year's Day, 1562, and the Queen attended.
"The Dean,‡ having met with feveral fine engravings,
reprefenting the ftories and paffions of the faints and
martyrs, had placed them againft the epiftles and
gofpels of their refpective feftivals in a Common
Prayer Book, which he had caufed to be richly bound,
and laid on the cufhion for the Queen's ufe, in the
place where fhe commonly fat: intending it for a New

* Froude, *Hiftory*, viii. pp. 136, 137.   † *Ibid.*, vii. pp. 479, 541.
‡ Churton, *Life of Nowell*, pp. 71-73.

Year's Gift for her Majefty, and thinking to have pleafed her fancy therewith . . . When fhe came to her place, and had opened the book, and faw the pictures, fhe frowned and blufhed : and then fhutting the book (of which feveral took notice) she called for the verger, and bade him bring her the old book, wherein fhe was formerly wont to read.   After fermon, whereas fhe ufed to get immediately on horfeback or into her chariot, fhe went ftraight to the veftry, and applying herfelf to the Dean, thus fhe fpoke to him :

" ' Mr. Dean, how came it to pafs that a new fervice book was placed on my cufhion ?'

" To which the Dean anfwered, ' May it pleafe your Majefty, I caufed it to be placed there.'

" Then faid the Queen, ' Wherefore did you fo ?'

" ' To prefent your Majefty with a New Year's Gift.'

" ' You could never prefent me with a worfe.'

" ' Why fo, Madam ?'

" ' You know I have an averfion to idolatry, to images, and pictures of this kind.'

" ' Wherein is the idolatry, may it pleafe your Majefty ?'

" ' In the cuts refembling angels and faints ; nay groffer abfurdities, pictures refembling the Bleffed Trinity.'

" ' I meant no harm : nor did I think it would offend your Majefty, when I intended it for a New Year's Gift.'

" ' You muft needs be ignorant then. Have you forgot our proclamation againft images, pictures, and

Romiſh reliques in the Churches ?　Was it not read in your Deanery ?'

"' It was read.　But be your Majeſty aſſured I meant no harm, when I cauſed the cuts to be bound with the ſervice book.'

"' You muſt needs be very ignorant to do this after our prohibition of them.'

"' It being my ignorance, your Majeſty may the better pardon me.'

"' I am ſorry for it, yet glad to hear it was your ignorance, rather than your opinion.'

"' Be your Majeſty aſſured, it was my ignorance.'

"' If ſo, Mr. Dean, God grant you His Spirit, and more wiſdom for the future.'

"' Amen.　I pray God.'

"' I pray you, Mr. Dean, how came you by theſe pictures ?　Who engraved them ?'

"' I know not who engraved them.　I bought them.'

"' From whom bought you them ?'

"' From a German.'

"' It is well it was from a ſtranger.　Had it been any of our ſubjects, we ſhould have queſtioned the matter. Pray let no more of theſe miſtakes, or of this kind, be committed within the churches of our realm for the future.'

"' There ſhall not.' "

Elizabeth was about eight-and-twenty when this dialogue occurred, and Nowell, a man of ripe age, about fifty-four.　It is not an edifying ſpectacle, the Dean of Paul's, a grave and reverend divine, browbeaten by an imperious young woman, though ſhe was a Queen. In 1562 fhe rebukes him for the pictures in her Prayer Book ; in 1565, *varium et mutabile femper*, becaufe he fpoke againft images. It feems not unlikely that he really was pointing at the crucifix ftill ftanding in the Royal Chapel. His tranfition, he fays, which aroufed the Queen's difpleafure, was "from Dame Grace's books burned, to Images, termed the Books of Ideots, which I took as not altogether impertinent."*

He was received back, however, into the royal favour, for on Tuefday, the 20th of Auguft, 1588, he was felected to give the firft public notice, from Paul's Crofs, of the defeat of the Spanifh Armada ;† and again on the 8th of September, he performed a fimilar duty. Eleven enfigns, taken from the Spaniards, waved from the lower battlements of S. Paul's. A ftreamer, on which was painted the Virgin and Child, was held in a man's hand over the pulpit. On November 24th, the Queen herfelf, in a chariot of ftate, drawn by a pair of white horfes, came in folemn proceffion from Somerfet Houfe to S. Paul's, to return public thanks to Almighty God for the great victory. Aylmer, the Bifhop of London, and Dean Nowell received her at the Cathedral.

The mention of Aylmer's name recalls a remarkable and characteriftic letter written by the Bifhop in 1581 to the then Lord Mayor, Sir James Hervey, in which the prelate lectures the Lord Mayor fomewhat

* Churton, *Life of Nowell*, p. 111, note.　† *Ibid.*, p. 293.

ſeverely and rates him roundly upon ſome miſconduct
at Paul's Croſs. Biſhop Aylmer was evidently very
angry. He plunges at once *in medias res.* "My
Lord Maior," he ſays,* " I heare that yow deale very.
hardly with the preachers and Clergie, the ouerſight
of whome god and Her Majeſtie hath comitted unto
me. . . . Yow thou them, yow taunte them, yea ſuch
as by calling are Archedecons, by lawe not enferior
to yow when yow be out of your Maraltie. Your ſon
beknaueth them. Wherefore if any complaine, he is
like to anſwere it. . . . I paſſe ouer my ſelf, whome it
pleaſeth yow to tearme familiarly by the name of
Aelmer, as unreuerently as if I ſhold omitt the name
of your office and call yow Haruey, which, god will-.
ing, I will not doe, to teach yow good manners.
Yow ſay that when Aelmer was in Zurich, he thought
c^{li} a year was enoughe for any miniſter : and ſo
thought yow paraduenture in your prentiſhood, that
c^{li} a year had been well for a merchaunte. Yow are .
glaunſing at my houſe keping, and that the B. of
London feaſted the L. Maior and his bretheren : I
thinke that wonte was but once, and therefore. I
minde not to followe it as a preſident ; and as litle as
yow make of Aelmers hoſpitalitie, yet if yow com-.
pare v yeres of yours with v yeres of his, his may
chaunce to ouerreache your 4000 ^{li}." He proceeds in
a ſimilar ſtrain, making one very good point *en paſ-*
ſant, as regards the Lord Mayor's lack of courteſy :
" the nexte yere," he ſays, " I may remember it, when

---

* The letter was printed, I believe for the firſt time, in my
Documents, etc., pp. 128-130.

by gods grace I ame like to be as I ame and yow
fomewhat inferior to that that you are ;" and thus
he brings his vigorous letter to a clofe : "If yow
take this in good parte as coming from him that
hath charge ouer yow, I ame glad. If not, I muft
tell yow your dutie out of my chaire, which is the
pulpit at Poules croffe, where yow muft fitt not as a
iudge to comptrole, but as a fcholler to learne : and I
not as John Aelmer to be thwarted, but as John
London to teache yow and all London : and if you
ufe not your felf as an humble fcholler, then to diffip-
line yow as a teacher and prelate. Thus I bidd your
Lᴾ hartely farewell. Fullham this j. of March, 1581.
Your Lᴾˢ louing frend and Biffhop, John London."
Did the Lord Mayor reply to his "louing frend and
Biffhop"?   The anfwer would be worth reading.
There was evidently an old feud between the Bifhop
and the Chief Magiftrate.

Fuller fays* of Aylmer that he was "one of a low
ftature but ftout fpirit, very valiant in his youth and
witty all his life."   And he tells an odd ftory of him,
that "once when his auditory began at fermon to grow
dull in their attentions, he prefently read unto them
many verfes out of the Hebrew text, where at they
all ftarted, admiring what ufe he meant to make
thereof.   Then fhewed he them their folly, that
whereas they neglected English, whereby they might
be edified, they liftened to Hebrew, whereof they
underftood not a word."

It is even faid that on one occasion, when preaching

* Fuller, *Church Hiftory*, edit. J. S. Brewer, vol. v. pp. 200, 201.

at S. Paul's, the Bishop produced a skull from under his gown that he might stimulate the flagging attention of the congregation.*

The Paul's Cross preachers were wont to be received and entertained at the "Shunammite's House:" a house so called because "besides the stipend paid the preacher, there is provision made also for his lodging and diet for two days before, and one day after his sermon."† To this house, in or about the year 1581, came Richard Hooker wet, weary, and weather-beaten; worn out by his long ride upon an ill-paced horse which would not trot. The house was kept at that time by one John Churchman, sometime a draper of good note in Watling Street, but who had fallen into poverty. Mrs. Churchman nursed the great theologian carefully, gave him a warm bed, and proper food, and by her diligent attendance so far cured his cold that he was able to preach his sermon, whereof he had despaired. But her kindness was fatal to his peace. Mrs. Churchman deluded the good simple man— (Fuller‡ speaks of his "dove-like simplicity")—persuaded him "that he was a man of a tender constitution"—and "that it was best for him to have a wife, that might prove a nurse to him; such an one as might both prolong his life, and make it more comfortable"—nay, she went on to say, that "such an one

* Mackenzie Walcott, *Traditions and Customs*, p. 87.
† Walton's *Life of Hooker*, prefixed to Keble's edition of Hooker's *Works*, i. pp. 22, 23 (5th edit.).
‡ Fuller, *History*, v. p. 235.

ſhe could and would provide for him, if he thought fit
to marry." He was entrapped into a marriage with
Mrs. Churchman's daughter, who had "neither beauty
nor portion :" and, worſe ſtill, was of a ſhrewd temper.
She proved a thorough Xantippe. As Melanꞓthon
was ſeen by a friend with a book in one hand, whilſt
the other rocked a cradle ; ſo, when two of his college
friends came to viſit him, " Richard was called to rock
the cradle." Profound theological learning had not
made him a match for a deſigning mother and an ill-
conditioned daughter.

In 1595, November 17th, "a day of great triumph
for the long and proſperous raigne of her Majeſtie at
London, the Pulpit Croſſe in Paules Churchyard was
new ɩepayred, and partly incloſed with a wal of bricke,"
as Stow records in his *Annals*. " Doꞓtour Fletcher,
Biſhop of London, preached there in prayſe of the
queene." The trumpets ſounded upon the church
leads, the cornets winded, "the quiriſters ſung an
antheme ;" on the ſteeple many lights were burned,
the Tower ſhot off her ordnance, the bells were rung,
and bonfires made.

On May 30th, 1630, King Charles I., having attended
divine Service in S. Paul's Cathedral, "went into a
roome and heard the Sermon at Paules Croſſe."
Three years later, in 1633, the Sermons which uſually
had been preached at the Croſs were removed into
the Choir of the Cathedral.* The Vergers, in a Peti-

---

* Dugdale, *S. Paul's*, p. 91, note.

tion preferved amongft the State Papers,* fays that
"for the repaire of the Church the Sermons appointed
for the Crofs were remooved from the yard into the
Quire." There is good reafon to believe that about
this time the Crofs itfelf was taken down.

Dugdale ftates, very plainly, that in "1643, Ifaac
Penington being Lord Mayor, the famous Crofs in the
churchyard, which had been for many ages the moft
noted and folemn place in this nation, for the graveft
divines and greateft fcholars to preach at, was, with
the reft of the croffes about London and Weftminfter,
by further order of the faid Parliament pulled down to
the ground."† This is a very clear and definite ftatement; but is it accurate? It has been repeated
without queftion again and again.‡ There is a view
in Wilkinfon's *Londina Illuftrata* reprefenting the
pulling down of *Cheapfide Crofs*, and on the plate is
engraved a fhort account which ftates that it was
pulled down on the 2nd of May, 1643, and that on
May 10th, the Book of Sports was burnt by the
common hangman on the place where the Crofs had
ftood. It is ufually fuppofed that Paul's Crofs fell at
the fame time, but Profeffor Gardiner has brought
under my notice a paffage from a fomewhat rare tract,
*A dialogue between the Croffe in Cheap and Charing
Crofs*, publifhed in 1641, which ferves to caft confiderable doubt upon the commonly received opinion.

* Printed in my *Documents*, pp. 140, 141.
† *S. Paul's*, p. 109.
‡ I have lately repeated it (alas!) in *Documents*, etc. (Camden
Society).

The Crofs in Cheap and Charing Crofs are holding a converfation, and the following words are fpoken :

" *Char.* Paul's Croffe, the moft famous preaching place, is downe and quite taken away.

" *Cheap.* It is true, but with an intent to be built fairer and bigger when the Church fhall be finifhed."

If Paul's Crofs was " downe and quite taken away " in 1641, it is exceedingly improbable that it was re-erected in time to be pulled down by the Lord Mayor in 1643. It was certainly down on May 16th, 1643, for on that day a Court was holden under the prefidency of Sir Ifaac Pennington, when a petition was read from the Parifhioners of " ffaithes vnder Paules Church," in which complaint is made that the " Stones, rubbifh, pales, and fheds " in the Churchyard are of much detriment to the Parifhioners and are a hindrance to the entrance of light into their houfes. The Court orders that the obftructions be removed ; and further appoints Sir John Gayre, Knight and Alderman, and Mr. Alderman Gibbs, " to confider of a convenient and fitt place within the faid yard for a pulpitt to ftand in, and alfo of a convenient place for the Lord Maior and Aldermen to fitt in to heare the Word of God preached as heretofore hath byn accuftomed vpon the Lords day." The faid Aldermen are " to certefie vnto this Court theyre doeings and opinions."*

It muft be confeffed that Sir Ifaac Pennington has been wronged in this matter. Certainly his other

* Records in the Guildhall. Repertory, 56, 1642-43 (unpub-lifhed).

deeds would not lead one to think that he would have
had any diſlike to pull down a Croſs ; but probably
Paul's Croſs had nothing about it to offend him, ſave,
indeed, the Croſs at its ſummit.   No figures of ſaints,
no effigy of the Virgin and Child, as at Cheapſide
Croſs, would have ſtirred his wrath : Paul's Croſs was
but an outdoor pulpit.

If the evidence of the tract juſt cited is to be
believed—and there ſeems no reaſon to doubt it—the
Croſs had been taken down only in order that it
might be rebuilt " fairer and bigger " when the Church
was finiſhed.

Dugdale, however, who died on February 10th,
1685—and worthy Thomas Fuller, who died Auguſt
16th, 1661—might fairly have been ſuppoſed to give
us good teſtimony upon a contemporary event.   The
latter ſays, " No zealot reformer (whilſt Egypt was
Chriſtian) demoliſhed *the Pyramids* under the notion
of Pagan Monuments."*   And afterwards, regretting
the deſtruction of Paul's Croſs, he ſays, " Methinks,
though idle croſſes, ſtanding only for ſhow, were publiſhed for offenders, this uſeful one which did ſuch
ſervice, might have been ſpared.   But all is fiſh which
comes to the net of ſacrilege."   It was " guilty of no
other ſuperſtition ſave accommodating the preacher
and ſome about him with convenient places."†

The *Charge Books* of the Cathedral throw ſome
light upon this difficult point : for in June, 1635,

* *Pisgah-Sight*, iiv. p. 83.   See Mr. J. E. Bailey's excellent
Life of Fuller, p. 442.

† Fuller's *Worthies of England*, edit. 1840, ii. pp. 136, 137.

labourers were employed in carrying away "the Lead, Timber, &c., that were pull'd downe of the Roomes where the Prebends of the Church, the Doctors of the Law, and the Parifhioners of St. ffaith's did fett to heare Sermons at St. Pauls Croffe." Extenfive repairs were, at this time, being carried out at the Eaftern end and Northern fide of the Cathedral. The volume* from which the above paffage is taken is one of the *Charge Books*, finely tranfcribed on vellum ; the laft page bears, amongft other fignatures, thofe of Archbifhop Laud, Bifhop Juxon, Lord Arundel and Surrey, Lord Manchefter, Inigo Jones, and Windebank. Succeeding entries in the fame volume render it highly probable that the Crofs had previoufly been taken down, and that preparations were being made for its re-erection.

Certainly the Crofs had been moft impartial. Every phafe of religious opinion had found expreffion there. Hear what Carlyle† fays : " Paul's Crofs was a kind of Stone Tent, with leaden roof, at the N.E. corner of Paul's Cathedral, where fermons were ftill, and had long been, preached in the open air ; crowded devout congregations gathering there, with forms to fit on, if you came early. Queen Elizabeth ufed to ' tune her pulpits,' fhe faid, when there was any great thing on hand ; as Governing Perfons now ftrive to tune the Morning Newfpapers. Paul's Crofs, a kind of *Times Newfpaper*, but edited partly

---

* Preferved amongft the archives of the Cathedral. Preffmark, W. F. 4.

† *Letters and Speeches of O. Cromwell*, edit. 1873, i. pp. 55, 56.

by Heaven itſelf, was then a moſt important entity !"

In proceſs of time the preciſe ſite of Paul's Croſs was forgotten. It was reſerved for Mr. Penroſe, the Cathedral Surveyor,* to ſearch diligently for it and to find it. The outline of the octagonal baſe may now be ſeen, in the churchyard, at the N.E. angle of the Choir of the preſent Cathedral. A portion of the *podium* coincides with the wall of the exiſting church : it would have been about twelve feet diſtant from the walls of old S. Paul's. Mr. Penroſe has favoured the writer with a ſketch of his diſcoveries, from which it appears that the octagonal baſe meaſured about thirty-ſeven feet acroſs. The ſides of the octagon were not parallel to the axis of the old Cathedral, but four of the ſides faced very nearly to the four cardinal points. The platform itſelf was ſupported by a vault. A brick wall was found which probably carried the timber ſupports of the pulpit proper. The probable diameter of the pulpit itſelf was eighteen feet.

* On April 2, 1879, I had the great pleaſure of receiving a note from Mr. Penroſe, in which he wrote, " We have found the foundation of S. Paul's Croſs."

CHAPTER XIII.

PAUL'S WALK.

THE grand and fpacious Nave of the Cathedral obtained the name of Paul's Walk : a name only too fuggeftive of the profanations of which it became the fcene. It was the common lounge of the idler, the Fop's Alley of the day. It will be remembered that there were two doors exactly oppofite to each other, piercing the north and fouth walls, about the middle of the Nave ; and that there were grand entrances at each of the tranfepts. Thefe two fets of doors, immediately oppofite to each other, were only too fuggeftive to the profane of the eafe with which a fhort cut might be made from one fide of the churchyard to the other. A common thoroughfare was foon eftablifhed. Prefently men were not fatiffied with merely paffing through the Church. The porter with his heavy burden on his fhoulders, the water-carrier with his buckets, found it pleafant enough to fet down their burdens, and to reft in the cool fhade of the maffive

pillars. Nor was this all, for both men and women
foon began to bring their wares into the holy place,
and to buy and fell and get gain. As early as the
year 1385, Bifhop Braybrooke, from his Palace hard
by the Cathedral, writes a very vigorous letter to his
faithful laity upon the fubject of the buyers and fellers
in the Church of S. Paul.* He calls to mind the example of the Divine Redeemer, who vifited the Temple
at Jerufalem, and "feeing that the people were more
intent on buying and felling than on prayers," caft out
the offenders, and proclaimed that they had made the
Houfe of God a den of thieves. So, alas, it had come
to pafs that in the very Cathedral of S. Paul on
ordinary days, and ftill more on feftival days, men
and women thronged to the holy place with their
merchandife. There, at their feveral ftanding places,
juft as in a public market, they expofed their wares.
Other pollutions took place which revealed themfelves
not only to the eyes but alfo to the noftrils of the
faithful. Some took delight in hurling ftones at the
crows, pigeons, and other birds, which built their nefts
about the towers and battlements ; whilft fome, more
daring ftill, fhot at them with arrows and crofs-bow
bolts, breaking the pictured windows, and even the
ftatues which graced the exterior. Solemn monition
is to be given by all Rectors, Vicars, Curates, and
other Clergy throughout the City of London to their
people, abfolutely forbidding fuch profanations, under
pain of the Greater Excommunication. And if, after

---

* I have printed the letter, from the original entry in Bifhop
Braybrooke's Regifter, in my *Statuta S. Pauli*, pp. 391-2.

the monition had been thrice repeated, any were fo
bold as to tranfgrefs, the offenders were to be publicly
excommunicated in due form, with bells, candles, and
crofs.

The Statutes of the Cathedral, however, prove that
the abufes continued. One Statute, in particular,
provides that if the buyers and fellers defpifed the
ecclefiaftical cenfures, the vergers fhould feize upon
their wares and caft them on the pavement.* Nor
muft it be fuppofed that fuch evil practices were
peculiar to S. Paul's. The ancient Statutes of Wells
Cathedral contain a fimilar clause,† and the like
abufes were common enough elfewhere. At Exeter it
was the firft act of Seth Ward (afterwards Bifhop of
Salifbury) on his appointment as Dean in 1661, to
"caft out of the Temple the Buyers and Sellers, who
had ufurp'd it, and therein kept diftinct fhops to vent‡
their Ware," as Dr. Walter Pope, his biographer,
records. "At Durham there was a regular thoroughfare acrofs the nave until 1750, and at Norwich until
1748, when Bifhop Gooch ftopped it. The naves of
York and Durham were fafhionable promenades.
The Confeffor's Chapel made, on occafion, a convenient play-ground for Weftminfter Scholars, who
were allowed, as late as 1829, to keep the fcenes for
their annual play in the triforium of the north
tranfept."§

* *Statuta S. Pauli*, p. 79.

† *Statuta Wellens:* Lambeth Library, MS. No. 929, p. 60.

‡ So in original. Pope's *Life of Seth Ward*, 8vo, London,
1697, p. 55.

§ Abbey and Overton's *Englifh Church in the Eighteenth
Century*, ii. p. 419.

If ſuch flagrant abuſes were common before the Reformation, when the Church was full of Altars, venerated images, ſhrines, and paintings, it can hardly be matter of ſurpriſe that they were greatly augmented when the Altars were deſtroyed and the ſculpture and painting were alike removed. The Divine Service was ſaid for the moſt part in the Choir, which was ſhut off from the reſt of the Church by its cloſe ſcreen. The broad nave and tranſepts ceaſed to be regarded as holy.

In 1598, Biſhop Bancroſt held a Viſitation of the Cathedral ; ſome of the returns made by the Clergy and Officials are ſtill preſerved in the Cathedral Record Room.* They diſcloſe a lamentable ſtate of things. One of the Vergers' ſtates that the Nave was "a comon paſſage and thorowfaire for all kinde of Burden-bearing people, as Colliers with ſacks of Coles, Porters with Baſkettes of fleſhe, and ſuch like." Another perſon complains "that Porters, Butchers, Water-berers, and who not? be ſuffred, in ſpeciall in tyme of ſervice, to carrye and recarrye whatſoever, no man withſtandynge them or gaynſayenge them." Even the choriſter boys, "the children of the queer," were eager in ſearch of ſpur money ; and there was "ſuche noyſe of children and others in the ſide chaples and churche at the devine ſervice and ſermondes that a man may ſcarce be hearde for the noyſe of them." Spur-money was a fee claimed by

---

* I have printed a ſelection from theſe in *Statuta S. Pauli,* pp. 276-278.

chorifter boys from any perfon entering the church wearing fpurs. The perfon from whom it was claimed had, however, the right of calling on the youngeft chorifter to fing his gamut ; if he failed to do fo, the fpur-wearer efcaped fcot-free. It is faid that the Duke of Wellington was challenged by one of the boys at the Chapel Royal, but that he efcaped by this device. The cuftom lingered at Peterborough as late as 1847.* In the Privy Purfe Expenfes of Henry VII. occurs this entry :

"1495. Oct. To the children, for the King's fpoures 4s.": from which it would appear that even Kings were not exempt from the payment.

The allufions to Paul's Walk in the literature of the fixteenth and feventeenth centuries are very frequent and are well known. A few only fhall be cited here.

In *The Burnynge of Paules Church*, a rare little book, printed in 1562-3, Bifhop Pilkington fays : " The South Alley for Ufurye and Popery, the North for Simony, and the Horfe Faire in the middeft for all kind of bargains, metings, brawlinges, morthers, confpiracies, and the Font for ordinarie paymentes of money, are fo well knowen to all menne as the begger knowes his difhe."†

There was a " Serving man's pillar," where fervants out of place waited to be hired. Falftaff, it will be remembered, engaged Bardolph as his fervant in Paul's :

* *Statuta S. Pauli*, p. 275, note.
† *The Burnynge,* etc. G. iiii.

" *Fal.* Where's Bardolph ?
Page. He's gone into Smithfield, to buy your worship a horse.
Fal. I bought him in Paul's, and he'll buy me a horse in Smith-
field."*

Ben Jonson lays the scene of the third Act of his play, *Every Man out of his Humour*, in Paul's Walk.

John Chamberlain, son of an Alderman of London, interchanged a good deal of correspondence with Dudley Carleton, afterwards Lord Viscount Dorchester, and the following passages from the letters that passed between them will show that in the year 1600 Paul's Walk was the common place of meeting and of gossip for London loungers :†

" Nobody in Powles, *solitudo ante ostium* in Little Britain, and all as close and quiet as if it were midnight."

" Powles is so furnisht that it affords whatsoever is stirring in France, and I can gather there at first hand to serve my turne sufficiently."

" Here is nobody to talk with, for Pauls is as empty as a barn at Midsummer."

Bishop Corbet, who loved the Cathedral, and delivered a very quaint and forcible Charge to the Clergy of his Diocese of Norwich,‡ urging them to contribute to its restoration ; yet could speak in such terms as these in his *Elegie written upon the death of Dr. Ravis, Bishop of London*, who died in 1609 :

* *Henry IV.*, Pt. 2, A. i. Sc. 2.
† *Chamberlain's Letters*, pp. 88, 176 ; and *Calendar of State Papers*, Eliz., vol. 275.
‡ Printed in my *Documents*, etc. pp. 134-139.

"When I paſt Paules, and travell'd in that walke
Where all oure Brittaine-ſinners ſweare and talke ;
Ould Harry-ruffians, bankerupts, ſuthe ſayers,
And youth, whoſe couſenage is as ould as theirs."

Samuel Speed, in *The Legend of his Grace Humphrey, Duke of S. Paul's Cathedral Walk*, ſays, in 1674 :

"Some with their beads unto a pillar crowd,
Some mutter forth, ſome ſay their graces loud ;
Some on devotion come to feed their muſe ;
Some come to ſleep, or walk, or talk of news."

But Biſhop Earle—he was Biſhop, ſucceſſively, of
Worceſter and of Saliſbury, and a ſtaunch royaliſt—
gives a ſingularly graphic account of Paul's Walk in
his very quaint and remarkable book, *Microcoſmo-
graphy*, firſt publiſhed in 1628. It is really worth
while to extract the whole paſſage.*

"*Paul's Walk* is the land's epitome, or you may call
it the leſſer iſle of Great Britain. It is more than this,
the whole world's map, which you may here diſcern in
its perfecteſt motion, juſtling and turning. It is a
heap of ſtones and men, with a vaſt confuſion of lan-
guages ; and, were the ſteeple not ſanctified, nothing
liker Babel. The noiſe in it is like that of bees, a
ſtrange humming or buzz mixed of walking, tongues,
and feet : it is a kind of ſtill roar, or loud whiſper. It
is the great exchange of all diſcourſe, and no buſineſs
whatſoever but is here ſtirring and afoot. It is the
ſynod of all pates politick, jointed and laid together
in moſt ſerious poſture, and they are not half ſo buſy

* From the edition edited by Dr. Bliſs in 1811, pp. 116–119.

16

at the parliament. It is the antick of tails to tails,
and backs to backs, and for vizards you need go no
farther than faces. It is the market of young lecturers,
whom you may cheapen here at all rates and fizes.
It is the general mint of all famous lies, which are
here, like the legends of popery, firft coined and
ftamped in the church. All inventions are emptied
here, and not few pockets. The beft fign of a
temple in it is, that it is the thieves' fanctuary, which
rob more fafely in the crowd than a wildernefs, whilft
every fearcher is a bufh to hide them. It is the other
expence of the day, after plays, tavern, and a bawdy-
houfe; and men have ftill fome oaths left to fwear
here. It is the ear's brothel, and fatiffies their luft
and itch. The vifitants are all men without exceptions, but the principal inhabitants and poffeffors are
ftale knights ,and captains* out of fervice; men of
long rapiers and breeches, which after all turn merchants here and traffic for news. Some make it a
preface to their dinner, and travel for a ftomach; but
thriftier men make it their ordinary, and board here
very cheap. Of all fuch places it is leaft haunted
with hobgoblins, for if a ghoft would walk more he
could not."

Certainly the Bifhop writes with an unfparing pen.
It has been thought better to prefent the picture
exactly as he has drawn it, without foftening the
more repulfive features.

Other allufions to the fubject will be found in *The*

* In the *Dramatis Perfonæ* to Ben Jonfon's *Every Man in
his Humour*, Bobadil is ftyled a *Paul's Man.*

Meeting of Gallants at an Ordinarie; or, The Walkes in Powles, a unique tract; the only copy known is in the Bodleian Library. It was printed in 1604, and was reprinted by Mr. Halliwell-Phillipps for the Percy Society in 1841.* The following paffage occurs in it:

"But fee yonder Signior Stramazoon and Signior Kickfhawe, now of a fuddaine allighted in Powles with their durtie Bootes. Lets encounter them at the fift Pillar; in them you fhall finde my talke verified, and the fafhion truly pictured. . . Mee thinkes, Signiors, this middle of Powles lookes ftrange and bare, like a long-hayrde Gentleman new powlde, wafht and fhaued. And I may fitly fay fhaued, for there was neuer a lufty Shauer feene walking here this halfe yeare; efpecially if he loued his life, hee would reuolt from Duke Humfrey, and rather bee a Wood-cleauer in the Countrey, then a cheft-breaker in London. But what Gallants march vp a pace now, Signiors; how are the high waies fild to London ?"

Even the very dreffes of the Gallants are thought worthy of notice:

"But fee how we haue loft our felues. Powles is changde into Gallants, and thofe which I faw come vp in old Taffata Doublets yefterday are flipt into nine yardes of Sattin to-day."

Our laft reference fhall be to Thomas Decker's *The Gul's Horn-booke*, imprinted at London in 1609.† A

---

* The reprint itfelf has now become fcarce. The paffages cited will be found at pages 11 and 14 of the Reprint.

† The quotations are taken from the reprint edited in 1872 by Charles Hindley.

whole Chapter in this book (Chapter IV.), is devoted to the fubjeƈt, " How a Gallant fhould behave himfelf in Paul's Walks ;" and if our extraƈts be rather lengthy, there will be fome excufe for the length, in the minute-nefs and value of the details that are given.

" Your mediterranean ifle* is then the only gallery, wherein the piƈtures of all your true fafhionate and complemental Gulls are and ought to be hung up. Into that gallery carry your neat body ; but take heed you pick out fuch an hour, when the main fhoal of iflanders are fwimming up and down. . . .

" Be circumfpeƈt, and wary what pillar you come in at ; and take heed in any cafe, as you love the reputa-tion of your honour, that you avoid the ferving-man's log, and approach not within five fathom of that pillar : but bend your courfe direƈtly in the middle line, that the whole body of the Church may appear to be yours ; where, in view of all, you may publifh your fuit in what manner you affeƈt moft, either with the flide of your cloak from the one fhoulder; and then you muft, as 'twere in anger, fuddenly fnatch at the middle of the infide, if it be taffeta at the leaft ; and fo by that means your coftly lining is betrayed, or elfe by the pretty advantage of compliment. But one note by the way do I efpecially woo you to, the negleƈt of which makes many of our gallants cheap and ordi-nary, that by no means you be feen above four turns ; but in the fifth make yourfelf away, either in fome of the feamfter's fhops, the new tobacco-office, or amongft the book fellers, where, if you cannot read, exercife

---

* The middle aifle (as people incorreƈtly call it) of the Nave.

your fmoke, and enquire who has writ againft this divine weed. For this withdrawing yourfelf a little will much benefit your fuit, which elfe, by too long walking, would be ftale to the whole fpectators; but howfoever, if Paul's Jacks* be once up with their elbows, and quarrelling to ftrike eleven, as foon as ever the clock has parted them and ended the fray with his hammer, let not the Duke's gallery† contain you any longer, but pafs away apace in open view. In which departure, if by chance you either encounter, or aloof off throw your inquifitive eye upon any knight or fquire, being your familiar, falute him not by his name of Sir fuch a one, or fo; but call him Ned, or Jack, &c. This will fet off your eftimation with great men. And if, though there be a dozen companies between you, 'tis the better, he call aloud to you, for that is moft genteel, to know where he fhall find you at two o'clock; tell him at fuch an Ordinary, or fuch : and be fure to name thofe that are deareft, and whither none but your gallants refort. After dinner you may appear again, having tranflated yourfelf out of your Englifh cloth cloak into a light Turkey grogram, if you have that happinefs of fhifting. And then be feen, for a turn or two, to correct your teeth with fome quill or filver inftrument, and to cleanfe your gums with a wrought handkerchief : it fkills not whether you dined or no, that is beft known to your ftomach ; or in what place you dined, though it were with cheefe of your own mother's making, in your chamber or ftudy.

" Now if you chance to be a gallant not much croffed

* Figures ftriking the hours.
† An allufion to Duke Humfrey.

among citizens; that is, a gallant in the mercer's books, exalted for ſatins and velvets; if you be not ſo much bleſſt to be croſſed; (as I hold it the greateſt bleſſing in the world to be great in no man's books) your Paul's Walk is your only refuge; the Duke's tomb is a ſanctuary, and will keep you alive' from worms, and land rats that long to be feeding on your carcaſe. There you may ſpend your legs in winter a whole afternoon; converſe, plot, laugh, and talk anything: jeſt at your creditor, even to his face, and in the evening, even by lamplight, ſteal out, and ſo cozen a whole covey of abominable catchpoles. Never be ſeen to mount the ſteps into the Choir but upon a high feſtival day, to prefer the faſhion of your doublet: and eſpecially if the ſinging-boys ſeem to take note of you, for they are able to buzz your praiſes above their anthems, if their voices have not loſt their [freſhneſs]. But be ſure your ſilver ſpurs dog your heels, and then the boys will ſwarm about you like ſo many white butterflies; when you in the open choir ſhall draw forth a perfumed embroidered purſe, the glorious ſight of which will entice many countrymen from their devotion to wondering, and quoit ſilver into the boys' hands that it may be heard above the firſt leſſon, although it be read in a voice as big as one of the great organs.

"This noble and notable act being performed, you are to vaniſh preſently out of the Choir and to appear again in the Walk. But in any wiſe be not obſerved to tread there long alone, for fear you be ſuſpected to be a gallant caſhiered from the ſociety of captains and fighters. . . .

" All the difeafed horfes in a tedious fiege cannot fhow fo many fafhions as are to be feen for nothing every day in Duke Humphrey's Walk. If, therefore, you determine to enter into a new fuit, warn your tailor to attend you in Paul's, who, with his hat in his hand, fhall like a fpy difcover the ftuff, colour, and fafhion of any doublet or hofe that dare be feen there : and, ftepping behind a pillar to fill his table-books with thofe notes, will prefently fend you into the world an accomplifhed man : by which means you fhall wear your clothes in print with the firft edition. But if fortune favour you fo much as to make you no more than a mere country gentleman, or but fome degrees removed from him, (for which I fhould be very forry, becaufe your London experience will coft you dear before you fhall have the wit to know what you are) then take this leffon along with you : the firft time that you venture into Paul's, pafs through the body of the Church like a porter, yet prefume not to fetch fo much as one whole turn in the middle ifle, no nor to caft an eye to *Si quis* door, pafted and plaftered up with ferving-men's fupplications, before you have paid tribute to the top of Paul's Steeple with a fingle penny. . . . Before you come down again. I would defire you to draw your knife, and grave your name, or, for want of a name, the mark which you clap on your fheep, in great characters upon the leads, by a number of your brethren, both citizens and country gentlemen. And fo you fhall be fure to have your name lie in a coffin of lead, when yourfelf fhall be wrapped in a winding-fheet ; and, indeed, the top of Paul's contains more names than Stow's *Chronicle.*

"These lofty tricks being played, and you, thanks to your feet, being fafely arrived at the ftairs' foot again, your next worthy work, is to repair to my lord Chancellor's tomb ;* and, if you can but reafonably fpell, beftow fome time upon the reading of Sir Philip Sidney's brief epitaph.† In the compafs of an hour you may make fhift to ftumble it out. The great dial is your laft monument : there beftow fome half of the threefcore minutes to obferve the faucinefs of the Jacks that are above the man in the moon there ; the ftrangenefs of the motion will quit your labour. Befides, you may here have fit occafion to difcover your watch, by taking it forth, and fetting the wheels to the time of Paul's ; which, I affure you, goes truer by five notes than S. Sepulchre's chimes. The benefit that will arife from hence is this, that you publifh your charge in maintaining a gilded clock, and withal the world fhall know that you are a time-pleafer. By this, I imagine, you have walked your bellyful : and thereupon being weary, or, which rather I believe, being moft gentlemanlike hungry, it is fit that I brought you into the Duke ; fo becaufe he follows the

* The huge monument to Sir Chriftopher Hatton, K.G., Lord Chancellor.

† The epitaph as given by Dugdale (p. 72) comprifes only eight lines of Englifh verfe :

"England, Netherlands, the Heavens and the Arts,
  The Souldiers and the World, have made fix parts
    Of noble Sidney ; for none will fuppofe
    That a fmall heape of ftones can Sidney enclofe.
  His Bodie hath England, for fhe it bred,
  Netherlands his Blood in her defence fhed,
    The Heavens have his Soule, the Arts have his Fame,
    All Souldiers the grief, the World his good Name."

faſhion of great men, in keeping no houſe, and that therefore you muſt go ſeek your dinner; ſuffer me to take you by the hand and lead you into an Ordinary."

The quotation is of great length; but the light which it caſts upon Paul's Walk juſtifies its introduction here. It might be thought that as Decker, its author, was a playwright, he has given us more of fancy and imagination than of real hiſtory. But the previous extracts from official documents, ſuch as preſentments at an epiſcopal viſitation; the paſſages from private letters; the unbiaſſed evidence of Biſhop Corbet, and, indeed, the concurring teſtimony of contemporary literature—all tend to ſhow that the picture is not overdrawn. Paul's Walk was, as was ſaid at the beginning of this chapter, the Fop's Alley of the day: and the noiſe and buſy profanity of the Nave even ſurged in upon Divine Service in the Choir.

Biſhop Hall has much to ſay about *Si Quis* Door :*

" Saw'ſt thou euer *Siquis* patch'd on Paul's Church Dore,
   To ſeek ſome vacant Vicarage before ?
   Who wants a Churchman that can ſeruice ſay,
   Read faſt and faire his monthly Homiley ?
   And wed, and bury, and make Chriſten-ſoules ?
   Come to the left-ſide Alley of Saint Poules.
   Thou ſeruile Foole : why could'ſt thou not repaire
   To buy a Benefice at Steeple-Faire ?
   There moughteſt thou for but a ſlender price
   Aduowſon thee with ſome fat benefice :
   Or if thee liſt not wayt for dead mens' ſhoon,
   Nor pray ech morn th' Incumbents days wer done :
   A thouſand Patrons thither ready bring
   Their new-falne Churches to the Chaffering ;

---

* *Virgidemiarum*, 12mo., London, 1597, Lib. ii. Sat. 7, quoted in Dugdale, p. 107.

> Stake three yeares Stipend ; no man aſketh more :
> Go, take poſſeſſion of the Church-Porch-doore,
> And ring thy bels : lucke-ſtroken in thy fiſt :
> The Parſonage is thine, or ere thou wiſt.
> Saint Fooles of Gotam mought thy pariſh bee,
> For this thy baſe and feruile Symonie."

It would appear that even ſo late as 1711, when
Pope publiſhed his *Eſſay on Criticiſm* there was ſtill
great room for amendment.   For he ſays :

> " No place ſo ſacred from ſuch fops is barr'd,
>   Nor is Paul's Church more ſafe than Paul's Churchyard :
>   Nay, fly to altars ; there they'll talk you dead ;
>   For fools ruſh in where angels fear to tread."*

Even in 1724 when Biſhop Gibſon viſited the
Cathedral, he records that " There hath grown an evil
cuſtom of great numbers of perſons walking and talking in the body of the Cathedral Church during the
time of Divine Service in the Choir, and more eſpecially on the Lord's Day, to the great diſturbance of
the ſaid Service, and the profanation of the houſe of
God, and the offence of many ſerious and good
Chriſtians."   And he enjoins the Dean and Reſidentiaries " to prevent the ſame for the future," and if
neceſſary, to put in action the ſtatute made in the firſt
year of William and Mary, *cap.* 18, againſt any who
" willingly and of purpoſe maliciouſly and contemptu-
ouſly come into any Cathedral or Pariſh Church, and
diſquiet or diſturb the ſame."†   It is to be ſuppoſed
that the vigorous courſe of action recommended by
the Bishop produced its natural effect.

* *Eſſay*, vv. 623-626.   † *Statuta*, p. 311.

S. PAUL'S DURING THE INTERREGNUM.

CHAPTER XIV.

THE firſt edition of Sir William Dugdale's *Hiſtory of S. Paul's Cathedral* was iſſued in 1658 ; "making therefore its period," as its author ſays in the preface to the ſecond edition (printed in 1716), "with the commencement of the late wicked Rebellion raiſed by the Sectaries and their Adherents." He, naturally enough, does not enlarge very much upon the fortunes of the Cathedral during the times of the Interregnum. If he ſays but little, however, that little is worthy of attention. We are able, from other ſources, from Documents preſerved at the Record Office and elſewhere, to add ſome details of conſiderable intereſt to thoſe who, having ſeen the Cathedral in its ſplendour, can bear to look upon it in its humiliation.

Charles I. ſuffered on Tueſday, 30th January, 1648-9, and Oliver Cromwell was not proclaimed Protector till 16th December, 1653. Long before the death of the King the troubles began.

From time to time there were ſerious diſturbances cauſed by the unruly ſoldiery. In a letter ſent from London by one Andrew Newport to Sir Richard Leveſon,* 28th January, 1639-40, the writer ſays that "a troop of horſe and a company of foot laſt night broke open the houſe of a draper in Paul's Church-yard, and carried away £4000 to Whitehall, for which they would ſhow the draper (a Common Councilman) no order. To-day the man was attending at the Parliament door, but what ſatiſfaction he hath I do not yet hear." Drapers, at that time, had their head-quarters in Paternoſter Row : "this ſtreet, before the Fire of London, was taken up by eminent mercers, ſilkmen, and lacemen."† Pepys has recorded, amongſt other matters of equal importance, that on 17th May, 1662, he and his wife, with Lady Sandwich, went "on foot to Paternoſter Row, to buy a petticoat againſt the Queen's coming, for my lady, of plain ſatin."

Sectaries and fanatics propounded their opinions in public places. Amongſt the Acts of the Court of High Commiſſion in the year 1640 is an entry relating to one James Hunt, of Sevenoaks, Kent. "The Court being informed that Hunt was a fanatic and frantic perſon, a huſbandman, and altogether illiterate, who took upon him to preach and expound the Scriptures, and was lately taken abſurdly preaching on a ſtone in S. Paul's Churchyard, ordered him to be committed to Bridewell and remain there till further orders."‡

* Duke of Sutherland's MSS., *Hiſtorical MSS. Commiſſion,* vol. v. p. 132, *a.*

† Strype's *Stow,* Book iii. p. 195.

‡ *Calendar of State Papers, Domeſtic,* 1640 p. 415.

In November of the fame year, John Rous, Incumbent of Santon Downham, Suffolk, writes : " In Paules Church lately, a great tumult againſt Dočtor Ducke and others in the High Commiſſion within the Conſiſtory ; who eſcaping, much outrage was ſhewed in the Conſiſtorie to the feates, &c. The Biſhops, guarded with muſket-men, came to the Convocation-houſe."* This is, in all probability, a brief notice of the ſerious riot more fully recorded by Collier† under the date 21ſt Očtober, 1640. " When the High Commiſſion fat at S. Paul's, about two thouſand Browniſts inſulted the Court, pulled down all the benches in the Conſiſtory, and cried out they would have no Biſhops and no High Commiſſion. Thus the king, by this tumult, was put to the expenſe of ordering a guard for S. Paul's, as he had done before at Weſtminſter, for the protečtion of the Convocation. On the 3rd of November, the Long Parliament, which proved ſo fatal to the King, met at Weſtminſter."

Preachers thought it neceſſary to allude to the troubles of the times in their public ſermons. " Upon Tueſday, Nov. 17," ſtill in the year 1640, " when the faſt was kept at London for the Parliament, &c., I was at S. Paul's Church," ſays John Rous‡ " where one Mr. Stanwicke (or Kanwicke), a Chaplain to my lord of Ely, preached on Nehemiah i. verſe 4, who, upon juſt occaſion, in opening the ſtory of the Jewiſh preſſures and calamities which cauſed Nehemiah to faſt,

---

* *Diary of John Rous* (Camden Society), p. 99.
† *Eccleſiaſtical Hiſtory of Great Britain*, vol. viii. p. 184.
‡ *Diary of John Rous*, p. 103.

&c., did ſay that the care of the Jews to have Jeru-
ſalem rebuilded in her walls and the gates ſet up, *was
not to mainteine rebellion and keepe out the King's
authority*, but to defend themſelves againſt Tobiah,
Sanballah, and ſuch great men as under the King
(whom they flattered with lies) ſought to oppreſſe
them." Vigorous preaching that! and going ſtraight
to the mark.

In 1642 "a deſign was now forming in the Parliament for lopping the revenues of the Church, and
ſuppreſſing the Deaneries and Chapters." Dr. John
Hacket, prebendary of S. Paul's and archdeacon of
Bedford, was ſelected by the Clergy to plead their
cauſe before the Houſe of Commons. The heads of
his ſpeech may be read in Collier.* He commenced
with a brief apology; he was ſtraitened in time—
the buſineſs had been put upon him only the afternoon before—the objections to be offered againſt the
Cathedral bodies had not been ſubmitted to him. He
defended the public prayers of the Church, and ſhowed
the benefit of preaching in Cathedrals, on weekdays
as well as on Sundays—which indeed had been the
cuſtom ever ſince the Reformation, in accordance with
the Statutes of theſe mother Churches. Each Cathedral was a ſort of univerſity in little and a ſchool of
learning; he offered to produce, in proof, a liſt of
learned dignitaries; the very thought of the ſuppreſſion of Cathedrals had "ſtruck a damp into the book-
ſellers' buſineſs." The buildings themſelves were the

---

* *Eccleſiaſtical Hiſtory of Great Britain*, viii. p. 207.

moſt ancient monuments of Chriſtianity in the country. Many thouſands of perſons depended on theſe grand inſtitutions for their ſuſtenance. The Deans and Canons had been liberal landlords—the tenants affirmed this with conſentient voice. The Engliſh laity lived in plenty, why ſhould the clergy be made, like Jeroboam's prieſts, the "loweſt of the people ?" The Papiſts would be delighted by the overthrow. And, above all, he warned his audience againſt the ſin of ſpoliation—" Thou that abhorreſt idols, doſt thou commit ſacrilege ?" Withdraw the encouragements of learning, and ignorance would reign : ignorance would carry us to profaneneſs and confuſion.

The ſpeech was eloquent and forcible, and " handſomely delivered," and had the queſtion been immediately put to the vote, it was thought that the Clergy would have had a majority of one hundred and twenty. In the afternoon, Dr. Cornelius Burges pleaded the cauſe of the Puritan party, and delivered a violent invective againſt the Deans and Chapters. If his ſpeech is rightly reported, he would have caſt out the clergy but retained the endowments. Dr. Burges' ſervices were not forgotten ; in due time he ſwept into his purſe ſome of the money which was confiſcated.

Biſhop after Biſhop was impeached. It was ſeriouſly propoſed, though it muſt be added that the bill was thrown out, " that every biſhop, being in his dioceſe, and not diſabled by ill health, ſhould preach every Sunday, or pay five pounds to the poor, to be levied by the next juftice of peace, and diftrefs made by the conftable."* So that the conftable and the juftice would have been the bifhop's metropolitans. Archbifhop Williams, of York, is credited with this abfurdity.

On September 10th and 11th, 1642, a bill was paffed for the abolition of Bifhops, Deans, and Chapters:† and its effect was foon felt at S. Paul's. A letter from Stephen ·Charlton to Sir Richard Levefon,‡ 25th October, 1642, fpeaks of an "Order by Parliament yefterday that Paul's fhall be kept fhut, and that all trades fhall fhut up their fhops for a fmall time, and all prifoners that are in Tower or Gate Houfe fhall be kept clofe prifoners."

A few days later, 1ft November, 1642, the Dean and Chapter petition the Houfe of Lords upon the fubject.§ "The Lord Mayor, alleging an Order in that behalf from their Lordfhips, has fhut up the doors of the Church and taken the keys into his cuftody ; by which many well-affected perfons cannot enjoy the frequent ufe of prayer, and fome cannot bury their deceafed friends by their anceftors as they defire. They pray that the Church may be again opened for thefe purpofes."

Even fo late as 1660 the relations between the Cathedral and the City appear to have been of by no

---

* Collier, viii. p. 214.

† Dugdale, *S. Paul's*, p. 109.

‡ Duke of Sutherland's MSS., *Hiftorical MSS. Commiffion*, v. p. 161, *a.*

§ Houfe of Lords' Calendar, *ibid.*, v. p. 56, *a.*

means a too friendly character. Mr. Edward Gower writing to Sir R. Levefon fays (the date of the letter is, probably, November 22nd), "This Lord Mayor of London is troublefome to the Clergy of the old ftamp. The Bifhop fent to him that the Church might be fitted decently, and he would provide minifters to preach there. His anfwer was, that he would make no provifion for any of the finging-men, and when he faw the names of thofe he [the Bifhop of London] intended for Preachers, if he liked them they fhould have admittance."* The Bifhop was Gilbert Sheldon, who had been elected to the fee of London 23rd October, and confecrated at Weftminfter on the 28th of the fame month: and who on the death of Archbifhop Juxon was tranflated to Canterbury. The Lord Mayor was Sir Thomas Alleyne. His claim to revife the lift of preachers appointed by the Bifhop feems fufficiently prepofterous.

The high-handed dealing of Parliament with the Cathedrals foon made itfelf felt in the infliction of great fuffering and diftrefs upon the Clergy and upon the Officers attached to thefe time-honoured fanctuaries. On Auguft 9th, 1644, a Petition was prefented to the Lords and Commons by the Minor Canons, Vicars Choral, and other officers of S. Paul's. It ftates that the Petitioners "having fpent their days in the performance of the duties and offices of the Church, are unfit for other ways of procuring their livelihood, and, the rents and revenues of the Church

* Duke of Sutherland's MSS., *Hiftorical MSS. Commiffion,* v. p. 200, *b.*

being ſequeſtered, they are likely to be utterly im-
poveriſhed." They pray " that they may enjoy during
their lives all the rents and dues which they formerly
had from the Dean and Chapter." The Petition was
referred to the Committee for Sequeſtrations.*

On April 26th, 1645, the workmen lately employed
upon the repairs of S. Paul's ſend in *their* Petition.
Divers ſums of money are due to them; they are
ready to periſh for want. They pray that ſome
ſcaffolding ſtuff and other materials belonging to the
Church, "which, as the work goes not forward, will
decay and be loſt, may be ſold for their benefit."† The
workmen, naturally enough, were not ſlow to learn
the leſſons of confiſcation and of ſacrilege.

At the end of the *Interregnum* only one Minor
Canon, fully admitted as a Member of that ancient
College, could be found; two others had been admitted as Probationers. When Dean Barwick under-
took the " difficult charge " of the Deancry, his firſt
care was " what it had alſo been at Durham, to reſtore
the Celebration of Divine Service by the ſacred Muſic
of a Choir." One minor Canon only remained at S.
Paul's; and he, it would ſeem, muſt have been intruded
into the office during Puritan times, for there was no
evidence that he had ever been admitted into Prieſts'
Orders, "which, yet by the Statutes, all the Canons of
this Church were obliged to be." He proved to be a
worthy diſciple of Dr. Burges, for he laid claim to the

* Houſe of Lords' Calendar, *Hiſtorical MSS. Commiſſion*, vi.
p. 22, *a.*
† *Ibid.*, vi. p. 56, *a.*

whole revenues of the College of the Minor Canons, and had bought at a nominal rate, during the Troubles, fome of the fequeftered property of the College for his own ufe.*

The trials and miffortunes of the Cathedral Clergy are briefly related by John Walker in his *Sufferings of the Clergy* :† the phrafes which he ufes in defcribing the hardfhips endured by Bryan Walton, Prebendary of Twyford, " affaulted, fequeftered from his living, Plundered, Forced to fly, Barbaroufly ufed, grievoufly Harraffed," will apply to many more.   Walton was one of the moft learned men of the day.‡   The Cathedral Library poffeffes a magnificent *Large Paper* copy of his *Polyglot Bible*, moft fumptuoufly bound, a worthy monument of his labours.   But learning was out of fafhion.   The greedy Cornelius Burges found favour, and Bryan Walton was ejeɛted from S. Paul's.

On May 10th, 1645, Parliament paffed an Ordinance§ enabling the Lord Mayor and the Court of Aldermen to feize and fequefter into their hands all the Houfes, Rents, and Revenues, of the Dean, Canons, and other officers of S. Paul's Cathedral.   Dr. Burges alfo receives his reward : the houfe in which the Dean had lived, the old Deanery, is affigned to him as a refidence ; he is appointed " publike Leɛturer in the Church of Paul's, London " (it is *Saint* Paul's no longer); and " for his incouragement therein " there is

---

* *Life of Dean Barwick*, 8vo., London, 1724, pp. 311-316.
† Folio, London, 1714, pp. 47-54.
‡ After the Reftoration he was made Bifhop of Chefter.
§ Dugdale, pp. 415-417.

granted to him the ſum of £400 per annum. Very good pickings, Dr. Burges! You were wiſe in ſuggeſting that the endowments ſhould not be alienated : wiſe, that is, in your generation. Profeſſor Brewer, in his notes to quaint old Fuller,* aims at you a ſhaft which pierces through your harneſs, when he ſays that you were "A railer againſt biſhops, afterwards a purchaſer of biſhop's lands." He was, in faĉt, ſo large a purchaſer of theſe lands that, a little before the Reſtoration, he was offered and declined to take £20,000 for what he had acquired. (What a convenient word "acquired" is!) After the Reſtoration he was compelled to diſgorge his plunder ; he was reduced, he ſays, to want a piece of bread. He died in obſcurity in 1665, the anguiſh of his diſtreſs augmented by a terrible diſeaſe. Dr. Hacket's warnings were not in vain.

On March 13th, 1640, three noble Lords were in a boat upon the Thames ; Robert Greville, Lord Brooke, was in their company ; they were on their way to dine with Lord Herbert at his new houſe at Fox Hall. As they were paſſing S. Paul's, the converſation naturally turned upon the commitment of Laud. One of the company ſaid, that he was ſorry for it, "becauſe the building of S. Paul's went ſlow on therewhile." Lord Brooke replied, "I hope ſome of us ſhall live to ſee no one ſtone left upon another of that building." A note of the occurrence is found in Laud's *Diary.* Two years afterwards, on March 2nd, 1642, Laud opens his Diary again, and this is his entry : " Thurſday, S. Cedd's day. The Lord Brooke

* *Church Hiſtory,* vi. pp. 188, 203, notes.

• ſhot in the left eye, and killed in the place, at Lichfield, going to give the onſet upon the Cloſe of the
Church, he having ever been fierce againſt Biſhops
and Cathedrals: his beaver up, and armed to the
knees, ſo that a muſket at that diſtance could have done
him but little harm. Thus was his eye put out, who
about two years ſince ſaid, he hoped to live to ſee at
S. Paul's not one ſtone left upon another."* The com-
ment is Archbiſhop Laud's. The eloquent Dr. South
makes very forcible uſe of the incident, and adds ſome
details. He ſpeaks "of a commander in the parliament's rebel army, who, coming to rifle and deface the
Cathedral at Lichfield, ſolemnly at the head of his
troops begged of God to ſhow ſome remarkable token
of His approbation or diſlike of the work they were
going about. Immediately after which, looking out
at a window, he was ſhot in the forehead by a deaf
and dumb man. And this was on S. Chad's day, the
name of which Saint that Church bore, being dedicated to God in memory of the ſame. Where we ſee,
that as he aſked of God a ſign, ſo God gave him one,
ſigning him in the forehead, and that with ſuch a mark
as he is like to be known by to all poſterity. There
is nothing that the united voice of all hiſtory pro-
claims ſo loud as the certain unfailing curſe that has
purſued and overtook ſacrilege."†

The Houſe of Commons was by no means inatten-
tive to S. Paul's Cathedral. On January 2nd, 1642-3,

* *The Diary of the Life of Archbiſhop Laud*, Works, iii. pp.
241, 249.
† South, *Sermons*, edit., London 1859, i. p. 55.

they refolve "that my Lord Petre's Houfe in Alderf- •
gate Street, and the Dean of Paules his Houfe near
Paules, fhall be appointed Prifons to receive the
Prifoners that are coming from Chichefter, and,"
(ominous addition !) "fuch other prifoners as the
Houfes fhall appoint: and that Mr. White be ap-
pointed Keeper of my Lord Peter's Houfe, and Mr.
Dillingham, Keeper of the Dean of Paules his Houfe."
The Deanery, in which fuch men as Colet, Nowell,
Overall, and Donne, had lived is turned into a Prifon.

In the Journal of the Houfe of Lords, 5th January,
1642-3, are three draft Orders directing that Lord
Petre's houfe in Alderfgate, and the Bifhop of
London's Palace near S. Paul's, and "Lambeth
Houfe," fhould be ufed as Prifons. Two days later
we find in the records of the Houfe of Lords a *Lift of
the Prifoners in Lambeth Houfe.**

What remained of the treafures of the Cathedral
alfo engages the very earneft attention of the Houfe.
They refolve on April 17th, 1644, "that the Cheft, or
Silver Veffel, in Paul's, fhall be fold for the beft advantage, and employed towards the providing of necef-
faries for the Train of Artillery, by the Committee at
Grocers Hall." Seven days later, it is ordered, "that
the materials informed of by Sir Robert Harley, be
forthwith fold by Sir Robert Harley, viz., the Mitre
and Crozier-ftaff found in Paul's Church London ;
and the brafs and iron in Hen. VII. Chapel in Weftminfter ; and the proceed thereof (the neceffary charges

* Houfe of Lords' Calendar, *Hiftorical MSS. Commiffion,*
v. p. 67, a.

deducted) be employed according to the direction of this Houfe."*

Were any of thefe treafures ever reftored ? One or two, "rari nantes in gurgite vafto," found their way back. The Calendars of State Papers (Chas. II., vol. 109) preferve a Report by one Mr. Garret in 1664, "that Carey, late Verger of S. Paul's fays that Alderman Pack of Blackwell Hall, or Mr. Jermyn the City Carpenter in Little Moorfields, can difcover the Will of Hen. VII. with feals affixed in filver boxes ; alfo a Chalice, Crofier-Staff and other things formerly belonging to S. Paul's, in which Warner a verger may affift." The (so called) Will of Henry VII., fumptuoufly bound in velvet, with boffes glowing with enamel, is now in the Cathedral Library : but the Chalice, and the Crofier-Staff, where are they ?

The floodgates were opened and the waters rapidly fpread. All repairs at the Cathedral ceafed. It had been the defire of Laud's heart to fee it reftored to its priftine grandeur. Amongft the " Things which I have projected to do, if God blefs me in them," the Archbifhop writes, fifth in order, "to fet upon the repair of S. Paul's Church in London." All kinds of encroachments had been allowed about the Cathedral. A temporary houfe had been built up againft the Weft end of it for the purpofes of a lottery : and after the lottery ended, was "finifhed up into a dwelling houfe to the great annoyance of that church ; the Bifhops, and Dean, and Chapter being afleep while it was done." Laud boldly and refolutely charges them with

* Dugdale, p. 110.

their ſupineneſs, and with increaſing their rents by a
ſacrilegious revenue.   His own love for the Cathedral
ſhowed itſelf not merely in words but in liberal gifts.
He was able to ſay at his trial, that his perſonal outlay
upon S. Paul's had coſt him "above one thouſand and
two hundred pounds" out of his own purſe.   He remembered the work even in the time of his impriſon-
ment, and left a legacy, "a bleſſing," as he phraſes it,
"of £800," to be truly paid in for that work "if ever
it go on while the party truſted with it lives."*

The works at the Cathedral were ſuſpended.   Some
part of the materials gathered together were given by
Parliament in 1645 to the Pariſhioners of S. Gregory's
to rebuild their Church, which had been pulled down
becauſe it was thought to be an eyeſore to the Cathedral.†   The vaſt ſcaffoldings which had been erected
for the repair of the tower and the adjacent parts,
were aſſigned to Colonel Jephſon's regiment, for
£1746 15s. 8d. due thereunto from the ſaid Parliament, and in arrear.   The *Calendars of State Papers*
ſhow how intereſting were the queſtions which aroſe
about theſe ſame ſcaffoldings.‡   Dugdale ſays that
pits were dug in the Church itſelf, even where the
bones of reverend biſhops lay, as ſawpits to cut up the
great timbers.§   The body of the church was frequently converted into horſequarters for ſoldiers.   Part
of the Choir, the eaſtern part, was ſhut off by a parti-
tion wall, and made into a preaching place for Dr.

---

* *Works of Archbiſhop Laud,* iii. p. 253; iv. pp. 92, 96.
† Dugdale, p. 110.
‡ See *Documents,* liii., liv.   § Dugdale, p. 110.

Burges : an entrance being made to it, through the uppermoft window on the north fide, eaftwards.

On December 18th, 1648, good John Evelyn makes this entry in his *Diary,** " Since my laft, foldiers have marched into the City. . . They have garrifoned Black-friars (which likewife they have fortified with artillery) ; Paul's Church, which with London Houfe they have made ftables for their horfes, making plentiful fires with the feats." It appears from Dugdale that the Choir Stalls and the Organ-loft were about this time totally deftroyed.

The City authorities had negleﬆed to pay their affeffments to the army, wherefore General Fairfax fent Colonel Dean with fome troops into the City, on Friday, December 8th, 1648, to feize the treafures of the Goldfmiths', Haberdafhers', and Weavers' Companies. The two former Companies had removed their wealth, but at the Weavers' a rich booty of £35,000 was feized and carried off. The Lord Mayor was warned that the troops would be quartered upon the citizens till all the arrears were paid. " So for the prefent His Forces Quarter upon the Citizens, keeping ftrong Guards in *London Houfe, Creed Church, Ludgate Church*, and all the *Gates* of the *City :* And that *facred Temple* dedicated to *S. Paul* and heretofore fet apart and kept in all poffible *decency* for the *fervice* and *worfhip* of *God*, they have now converted into a moft filthy *Stable*, and filled it with Hay and Horfes, &c., fo that of a *Houfe of Prayer it is become a Den of Thieves.*" So fays the fecretly printed Royalift paper

* Evelyn, *Diary and Correfpondence*, iii. p. 33, edit. 1863.

the *Mercurius Eleucticus.** A few weeks later,†
a still more suggestive passage occurs: " The Saints in
Pauls were the last weeke teaching their Horses to
ride up the *great Steps*, that lead into the *Quire*, where
(as they derided) they might perhaps learne to *Chaunt*
an *Antheme:* but one of them fell, and broke both his
Leg and the *Neck* of his Rider, which hath spoiled his
Chaunting, for he was buried on *Saturday* night last.
A just *Judgement* of God on such a prophane and
Sacrilegious wretch."   One can hardly wonder at the
writer's strong language: he was contemporary, possibly
an eye-witness, and in such times men are not over-nice
in their phrases.

In the *Rump Songs* are some references to these
profanities.   In a composition, it can hardly be called
a poem, entitled *The Publique Faith*, the writer says:

> " *Paul's* shall be opened then, and you conspire
>   No more against the Organs in the Quire,
>   Nor threat the Saints i' th' Windows, nor repair
>   In Troops to kill the Book of Common Prayer :
>   Nor drunk with Zeal, endeavour to engroffe
>   To your own use, the stones of Cheapside Croffe."

The same volume is eloquent as to the misdeeds of Sir
Isaac Pennington the then Lord Mayor, and contains
the following lampoon :

> " 1643.
>
> *A Bill on St.* Paul's *Church Door.*
>
>   This Houfe is to be let,   .
>   It is both wide, and fair ;
>   If you would know the price of it,
>   Pray afk of Mr Maior.
>
>   *Ifaack Pennington.*"

And a Ballad contained in the fame volume, fays:

> "Then S'· *Paul's* the Mother-Church of this City and Nation,
> Was turn'd to a Stable, O ftrange Profanation!
> Yet this was one of their beft fruits of Reformation,
> Which no body can deny."

The work of defecration continued; the ftately Portico with its beautiful Corinthian pillars—a ftructure fair and exquifitely proportioned, though moft inappropriately annexed to a Norman Nave—was "converted to fhops for feamftreffes and other trades, with lofts and ftairs afcending thereto; for the fitting whereof to that purpofe thofe ftately pillars were fhamefully hewed and defaced for fupport of the timber work."*

There is a ftrange ftory, hardly worth repetition, that Cromwell defired and propofed to fell the ufelefs building to the Jews. D'Bloffiers Tovey, in his *Anglia Judaica*, ftates very plainly that "as foon as *King Charles was murther'd*, the *Jews* Petition'd the *Council of War* to endeavour a Repeal of that Act of Parliament which had been made againft them; promifing, in Return, to make them a prefent of *five hundred thoufand Pounds:* Provided that they cou'd likewife procure the Cathedral of S⸺ *Paul* to be affigned them for a *Synagogue*, and the *Bodleian* Library at *Oxford*, to begin their Traffick with. Which Piece of Service, it feems, was undertaken by thofe *Honeft Men*, at the Solicitation of *Hugh Peters*, and *Harry Marten*, whom the *Jews* employ'd as their Brokers: but without any fuccefs."† Robert Monteith, of Salmonet,‡ adds

---

* Dugdale, p. 115.   † *Anglia Judaica*, pp. 259, 260.
‡ *Hiftory of Great Britain*, folio, London, 1735, p. 473.

fome further details, ſtating that the Jews "offer'd five hundred thouſand Pounds, but the Council of War would have eight." Theſe ſtatements have a very circumſtantial air about them, and the mention of names and figures gives them the look of hiſtory : but a tolerably careful ſearch has failed to diſcover any corroborative evidence. There is, indeed, in the Record Office, a copy of a *Remonſtrance* addreſſed to Charles II., in which the writer ſays, that the Jews "(as countenanced by the ſaid late Uſurper), endeavoured in his time (as frequently it was reported) to buy the famous Cathedral Church of Pauls to have made yᵐ a Synagogue, as alſoe your moſt renowned Court of Whitehall for ſome Imployment."* But the *Remonſtrance* is anonymous, it is undated, and if nothing more can be ſaid for the ſtory than "as frequently it was reported," the fable had better be conſigned to the hiſtorian's waſte-paper baſket. If the Cathedral had ever been offered for ſale, very poſſibly ſome

> "Jews from S. Mary Axe, for jobs ſo wary
> That for old clothes they'd even axe S. Mary,"†

might have been found amongſt the bidders ; but it can hardly be ſaid by the moſt earneſt hater of Cromwell that there is a particle of real evidence in favour of the ſtory.

The ſoldiers lodged in the City were not, as we have already ſeen, always very eaſily managed. Carlyle, in his *Letters and Speeches of Oliver Cromwell* ‡ tells a

---

* See *Documents*, pp. lxiii., lxiv.

† The *Rejeɛted Addreſſes*.

‡ Vol. ii. pp. 121, 122, five volume edition.

chara&cteriftic ftory, and tells it in his own inimitable fafhion. "This night," Thurfday, April 26th, 1649, "at the Bull in Bifhopfgate, there has an alarming mutiny broken out in a troop of Whalley's regiment there. Whalley's men are not allotted for Ireland; but they refufe to quit London, as they are ordered; they want this and that firft: they feize their Colours from the Cornet, who is lodged at the Bull there:—the General and the Lieutenant-General have to haften thither; quell them, pack them forth on their march; feizing fifteen of them firft, to be tried by Court-Martial. Tried by inftant Court-Martial, five of them are found guilty, doomed to die, but pardoned; and one of them, Trooper Lockyer, is doomed and not pardoned. Trooper Lockyer is fhot, in Paul's Churchyard, on the morrow. A very brave young man, they fay; though but three-and-twenty, 'he has ferved feven years in thefe Wars,' ever fince the wars began. 'Religious' too, 'of excellent parts and much beloved;' but with hot notions as to human Freedom, and the rate at which the Milleniums are attainable, poor Lockyer! He falls fhot in Paul's Churchyard on Friday, amid the tears of men and women. Paul's Cathedral, we remark, is now a Horfe-guard; horfes ftamp in the Canons' ftalls there: and Paul's Crofs itfelf, as fmacking of Popery, where in fa&ct Alablafter once preached flat Popery, is fwept altogether away, and its leaden roof melted into bullets, or mixed with tin for culinary pewter. Lockyer's corpfe is watched and wept over, not without prayer, in the caftern regions of the City, till a new week come." His funeral takes place on Monday.

On May 30th, 1649, ſays Evelyn,* "Unkingſhip was proclaimed, and his Majeſty's ſtatues thrown down at S. Paul's Portico and the Exchange."

We ſoon hear again of the ſoldiers quartered in S. Paul's Churchyard, for in May, 1651, a Proclamation was iſſued to regulate their conduct. As it is very brief and at the ſame time inſtructive, it may well be tranſcribed *in extenſo.*

"May 27, 1651.

"For as much as the Inhabitants of Paul's Church-yard are much diſturbed by the ſouldiers and others, calling out to paſſingers, and examining them (though they goe peaceably and civilly along) and by playing at nine pinnes at unſeaſonable houres ; theſe are therefore to command all Souldeirs and others whom it may concerne, that hereafter there ſhall be no examining and calling out to perſons that go peaceably on their way, unleſſe they doe approach their Gaurds, and likewiſe to forbeare playing at nine pinnes and other ſports, from the houre of nine of the clocke in the evening, till ſix in the morning, that ſo perſons that are weake and indiſpoſed to reſt, may not be diſturbed. Given under our hands the day and yeare above written.

"*John Barkeſtead,*
"*Benjamin Blundill.*"

The original of this Proclamation is preſerved in the Britiſh Muſeum.† The reader may obtain from it a

---

* *Diary,* ii. p. 5.   † *Documents,* p. 150.

glimpfe of the liberty which the "Inhabitants of Paul's Churchyard" were at this time enjoying. Turbulent and ill-difciplined foldiers purfued their fports and paftimes under the venerable walls of the Cathedral, and alarmed peaceable citizens by their rude challenges and examinations.

In 1653, on June 18th, the Council of State made an Order, upon the reading of the Petition of Captain Chillendon, "That the Chappell, on the Eaft fide of the North end of Pauls commonly called the Stone Chappell," (the proper name was S. George's Chapel, but S. George was out of fafhion, and England was no longer merry) " be allowed to the congregation whereof Captaine Chillendon is a Member, wherein they are to meet without interruption for the exercifeing of religious duties."* This appropriation, however, of one of the Chapels did not pafs unchallenged. On Sunday, October 16th, a tumult "hapned in Pauls, upon occafion of the meeting of a congregation in the Stone Chappell in the faid Church and their exercifeing there." Colonel Mountagu, Colonel Bennet, and Mr. Broughton, or any two of them, are appointed a Committee to enquire into this matter ; and particularly to examine what was the "Carriage of the Officers of the City," as well as of the congregation and of thofe who made the tumult. The latter were to be committed to the cuftody of my Lord Mayor.†

Dr. Burges being fettled in the eaftern part of the Choir, and Captain Chillendon's congregation being quartered in S. George's Chapel, it might have been thought that the dominant party would have refted

* *Documents*, p. 151. † *Ibid.*, p. 152.

fatiffied. More was, however, to be done. The Council of State met on Thurfday, September 24th, 1657. "His Highnefs" himfelf is prefent, with General "Difbrowe," and others. There is another congregation, "whereof Mr. John Simpfon is Teacher," and thefe have no "local habitation." No place will fuit them but S. Paul's. There is a piece of wafte ground at the Weft end of Paul's now vefted in the Truftees for Bifhops' lands: it is ordered that Colonel Webb, Surveyor-General for the faid Lands, do caufe the faid ground, "or any other place of Pawles fitt" for fuch a ufe, to be "forthwith furveyed, and the Survey thereof to bee returned to the Councell." Colonel Webb fends in a Report on November 12th. He does not recommend the ufe of the wafte ground at the Weft end of Paul's; but "upon perrufall of feverall unoccupied places about Pawles," he has feen the "parcell of grownd whereon yet ftandeth the Ruines of the Howfe commonly called the Convocation howfe, and of The Cloyfters thereto adjoyning." He thinks that this is the "moft privateft and convenienteft place to bee fitted and fet apart to the ufe aforefayd." The Chapter Houfe, fair and beautiful as it once was, had not been rebuilt fince the deftructive fire of 1561. The roof and floor had fallen to the ground, the windows were broken, "the iron and leade imbeziled," the whole building "exceeding ruinous and very dangerous." This is the place for the "Congregation that wallke with Mr. John Symfon." Colonel Webb fupplies a plan of the Cloifters and Chapter Houfe.* The Council of State

---

* *Documents*, pp. 153-155, where a copy of the Plan may be feen.

are of the fame opinion, and a Committee is appointed to fee that the matter be carried to an end.

The Chapter Houfe and the Upper and Lower Cloifters had been allowed to become receptacles for building materials. Boards of elm and deal, wainfcot, fir poles, large quantities of lead and iron, thoufands of quarries of glafs, were ftored here in 1644 :* as an original paper in the Dyce and Forfter Reading Room at the South Kenfington Mufeum, containing an Inventory of thefe materials, abundantly proves.

The words of worthy Thomas Fuller, written probably about the year 1662, fhould be ftudied by all who would underftand the wretched condition to which the once ftately Church of S. Paul had been reduced :

" This is the only Cathedral in Chriftendom dedicated folely to that faint. Great the pillars (little legs will bow under fo big a body), and fmall the windows thereof: darknefs in thofe days being conceived to raife devotion ; befides, it made artificial lights to appear with the more folemnity. It may be called the Mother Church indeed, having one babe in her body, S. Faith's, and another in her arms, S. Gregory's. Surely fuch who repair to divine fervice in S. Faith may there be well minded of their mortality, being living people, furrounded with the antiperiftafis of the dead both above and beneath them. For the prefent I behold S. Paul's Church as one ftruck with the dead palfy on one fide, the eaft part and quoir thereof being quick and alive, well maintained and repaired,

* *Documents*, pp. 142-145.

whilſt the weſt part is ruinous and ready to fall down. Little hopes it will be repaired in its old decays, which is decayed in its new reparations, and being formerly an ornament, is now an eye ſore to the city: not to ſay unto the citizens in general, ſome being offended that it is in ſo bad, and others that it is in no worſe, condition.

. "The repairing of this church was a worthy monument of the piety and charity of Archbiſhop Laud; not only procuring the bounty of others, but expending his own eſtate thereon. We deſpair not but that his majeſty's zeal, in commending this work to their care, will in due time meet with the forward bounty of the citizens. It is no ſin to wiſh, that thoſe who have plundered the cloak and cover of S. Paul's (not left behind *by*, but) violently taken *from* him, might be compelled to make him a new one of their own coſt; at leaſtwiſe to contribute more than ordinary proportions thereunto."* We may echo Dryden's words, when ſpeaking of the diſaſtrous fire of 1666, he ſays:

> "The daring flames peep'd in, and ſaw from far
>   The awful beauties of the ſacred Quire:
> But ſince it was profaned by Civil War,
>   Heaven thought it fit to have it purged by Fire."†

It cannot be denied, however ſad may be the confeſſion, that the appointed guardians of the Cathedral had, long before Cromwell's days, grievouſly neglected

---

* Fuller, *Worthies of England,* vol. ii. pp. 335, 336, edit. 8vo., London, 1840.

† Dryden, *Annus Mirabilis,* verſe 276.

their facred truft. The Manufcript Returns at Bifhop Bancroft's Vifitation in 1598,* ftill preferved in the Cathedral Record Room, are very melancholy reading. The fervices were, in all probability, faid at the appointed times, but the evidences of negleét and careleffnefs are everywhere vifible. The Chorifters fpent their time in talk and in hunting after fpur-money, even in fervice time; "the hallowinge and hootinge above in the fteple is intollorable at dyvers tymes;" people walked about in the upper Choir, where the Communion Table doth ftand, with their hats on their heads, commonly, all the fervice time, no man reproving them; the Organs were fo mifufed in the blowing, and other ways with jogging the bellows, that the bellows were broken; S. Dunftan's Chapel was made a ftorehoufe for glafs, and the glafs was brought in even during fervice time; the wheels of cars fet againft the fteps of the South door had fo broken the fteps "that manye men and women have had fhrewde fawles dyvers tymes;" the fweepings of the church lay in it three and four weeks together till the fmell became "very noyfom;" the bell-ringers admitted perfons into the Organ-loft for money, to the decay of the inftrument, the pipes being many of them under foot, to the hazarding of the people underneath; the choir men came late to prayers, "which caufeth the fervice to continue beyonde his howre, or maketh them vnreverently to knitt yt vp;" they were irreverent in their behaviour, and did "vfe greate vndecencye in

---

° A feleétion from thefe will be found in the *Statuta S. Pauli*, pp. 272-280.

prayer time, as leaninge vpon theyr elbowes, ſleepinge, talkinge, and ſuch lyke to the ſcandale of the Church ;" the Chapels below the ſteps were much unglazed ; in S. George's Chapel lay old ſtones and a ladder; in Long Chapel old fir poles and other old lumber ; vaults under the Church were let to a Carpenter, others to ſtationers ; houſes and ſhops blocked up the windows of ſome of the Chapels; the Shrouds, and Cloiſters under the Convocation Houſe were let out to Trunk Makers, and "by meanes of their daily knocking and noyſe the Church is greatly diſturbed ;" certain Tenants had excavated the very buttreſſes of the Church " whereby the foundation is greatly indaungered by making of cellers." It is a long and weariſome indictment : long as it is, it might eaſily be extended. Would that it were not ſo.   But let the reader ponder well the following notices of Saliſbury, Worceſter, and Canterbury.

In *A Remembrance for the Church of Sarum in very many and neceſſary particulars* appended to the papers relating to Archbiſhop Laud's Viſitation, is a very ſad picture of the negligent attendance at the Cathedral Services which had grown up, apparently unchecked :

"Of 760 canonicall howers *per ann:*, they are not 60 in the Church ; of theſe 60, not 30 at ſecond leſſon ; of theſe 30, not 10 at the confeſſion, no not at communions. For this, though wee have expreſſe ſtatute agaynſt it, and pænaltye, yett wee plead cuſtome, and challenge and receyve commons. According to this neglect, our quyre and church ſeruice is vtterly deſtitute and naked of all cathedral ornaments, I might fay robbed, for about 40 yeares agone, they were folde and fowly."

What wonder if the laity cared little for the Cathedral Services, if the Clergy at Salifbury were fo remifs in attending, and fo flovenly and idle when they did attend.   No marvel that a day of fharp retribution came.   Laud did what man could do to revive the dying embers of religion.*

Dr. Chriftopher Potter, writing to Archbifhop Laud, 18th November, 1639, thus defcribes the condition of affairs at Worcefter :

"On Sunday mornings, before Sermon, during the Choral Service, fome walked and talked in the Nave, others gathered their auditors about them in the feats and read to them fome Englifh divinity, fo loudly as that the fingers in the Choir were much difturbed by them : all defpifing that fervice."†

In 1634, the like account is fent to Archbifhop Laud from Canterbury :

"Men both of yᵉ better & meaner fort, mechanicks, youths, & prentifes do ordinarily & moft vnreverently walk in our church in yᵉ tyme of devine fervice, & wᵗʰin hearinge of yᵉ fame, wᵗʰ their hattes on their heads.   I haue feene them from my feate (& not feldome) fo walkinge or ftandinge ftill, & lookinge in vpon vs, when we haue byn on our knees, at yᵉ Letany

---

* *Hiftorical MSS. Commiffion, Fourth Report*, p. 131.

† *Calendars, Domeftic*, 1639-40, p. 106, edited by Mr. W. D. Hamilton.

& yᵉ comandmᵗˢ. I earneftly & humbly defire fome
effectuall courfe may [be] taken for redreffe. As alfo
for yᵉ ordinarie trudginge vp & downe of youths, &
clamours of children, to yᵉ greate difturbance of yᵉ
preachers in their fermons. The vergerers & other
officers haue had a charge to look to this; but to
little or no purpofe. Dʳ. Barfton, Dʳ. Hinchman, &
myfelf haue byn fayne to ryfe, & goe out of our feates
to fee & ftay yᵉ diforders. But I never (to my vtter-
moft remembrance) fawe Barfoot yᵉ vergerer (who fits
in my fight) to ryfe at yᵉ greateft noyfe.

" By mee, JOHN LEE."*

Alas, we need not end even here. Many another
grand Cathedral had the fame fad tale to tell : the
fame wearifome ftory of pluralities and non-refidence ;
of overwhelming greedinefs and felf-feeking ; of rampant nepotifm ; of defecrated Naves, and of deferted
Choirs ; of dignitaries receiving great revenues, and
rendering no fervice in return ; of cold hearts. The
way was paved for ftill greater defecrations, and they
came. Horfes neighed in the Canons' Stalls : and
Dr. Cornelius Burges, with his twenty thoufand pounds
of plunder, preached in the ruined Choir.

We may not conclude with words of fadnefs. Nor
is there need. The renewed life of Cathedrals is one
of the moft ftriking features of the great Religious

* *Houfe of Lords' Calendar, Hiftorical MSS. Commiffion,*
vol. iv. p. 135 b.

Revival of our day. S. Paul's has abundantly fhared in that regeneration. Let the largely attended daily fervices, the crowded Sunday fervices, the daily celebration of the Holy Euchariſt, be witneſſes of the throbbing life that beats in the great heart of the old Sanctuary. And let the reverent thouſands gathered in its vaſt dome area, its long-drawn Nave, its ſpacious Tranſepts, filling every part, ſilent, liſtening eagerly laſt Dedication Feſtival to the grand muſic of Mendelſſohn's *S. Paul*, remind us that the Cathedral is ſomething more than a " petrifaction of religion."

May GOD profper its work a thoufand fold !

NOTES.

Note to Page 21.

The original words of the *sequence* here rendered into Englifh, are thefe :

> Erkenwalde, Chrifti lampas aurea,
> Tua fancta prece noftra dele facinora,
> Quatenus te collodantes ftellata
> Gratulari tecum pofcimus in palacia,
> Ubi nova Domino reboantes cantica
> Confona voce jubilemus Alleluja.

Note to page 116.

In a Report by Inigo Jones upon the repairs of S. Gregory's Church, which adjoined S. Paul's, he fays that the Church is "in no way hurtful to the foundation or walls of S. Paul's, nor will it take away the beauty of the afpect when it fhall be repaired. It abuts on the Lollards' Tower, which is anfwered on the other fide by another Tower unto which the Bifhop's Hall adjoins. Conceives that neither of them is any hindrance to the beauty of the Church." The Report is dated 14th June, 1631. (*Calendar of State Papers*, vol. 193.) This paffage would feem to indicate that Inigo Jones would not be likely to make any great alterations in the Towers.

Note to page 142.

By Mr. Chappell's kind permiffion, I am able to prefent to my readers the tune called *Paul's Steeple* in modern notation. It is here reprinted from his moft interefting work, *Popular Mufic of the Olden Times*, vol. i. p. 120. The Irifh *Cruifkeen Lawn*, and the Scotch *John Anderfon my Jo*, are modifications of this ancient Englifh tune.

PAUL'S STEEPLE.

W. CHAPPELL, *Popular Music of the Olden Times*, vol. i. p. 120.

In a fcarce book called *The Dancing Mafter*, "printed for John Playford at his fhop in the Inner Temple, near the Church Door," in 1652, we find that the tune *Paul's Steeple* was ufed as a Country Dance Tune. The figures of the Dance are here given :*

Paul's Steeple.   *Longwayes for as many as will.*

Lead up all a D. forward and back, fet and turn S. . That again :
Firft man take his Wo. in his left hand, lead her down to the 2. Wo. take the 2. Wo. in his right, and flip up with them into the firft place, caft off the 2. Wo. and then his own, and turn off into his place . This forward to all the We. :
Sides all and turn S. . That again :
Firft man take his Wo. in his left hand, lead her down to the 2. Wo. take the 2. Wo. in his right hand, and flide up with them, kiffe the 2. Wo. hand then with your own Wo. hand and let them go, turning off into your place . This forward to the reft :
Arms, fet and turn S. . That again :
Firft man take his Wo. in his left hand, lead her down to the 2. Wo. take the 2. Wo. in your right hand, and fetting them back to back in the middle, kiffe the 2. then your own Wo. turning off into your places, this forward to the reft.

Note to page 145.

No mention has been made in the text of a Fire in the Cathedral which threatened to affume fomewhat dangerous proportions. It occurred on 27th February, 1698-99, according to a rare (if not unique) *Broadfide*, preferved in the Library of Lambeth Palace, and printed in my *Documents etc.*, pp. 158-60. The continuator of *Stow* gives the fame date : and fays, that "a fire broke out at the Weft end of the North ifle of the Choir, in a little room prepared for the Organ-builder to work in when the Choir was newly finifhed ; but, the communication between the faid work-room and organ-gallery being broke down, and all imaginable means ufed, the fire was happily got under, doing no other damage but to two pillars and an arch with enrichments, which are very artificially repaired, and the Church has no fign left of damage by that fire, except that the luftre of the gilding was thereby a little abated."†

* The figns used are explained *infra*, p. 294.
† Strype's *Stow*, vol. i. p. 649.

There is a fomewhat important manufcript in the Library at
Lambeth,* which dates this fire exactly ten years earlier.   The
Book is entitled " An Acco'. of Rebuilding the Cathedral Church
of S'. Paul's, London, from Sept. 1666 (when the Old Church
was deftroyed by the dreadful fire) to 29ᵗʰ Sept'., 1700." I am
not aware that the following details have ever been printed :

"Note, No. 98. That fire happen'd 27 Feb. 168⅞ and fuppofed to be by the careleffnefs of ...† Smith the Organ-maker.

" To the Charge of the repair fpecified may be added the
Scaffolding for it, & the wages to Labourers employ'd about it,
but both thefe being intermixt with other matters, a computation
cannot well be made.

" Repairing yᵉ damage by yᵉ fire, which happen'd at yᵉ Weft
end of yᵉ North Ifle of yᵉ Choir.

Gratuitys to Sevˡˡ. perfons who affifted to extinguifh the fire	11	15	6
Links, Candles, repairing borrowed Buckets, & expences in drink	6	6	8
Wine	2	1	6
	20	3	8
Mafon Rawlin			
For cutting out burnt ftone	19	7	6
New work by day	44	8	9
Dᵒ by agreem' including the Carving	599	6	9
	663	3	0
2 Tuns of Plafter of Paris.	5	7	6
Sundry Carpenters, Mafons, and Labourers	9	14	6
Iron Cramps	12	4	0¼
	27	6	0¼
	710	12	8¼"

It is clear from thefe figures that the damage done by the fire
was by no means inconfiderable. If we are to choofe between
the date given by Bateman's manufcript, and that given by

---

* *Lambeth Manufcripts*, No. 670.
† That is, of Bernard Smith, ufually called Father Smith.

Strype's *Stow* and the *Broadfide* and in Elmes' *Life of Wren*, I incline towards the latter three authorities. They agree in ftating that the fire occurred on 27th February, 1698-99.

Note to page 152.

John Chamberlain, in one of his Letters to Dudley Carleton, gives a fomewhat late example of penance at the Cathedral, under the date 12th February, 1612 :

"Moll Cutpurfe, a notorious beggar, has done penance in S. Paul's." (*Calendar of State Papers*, vol. 68.)

In another letter, to the fame perfon, he fays :

"Some books óf Suarez, the Jefuit, derogatory to Princes, burnt at Paul's Crofs." (*Ibid.*, vol. 75.)

And again, under date 27th July, 1620, he writes :

"Popifh books containing libels on Queen Elizabeth and her government, burnt in S. Paul's Churchyard." (*Ibid.*, vol. 116.)

In the *Letters of Lord George Carew* is a ftill more remarkable inftance of penance. He is writing in November, 1617 :

"The 30 day of this monethe, the Ladye Markham, wyfe to Sir Griffithe Markham (who yett lives), for maryenge one of her fervants, together with her late hufband, did pennance in white fheets at Pawles croffe ; the like they muft do at Yorke and ellfwhere, and are fyned in 1000 *li.* How they efcaped deathe (as the ftatute lately made° for that offence providethe) I cannott well deliver, and yett they were arraygned for itt vppon thatt ftatute." (*Letters*, etc., p. 132.)

Note to page 159.

In Wilkinfon's *Londina Illuftrata* is a view of Paul's Crofs "from an original Drawing in the Pepyfian Library, Cambridge." I have not feen the original drawing, and, in the abfence of any definite information about it in Wilkinfon, I addreffed a letter to F. Pattrick, Efq., Fellow of Magdalene College, Cambridge, afking feveral queftions as to its authorfhip and date. In the very courteous reply which Mr. Pattrick was fo good as to fend me, he fays that the engraving in the *Londina Illuftrata* appears to be a fac-fimile of the Drawing ; that there is no fufficient evidence as to the perfon by whom or the period at which the Drawing was executed ; and that no account of the

---

° 1 Jac. I. cap. 11.

·Crofs accompanies the Drawing. All that appears to be known about it is that it forms part of the feries of Drawings and Engravings gathered together by Samuel Pepys. " Pepys was the firft perfon to collect prints and drawings in illuftration of London topography. Thefe he left to his nephew, who added to the collection, and two thick volumes therefore came to the College with the other treafures." (Wheatley's *Samuel Pepys and the World he lived in*, p. 92.)

Note to page 216. ·

Very various indeed were the fubjects treated of in the fermons of the times. " The Bifhop of London," fays Chamberlain, " told his Clergy that the King had ordered them to inveigh vehemently in their fermons againft women wearing broad-brimmed hats, pointed doublets, fhort hair, and even fome of them poinards : and if pulpit admonition fail, another courfe will be taken." (Chamberlain to Carleton, 25th January 1620. *Calendar of State Papers*, vol. 112.)

Note to page 217.

An interefting account of the removal of the images from S. Paul's Cathedral is found in Wriothefley's *Chronicle*, vol. ii. p. 1 :

" The fixtenth daie of Nouember [1547] the Kinges Maiefties vifitors beganne that night to take downe the roode with all the images in Poules Church, which were clene taken awaie, and by negligence of the laborers certaine perfons were hurt and one flaine in the falling downe of the great croffe in the rode loft, which the papifh prieftes faid was the will of God for the pulling downe of the faid idolls. Likwife all images in euerie parifh church in London were pulled downe and broken by the commandment of the faid vifitors.

" The xxvii[th] daie of November, being the firft Soundaie of Aduent, preched at Poules Croffe, Doctor Barlowe, Bifhopp of Sainct Davides, where he fhewed a picture of the refurrection of our Lord made with vices [moveable joints], which putt out his legges of fepulchree and bleffed with his hand, and turned his heade ; and their ftoode afore the pilpitt the imag of Our Ladie which they of Poules had lapped in feerecloth, which was hid in a corner of Poules Church, and found by the vifitors in their vifitation. And in his fermon he declared the great abhomination of idolatrie in images, with other fayned ceremonies contrarie to fcripture, to the extolling of Godes glorie, and to the great compfort of the awdience. After the fermon the boyes brooke the idolls in peaces."

A little later, in May, 1548, Wriothefley records, that " Poules quire with diuers other parifhes in London fong all the fervice in Englifh, both mattens, maffe, and even-fonge ; and kept no maffe, without fome receaued the communion with the prieft."

It is eafy to underftand that the exhibition of thefe mechanical figures, fkilfully contrived to deceive the worfhippers, muft have greatly ftimulated the zeal of the Reformers.

Note to page 229.

The following extracts from the Journals of the Houfe of Commons* throw light upon two points of no little intereft : for they indicate (in the words "until that Place be prepared and fitted for that Purpofe") that, at the date of the Order, Paul's Crofs was no longer ftanding ; and they fhow the origin of the claim of the Lord Mayor to appoint Preachers at the Crofs.

12th May, 1643.

Ordered, That Mr. Vaffall and Mr. Ven do bring in an Ordinance to enable the Lord Mayor to appoint Preachers to preach the Sermons, given by the Charity of well-difpofed People, at Paul's Crofs, or elfewhere.

26th May, 1643.

Preacher in Paul's Church Yard.

Ordered, That the Lord Mayor and Aldermen of the City of London fhall have power and Authority to nominate and appoint fuch Minifters, as fhall hereafter preach in Paul's Church Yard upon the Lord's Day weekly; and that, in the Interim, until that Place be prepared and fitted for that Purpofe, the Lord Mayor and Aldermen may appoint fuch convenient Place for fuch Minifters to Preach, every Lord's Day weekly, before them, as they fhall think convenient: And likewife, that the Lord Mayor, for the time, may difpofe of the Allowance formerly

---

. * For which I am indebted to the courtefy of the Librarian, George Howard, Efq.

given to the Preachers at Paul's, upon fuch Minifters as fhall be
fo appointed to preach before the faid Lord Mayor and Aldermen, at the Place by them to be affigned, as aforefaid : Which
Difpofition and Appointment fhall not be accounted or reputed
any Breach or Violation of the Gifts or Devifes of any Donor,
or Perfon deceafed ; notwithftanding any former Ufage, Appointment, or Devife of any Bifhop's, Donor's, or otherwife, to
the contrary.

Note to page 231.

The *Charge Books* of the Cathedral, a long and very important
feries of volumes, extending from 1633 to 1749, contain much
valuable information as to the coft of labour and the price of
material.   At the period indicated in the text, 1635, the following are fome of the amounts paid for wages and material :

		s.	d.	
16 Labourers received		1	2	a day each.
1 Labourer	,,	1	4	,,
6 Carpenters	,,	2	0	,,
2 Apprentices	,,	1	10	,,
6 Mafons	,,	2	0	,,
1 Apprentice	,,	1	6	,,
3 Bricklayers	,,	2	0	,,
1 Plumber	,,	2	6	,,

Stone Sawyers 1½d. the inch ; and for Burford and
    Ketton Stone 1d. the foot.
Fir Timber, 32s. and 33s. the load.
Bricks, 12s. the thoufand.
Tiles, 2s. for a hundred and a quarter.
Lead, £12 4s. 6d. the fother.

Note to page 240.

Another paffage from Chamberlain's *Letters* may well be
added to thofe printed in the text.

19th November, 1602. " My laft to you was of the fourth or
fift of this prefent, fince which time here hath ben a very dull
and dead terme, or els I am quite out of the trade, which may
well be, by reafon of a new devifed order to fhut the upper
doores in Powles in fervice time, wherby the old entercourfe is
cleane chaunged, and the trafficke of newes much decayed."
(p. 162.)

From this letter it clearly appears that even during Divine Service the din of chattering tongues was ftill to be heard.

Note to page 265.

The manufcript called in the text the *Will of Henry VII.* is in reality the "Book of Penalties fer non-performance of the Covenants in the Indentures between Henry VII. and the Abbot of Weftminfter, and others." It is fumptuoufly bound in crimfon velvet ; and the feals, enclofed in filver fkippets, hanging by cords of purple and crimfon filk and gold, are appended to it. Each fkippet bears on its cover a gilt roundel with the name of the party whofe feal is enclofed infcribed in finely punctured letters. The covers are decorated with filver boffes and clafps. "The firft page is illuminated, red rofes on gold, and portcullifes on an azure field, being richly embroidered on the margin with the royal arms and fupporters. In the initial letter is a miniature of Henry VII. enthroned. Before him kneel ten perfons, the two prelates in front vefted in fcarlet copes. The Archbifhop (Warham) holds a crofs-ftaff in one hand, in the other the Book of Penalties in its crimfon forel. Behind thefe appear, amongft others, the Abbot and monks of Weftminfter ; the Mayor of London, alfo, in a fcarlet gown, furred, holding a fceptre terminating in a fleur-de-lis." The Indenture is feptipartite, and was made 16th July, 1504. The parties to it are the King ; the Archbifhop of Canterbury ; the Bifhop of Winchefter ; John Iflippe, Abbot of Weftminfter, and the Prior and Convent of the fame place : the Dean and Canons of S. Stephen's, Weftminfter ; the Dean and Chapter of S. Paul's ; and the Mayor and Commonalty of the City of London.

The manufcript in the Cathedral Library is one of the counterparts of this document : a fimilar copy is in the Britifh Mufeum, and the original is in the Record Office. The colours and gold of the illuminations of the S. Paul's MS. are in perfect prefervation, and the binding is remarkably beautiful.

The above notice is condenfed from a full account of thefe manufcripts in *The Archæological Journal*, vol. xviii. pp. 182, 278, 279.

Note to page 287.

The myfterious fymbols ufed by Playford in his *Dancing Mafter* are thus explained by himfelf :

    ☽ = Man.   ⊙ = Woman.
Wo. = Woman.   We. = Women.
    ⋅ = a ftrain played once.
    ⋮ = a ftrain played twice.
    S. = a fingle, that is, two fteps, clofing both feet.
    D. = a double, that is, four fteps forward or back, clofing both feet.

Note upon the manufcript from which a *fac-fimile* is given at page 49.

The manufcript from which our *fac-fimile* is taken is a fine folio volume, "written on very ftout vellum, in double columns, 44 lines to the page." It was "no doubt an original poffeffion of the author, and muft by him have been left among the archives of his Cathedral. It was there when Edward I. examined the treafures of the Cathedrals." Probably, it was tranfferred from S. Paul's to Lambeth foon after the Reformation. "It formed a part of the Archiepifcopal Library, when it was removed to Cambridge during the troubles of the Commonwealth, and was reftored at the Reftoration." (Profeffor Stubbs' *Hiftorical Works of Ralph de Diceto*, vol. i. pp. lxxxviii-xc.) In Lambeth Library the volume ftill remains, notwithftanding the infcription which it contains in very clear, legible writing :

LIBER ECCLIE SANCTI PAULI LONDON.

INDEX.

INDEX.

This Index contains about 700 references: every reference has been compared with the text since the compilation of the Index.

LONDON : ELLIOT STOCK.